THE ACCIDENT

GILLIAN JACKSON

BLOODHOUND
— BOOKS —

First published in 2022 by Bloodhound Books.

www.bloodhoundbooks.com

Print ISBN: 978-1-5040-8185-6

ALSO BY GILLIAN JACKSON

The Pharmacist

The Victim

The Deception

Abduction

Snatched

1

The day that changed everything for Hannah Graham started in the same way as any other. Not unusually she overslept, showered in record time and shouted at the kids at least twice before either of them took any notice. Kate slammed the bathroom door, and Sam shouted an obscenity he knew his mother hated. It was an unremarkable morning affording no clue to the life-changing event awaiting the Graham family.

'If you want a lift you need to be ready in twenty minutes!' Hannah yelled up the stairs. *What a nag I'm becoming*, she thought, frowning. Sam stomped into the kitchen in his boxers, reddish-brown hair mussed above a scowling face. Hannah's son was at an age where he appeared to be all arms and legs protruding from a skinny body, with features he'd not quite grown into yet. An embarrassing case of acne, which he hated anyone to mention, did little for his confidence.

'Kate's got in the bathroom before me again. She'll be ages!' he moaned. 'Why can't you wake me first?'

'If you'd get up when I call, you'd be there before your sister. Use the en suite if you like.'

'But all my stuff's in the bathroom.' Sam flopped down at the kitchen table and rested his chin in his hands.

'Have some breakfast while you wait and if you want a lift this morning, I need to be prompt. There's an early meeting at work.' Hannah placed a cup of coffee in front of her seventeen-year-old son.

'There's not a lecture until eleven, so I'm good.' Sam poured cereal into the bowl his mother passed him. 'Is Dad not home yet?'

'No. He rang to say he couldn't make it last night. He finished late and there are miles of road works on the M6 – the forecast's not good either so he decided to stay over another night.'

Hannah's husband, Mike, worked in sales and seemed to be constantly on the road, regularly staying away for up to three or four nights at a time. It wasn't ideal in the weather they were currently experiencing and Hannah worried for his safety. She hated him being away but had long since ceased to argue over the hours he worked. At almost eighteen, the twins were of an age where they could look after themselves, but Hannah still maintained Mike's unsocial hours were detrimental to their family life.

'What family life?' Mike would argue. 'They're teenagers; they don't want to be around us.' Hannah suspected it was actually her husband who didn't want to be around them, or maybe it was just her he wished to avoid. Perhaps this was how families evolved these days and it was natural for them all to do their own thing, but she was sadly aware that Kate and Sam would be going to university in a few months and these days children rarely came back home once they'd left. What kind of life would she and Mike have then?

Hannah supposed her work would take on greater importance and she did love her job as an office manager with a prominent estate agent. Unless Mike was home more often there'd be precious little else left when the twins were gone. Increasingly Hannah anticipated their leaving with mixed feelings. Frustrating though they were at times she adored having Kate and Sam at home and knew she'd miss them terribly.

On the other hand, Hannah secretly nursed the hope that when there was just her and Mike, they could perhaps recapture some of the sparkle which had escaped their marriage over the last few years. Devoting more time to each other could surely only improve their relationship. Maybe they could travel to some of those exotic places they dreamed about before the children came along, yet while Mike was working such long hours it seemed unlikely this would ever happen.

'Kate!' she shouted up the stairs. 'Do you want a lift this morning because I'm leaving in ten minutes?'

'No, I'm not in until lunch!' Kate replied.

They seemed to be hardly ever at the sixth form college. Hannah honestly didn't know how they'd get the required grades for university when they didn't appear to do any work. Still, they were old enough to know what they were doing, or were supposed to be.

Kate skidded into the kitchen as Hannah pulled on her coat. She was a pretty girl with rich auburn hair, like her mother's, framing a well-proportioned face with high cheekbones and lively green eyes. Mike said their daughter was the image of Hannah as she'd been when they first met. Kate was never short of admirers which both pleased and worried Hannah but she was a sensible girl and seemingly unaware of how attractive she was becoming.

'Can you leave me twenty pounds, Mum?' she asked, 'I need some new mascara.'

Hannah's eyes widened. 'You're not going to pay that much just for mascara, are you?'

'No, it's only twelve but I need money to get the bus into

town, unless you can drop me off before you go to work, it's freezing out there.' Kate looked disgusted that her mother would question the amount she asked for and rolled her eyes – an all-too-common expression which made Hannah smile – she'd perfected the same eye roll for her own mother's benefit when she was a teenager and knew precisely what her daughter was thinking.

'Sorry, love, but I can't take you to town or I'll be late. I've got an important meeting. What happened to your allowance?' Hannah was fishing in her bag for her purse, knowing her daughter went through money like it was going out of fashion.

Kate tutted. 'My allowance is barely enough to last the week.' She grabbed the twenty-pound note almost before her mother pulled it from her purse. 'Thanks, Mum!'

Hannah checked the time and hurried to the door. 'Remember to stack the dishwasher before you leave.'

Outside, the atrocious weather hadn't improved. After two days of heavy snow which was tightly packed on the roads, freezing rain was starting to fall. The temperature hovered below zero and it looked as if the gritting lorry hadn't made it again either. The council was quickly running out of salt for the roads.

They called the cold snap the Beast from the East, which seemed a spot-on description to Hannah who couldn't ever remember a colder start to February. The wind was biting, chilling her to the bone even though she'd only just left the warmth of the house.

Rachel, her neighbour and best friend, was also leaving for work. 'You still on for tonight, Hannah?' she called out. Hannah stopped, she'd forgotten agreeing to a girls' night out with Rachel and a couple of other friends.

'Oh, sorry but I'll have to pass on this one. Mike didn't get back last night so I can hardly go out and leave him when he hasn't been home for three nights.'

Rachel stood with her hands on her hips. Her breath clouding as it left her lips. 'Why not? He's big enough to fend for himself.'

'Next time, Rachel, promise! Anyway, it's hardly fit to venture out unless you have to.' Feeling a stab of guilt at letting her friend down, Hannah mouthed another sorry to Rachel and then hurried to the garage to get out of the freezing rain, clutching her coat to her neck against the bitter cold.

2

Hannah Graham hadn't always been stuck in the rut of domesticity. When she and Mike had married they delighted in making plans and promises, determined to always appreciate each other and their blessings whatever life threw their way. Midnight picnics, impromptu snowball fights and surprise gifts were just some of the little things which kept their relationship spontaneous, and laughter filled their home. There was no reason to think life would ever be any different.

Inevitably when the twins came along things changed. Hannah tried hard to keep the romance alive in her marriage, even throughout the constant exhaustion of those early years. It was difficult to pinpoint precisely when things started to change, yet she still considered their life to be good – they were financially stable with a healthy family and Hannah was always one to count her blessings. The magic of those early days had simply matured into something different. Contentment perhaps? Yes, that's what it was for her and hopefully for Mike too.

It took twenty minutes for Hannah to get to the office on a good day – on a bad one, nearer forty. She hoped for light traffic this morning yet the icy roads would probably slow things down. Heading towards the motorway, Hannah's thoughts again turned to Mike. It would soon be their twentieth wedding anniversary – she'd been tempted to surprise him by booking a holiday. But his reaction might not be what she hoped for, and the problem of getting time off work would undoubtedly cause more arguments.

It seemed that the longer Mike had been with the company, the more they expected of him although Hannah appeared to mind more than he did. In her opinion the firm took advantage of him and even on rest days there were calls at short notice, expecting him to drop everything and go wherever they asked. In the last month Mike had been away more nights than he'd been at home which was hardly a recipe for a healthy relationship. Hannah wished he'd assert himself more and say no to his boss rather than jumping every time they said 'go'.

The traffic was heavier than she'd expected and every light seemed to be against her, always the same when you were running late. The early meeting at work was to discuss a potential merger with another local estate agent and Hannah's thoughts switched to the prospect. Still undecided whether or not she was in favour of the union, it could offer her the chance of promotion or even a partnership, which would inevitably involve extra responsibility. Did she want that? If only Mike had come home last night they could have talked it through before the meeting. His opinion would have been welcome.

Niggling at the back of Hannah's mind was the thought that if Mike didn't cut down on his nights away, and when the time came for the twins to leave for university, she'd probably appreciate the extra work. Yet as much as she loved her job, being a homemaker had always been equally important to Hannah. Still, if it was going to be an empty home, what was the point? Why not support the merger and work towards a partnership?

She missed having Mike around to talk to and felt at a loss to know what he wanted out of life anymore. He seemed content to drift along rudderless, with no thought to their immediate or long-term future. How could she be expected to make decisions when he was never there?

A queue on the motorway slip road would probably add another five minutes to her journey – if only she hadn't overslept. With such atrocious weather it would have been a perfect day for staying at home. Hannah was due some leave, but the meeting was crucial and one she didn't want to miss.

Most of the local schools had been closed for the last three days, but a few days at home wasn't to be for Hannah and like many other people she braved the conditions and made every effort to get into work. Most of the vehicles joining the motorway were heavy goods traffic, their huge wheels throwing up icy slush. Hannah was behind two lorries and would most likely be flanked by others when she eventually joined the motorway. Snow was piled high at both sides of the road and freezing rain lashed violently onto the windscreen as if trying to get inside the car. Hannah shuddered. It sounded like bullets rapping on the roof.

Hannah hated this drive but the only alternative route added an extra seven miles and a further twenty minutes to the journey, so she suffered the motorway traffic every day. Suddenly the line of vehicles moved, a few stop-starts, then the road ahead cleared a little and she could see a gap coming up on the motorway. Slipping into first then second gear, Hannah moved carefully forward, willing the gap to stay open long enough for her to slot into it and join the motorway traffic.

The next thing she knew her car seemed to take on a mind of its own. The wheels skidded on the ice and the car veered forward, first to the right and then the left – Hannah had lost all control.

Panic rose inside, catching in her throat until she could

hardly breathe; she was utterly helpless as the car gathered momentum down the slope of the slip road. Hannah panicked. She tried to remember what she should do in such circumstances and steered into the skid but the steering wheel refused to respond.

Suddenly her Ford Focus spun 180 degrees, with no possible way for Hannah to avoid the rear of the car from smashing into the enormous back wheel of the lorry moving towards her at speed on the motorway. The little car was instantly filled with a horrendous grating noise – the sound of crushing metal, as it came to a sudden violent halt. Hannah's head was thrown backwards, and staring helplessly out of the front windscreen she was momentarily aware of a dark-coloured Range Rover heading straight towards her, the impending impact terrifyingly unavoidable.

For a split second, she made eye contact with the male driver whose face mirrored her horror at what was happening – what they were both powerless to prevent. Hannah briefly took in the frightened expression of the woman sitting beside the driver before hearing herself scream, a sound which seemed to come from somewhere outside of the car, an echo of sheer panic and raw fear.

Darkness and pain enveloped everything. Hannah's world became still, black and silent.

3

Joe Parker was convinced he was going through a mid-life crisis. He despaired whether this was the slippery slope to old age before the inevitable – the big 'D'. The mirror scared him these days but he couldn't resist studying his face in it and wondering what had happened to his once-firm jawline and taut skin. The reflection staring back at him was of a much older man whom he barely recognised – but Joe was only forty-three!

He supposed the mirror didn't lie. Loose skin sagged from his jaws and bags hung beneath his eyes; his skin was sallow too, with an unhealthy yellow tinge. Could it be the cigarettes? He'd tried so many times to kick the habit but his resolve crumbled after only a matter of days.

The booze probably wouldn't help either – he had a penchant for fine whisky and fancied himself as a bit of a wine buff, yet Joe liked to think he kept his drinking in moderation and he wasn't stupid. He knew the detrimental effect these things had on a person although he'd never considered it would happen to him. Joe had always enjoyed a smoke and a few drinks without seriously thinking of the damage they could do to his body. His hair was thinning as well, although he knew much younger men who would be glad to have the amount of hair he still possessed.

And then there was his mind – Joe was sure he was slowing down mentally. Only a couple of days before he'd been talking to someone in the pub, not a close friend but another regular whom he'd known to pass the time of day with for several years, and he couldn't remember the man's name. After a three-minute conversation the name still wouldn't come to mind and he'd left the pub frustrated and wondering if he was finally losing it.

Morning sounds from the kitchen rose up the stairs and Joe realised he'd better get a move on. Alison, his wife, was making toast and coffee, the same breakfast he ate every day, while she nibbled on fruit and yoghurt.

'You all right this morning, love?' she asked. 'You're looking a bit down.'

'I'm fine. Didn't sleep too well that's all. Have you taken Liffey out yet?'

'Yes, we've had a quick walk through the meadow but it's freezing, we were both ready to get back home. You haven't forgotten you're dropping me at Mum's this morning, have you?'

'Course not,' Joe lied as he slathered a generous helping of butter on his toast. He could have done without the detour on his way to work, especially in this weather, but at least if Alison visited her mum today he wouldn't be expected to take her at the weekend. *Every cloud*, he thought.

While his wife washed up the breakfast pots Joe went back upstairs to brush his teeth. He studied the yellowing teeth which had once been white and even. *I don't know why she stays with me*, he thought. Alison was trim and pretty at forty-two, and worked hard to keep her figure, with Pilates, swimming and a healthy diet. He knew he was too lazy to put in such effort and wondered if it was too late to change. Joe's waistline had thickened considerably in the last few years but Alison was great and never nagged him about it although he knew she harboured concerns about his health. Ali was the bright spot in his life, his 'reason for living' he called her – corny but true.

'Come on, love!' Joe called ten minutes later. 'We don't want to keep your mum waiting.'

Ali held on to his arm as they negotiated the icy path leading to the garage. 'I've never known such a long cold snap,' she grumbled. Even as a child when friends were out with sledges and building snowmen, Joe knew Alison didn't like the snow, preferring to stay in the warmth of her bedroom with a good book or her beloved 'My Little Ponies'. Cold feet and ice-caked mittens were never her idea of fun.

Once in the car with the heater warming them through, Joe asked, 'Do you think I should try to eat a little more healthily, Ali?'

'I think it's a great idea.' She smiled. 'I'm sure you'd like some of those recipes I get from my slimming magazines. We could both make an effort, work at it together.' Nothing more was said and Joe knew Alison would go about helping him in her quiet way; she was wonderful and in all honesty deserved better than him. Perhaps he'd even have another go at giving up smoking for both their sakes.

Joe and Alison had recently celebrated eighteen years of marriage, most of which had been blissfully happy with only one big regret – not having been blessed with children. As with every other setback in life, Alison simply got on with it without complaint, the painful subject barely referred to anymore now the chance had passed them by for good. Having briefly looked into the possibility of adoption, the lengthy process seemed so fraught with problems and red tape that they soon abandoned the idea and five years earlier decided to get a dog.

Neither of them was naive enough to think a dog could ever be the same as a child but they had love to give, a good home and plenty of time and patience, so after a visit to the local animal sanctuary, Liffey came into their lives. They fell in love with her as soon as they saw her sweet face, rich golden coat and large velvet brown eyes.

'This one was found abandoned on the streets of Ireland, frightened and hungry,' the manager told them. 'We think she's part golden Labrador, crossed perhaps with a lurcher.' Liffey had only been at the centre for a couple of days and hadn't settled well.

Alison was horrified to see blood on the poor dog's paws. 'What happened?'

'She's not taking to kennel life, I'm afraid, and barked and scratched through most of the night. If you were interested in her we'd want you to take her as soon as possible.'

Ali and Joe exchanged glances. There was no doubt they wanted this dog – they would find it very difficult to leave without her. Joe suggested naming her Liffey as a reminder of her Irish roots and so Liffey she became, and very quickly took centre stage in their household. Slim for a Labrador, which was probably the lurcher genes, they soon discovered that Liffey had issues.

Initially she was very nervous – they even wondered if she'd ever lived in a house before. Settling her in became a welcome focus for Alison and Joe, and over the first year Liffey became a central part of their lives – they doted on her. Joe liked to joke he had two women in the house bossing him around, but he loved every minute.

Not having children meant money wasn't tight for the Parkers like it was for many of their friends with families, and other than Liffey they weren't tied in any way. They'd taken some memorable, and perhaps some would say extravagant, holidays and been able to go to places they would never have afforded with a family. Still, Joe knew Alison would really have loved a child and so would he. Holidays could never compensate.

Joe had been pondering their childless status lately and felt envious of friends with children or grandchildren. He also worried about who would look after Ali when he was gone. True, she was an intelligent, capable woman but Joe had always taken delight in caring for her. It was he who paid the bills and he didn't think his wife even knew who their energy provider was, having lost interest after the second time he changed companies to save money. And who would maintain the car and mow the lawn?

Perhaps these thoughts were contributing to the way he'd been feeling of late. In reality, Joe knew his wife was far from helpless, but regrets can play heavily on the mind, or was he just depressed? If that was the case there was no reason for it; he was a lot better off than most people and so thought he should make an effort to pull himself together.

4

The traffic was slow and dropping Alison off at her mother's would make Joe late getting into work, but he was the department head and rarely took advantage of it – there would be no one waiting to reprimand him for tardiness. Joe's thoughts shifted to his mother-in-law, a woman he found very difficult to get along with.

Alison was a brick and went faithfully twice a week, often more, to do her mother's cleaning, washing, ironing, and shopping. He didn't mind, except that the old lady didn't appreciate it one iota and the more Ali did for her the more she expected without ever expressing a word of gratitude. Ethel Forester sat watching television from early morning until late at night, making no attempt to do anything for herself when she was more than capable of making an effort.

Joe drove carefully, never one to take risks and with the roads still covered in ice from the cold snap of the last week, he wasn't going to hurry. There was no let-up to this abysmal weather; he couldn't remember it ever being as bad as this. The wipers struggled to clear the freezing rain which was falling heavily, making visibility poor. Once on the motorway the conditions would hopefully improve and as they were approaching the slip road soon, he thought he should be able to go a little faster.

Joe's Range Rover was great in these conditions, another luxury he thought he should be thankful for, and very soon he manoeuvred smoothly into the flow of traffic on the motorway with only two miles to go until the next junction. The couple remained silent for a while, each with their own thoughts and Joe concentrating on driving.

'Shall we eat out tonight, Joe?' Alison asked. 'If I stay at Mum's until you finish work you can pick me up and we could go straight to The Mango Tree?'

'Yes, why not, a last splurge before you put me on a diet … what the hell!' Joe braked hard as the little Ford Focus careering down the slip road ahead of them came into his vision apparently having skidded on the ice and clearly out of control. Joe watched in horror as its wheels slid onto the motorway, the car spinning round – ending up with its back end smashed into a lorry approaching on the near side.

Suddenly the Range Rover slid out of his control. Panicking, Joe pumped the brakes frantically but the tyres couldn't find purchase on the ice beneath and they were heading towards the stricken Ford Focus, helpless to prevent the impending contact. An image of a screaming woman loomed in the windscreen as if magnified, but Joe was powerless to stop his car from hitting it head-on.

Alison screamed as the airbags activated on impact, obscuring their view as they smashed into the other vehicle. Joe's ears were filled with white noise as he gasped for breath, struggling against the fabric of the airbag and shouting to his wife.

'Ali, are you all right? Ali, Ali!'

There was no reply.

The car was jolted several times, grating noises assaulting his ears as Joe realised other vehicles must have crashed into the back of them. He fought frantically against the airbag to get out of the door, but it wouldn't open. The front wing had buckled on impact and the door was jammed. Clawing at the airbag, he managed to pull the voluminous folds of material down onto his knee until he could see his wife. Alison lay unconscious beside him, her head slack and drooping onto her right shoulder, a trickle of blood running from her mouth.

A feeling of utter helplessness engulfed Joe as he reached over to touch his wife, grasping for her hand as he repeated her name. The windscreen had shattered, preventing him from seeing the carnage outside the vehicle. With each movement his neck hurt. A stabbing pain shot into his head and down through his left arm as he struggled to see outside. Noises seeped into the car, the grating and grinding sounds of metal, screams, shouting and sobbing and the constant rhythmic drumming of the heavy icy rain pounding on the car roof.

Joe had no idea how many vehicles were now stationary – caught up in the tangled web of metal which only moments earlier were individual vehicles. Tears ran freely down his face as he waited, utterly powerless to do anything to help himself or his wife.

It seemed an eternity until sirens sounded in the distance and Joe prayed they would get to Alison in time. His eyes struggled to focus – his head swam. Joe wanted nothing more than to drift away into unconsciousness, but he knew he must keep awake for Alison. *Talk to her,* he told himself. *Keep her alive!*

'Alison … Ali, can you hear me, love?'

Silence – not a groan or a sob, just the most frightening silence, not even the sound of breathing while the noise outside was rising. Suddenly, a fireman pulled at the door, startling Joe who shouted to the black-uniformed figure. 'My wife!' he cried. 'My wife needs help, please!' The door opened with a sudden jerk and a strong arm reached in to help ease Joe out.

'Leave me, get Alison, please … she's unconscious!'

'It's okay, my colleague's working on getting her out now – let's get you to safety shall we?'

Joe's legs threatened to buckle beneath him as he was led towards the snow-covered verge. The pain was excruciating and he was unable to turn his head to see what was happening back at his car. His body trembled with cold and fear.

'Is she all right? My wife, Alison, is she all right?' Joe was becoming increasingly light-headed and almost collapsed into the fireman's arms, the acrid smell of burnt rubber making him feel nauseous. The next thing he knew he was inside an ambulance, wrapped in a silver foil blanket with his neck supported by an uncomfortable collar. Joe fought to keep his eyes open but it was such an effort.

The figure of a man was beside him, talking to him, asking him questions. 'Hi, mate, can you tell me your name?'

'How's my wife – Alison?' He wasn't sure if he'd got the words right but the man patted his knee.

'We're almost at the hospital now; your wife will either be there already or be arriving shortly. Can you tell me your name?'

'Joe, Joe Parker.'

'Well, you're doing fine, Joe, no obvious broken limbs but the pain you're in could indicate a problem with your collarbone. They'll check you out properly when we get to the hospital. An X-ray should show up any breaks.'

Joe closed his eyes again, tears escaping unchecked. He didn't care about himself – all he could think about was Alison – her head at such an awkward angle – blood from her mouth.

'Stay awake if you can, mate. Tell me where you were

going, can you?' The man's voice was quiet and even but persistent. Joe didn't want to talk. He wanted to sleep, to wake up and find this had all been a nightmare.

He wanted to see Alison – to make sure she was all right. She must be. Joe couldn't make it without her.

5

'Well, Joe, you've had a lucky escape.' The doctor studied his notes rather than look at Joe, who in all honesty felt anything but lucky and would much rather be dead, like his beloved Alison.

An X-ray had revealed a broken collarbone – the cause of the pain in his left arm and shoulder – and even trying to lift his head to drink made him wince. But lucky? No way! Joe's reason for living was gone, what did that mean for him now? Ali didn't deserve to die; it should have been him. She was so full of joy and energy, a truly good person who loved life. Joe didn't – not anymore – especially a life without Alison which stretched fearfully ahead of him, stark and stripped bare of all happiness.

It was over an hour after Joe's admission before someone had come to tell him his wife was dead, two hours during which he asked and pleaded for news to the point of becoming a nuisance. Initially the staff in Accident and Emergency were too busy to break off from tending the injured to enquire about his wife. The accident, declared a major incident, stretched the hospital's already strained and limited resources. From listening to the nurses' chatter, Joe learned there were three fatalities, two women and a teenage boy. In his heart he knew Alison must be one of them but he couldn't bear to accept it and clung to the gossamer thread of hope that she was still alive.

Joe was moved into a side ward where finally the chaplain and the ward sister came to see him.

'I'm so sorry, Joe, but it's not good news.' The sister took Joe's hand. 'Alison didn't make it. It was very quick; she wouldn't have been in pain.'

'No, you must be wrong! Not Alison!' Joe refused to believe it; surely it was another woman who'd died, not his wife, it couldn't be her! But in his heart he knew it was, and he wished it had been him who'd died instead of Alison.

'I'm really sorry, Joe.' The sister had tears in her eyes and Joe nodded, mumbling his thanks as she turned to go.

The chaplain remained. A severe-looking man, he stood at the side of the bed, his brow furrowed and his lips turned down at the corners as he placed his long slender fingers on Joe's good shoulder. His touch was cold, yet his words were warm, albeit hollow.

'Can I call anyone for you, Joe? A family member or good friend perhaps?'

But there was no one. Joe had a brother but they'd never been close. David lived somewhere on the south coast and he couldn't even remember the name the town. Alison's mother would need to be told, she'd wonder why her daughter hadn't arrived and would be unable to reach them on the phone. The chaplain said he'd speak to one of the police officers and they would go round to break the news. It wasn't an ideal way for the old lady to hear that her daughter was dead, but Joe was in no fit state to go himself and as yet didn't know how long they'd keep him in hospital. He gave the chaplain Ethel Forester's address and also his neighbours, to ask them to look after Liffey. He recited their phone number.

'They have a key and often have Liffey for us so it shouldn't be a problem,' Joe explained. 'Tell them I'll ring as soon as I know when I'll be home … and would you tell them about Alison please?'

Joe's neighbours were lovely people, salt of the earth, and almost as fond of Liffey as he and Alison were. They readily looked after Liffey when holidays came around and he knew his dog would be fine with them. Joe experienced a sudden longing for Liffey to be with him; her warm body and loving temperament would be a welcome comfort, perhaps she was the next most precious thing in his life, after Ali.

But Ali was gone.

The hospital staff struggled frantically to cope with the influx of casualties from the crash; nurses and doctors were called in from their days off. No one had time to answer the many questions stacking up in Joe's mind – questions about Alison. Even the chaplain moved on after promising to make the call to his neighbours – no doubt tasked with telling another man that his wife was dead too. Joe wondered if the other fatality was the woman in the Ford Focus into which his car had smashed.

Surely if Alison hadn't survived the impact, the other woman would also be dead; her car must have been squashed like a concertina into an unrecognisable mess. Would she leave a husband and children? Joe was suddenly struck with the depressing thought – he had no one. If they'd been fortunate enough to have children, he'd have someone with him, caring for him, another person to share his pain and shoulder the burden. Joe squeezed his eyes tight shut – it was futile wishing for the impossible.

After a seemingly endless day, the worst day ever, Joe spent an uncomfortable night in the stuffy hospital ward. A nurse offered painkillers but they couldn't ease the pain in his heart, the solid mass of emotion welling up in his chest at the thought of his wife, at the awful awareness that he'd never see her again, never hear her voice or touch her hand. It was unbearable.

Sleep refused to come, to afford him just a few hours' respite, and in the darkness tears fell readily. The neck brace he'd worn in the ambulance had been replaced with an arm sling, put on in such a way as to keep his arm immobilised so Joe could only lie on his back, which, even with pillows propping him up, was uncomfortable. But even without the pain and heavy sorrow he was experiencing, the unfamiliar night-time sounds of the busy ward would have been enough to keep him awake.

It was a welcome relief when dawn arrived. Joe forced himself to eat, wanting to build up his strength to enable him to go home as soon as possible.

A doctor appeared in the room later in the morning, bearing the signs of a man who hadn't slept. Dark circles encased his eyes yet his manner was professional and his voice kindly as he informed Joe he could be discharged.

'You really need to take this injury seriously. Keep the sling on for the next two weeks and then we'll do another X-ray to make sure the bone is knitting together and hasn't moved. It's a bad break and will be swollen and quite painful for a while, so you must be careful not to use your arm. If the X-ray's okay, you can begin some gentle exercise, swimming would be good, but we'll talk about that when I next see you. If you don't take care we may have to operate and fit a plate and screws, so in the long run it's better to give your body the time and rest it needs to heal. The sister will see to the paperwork for your discharge and I've prescribed some strong painkillers. I'm sorry for your loss, Mr Parker. Sister has some leaflets which might be of interest to you.' After his little speech the doctor smiled sadly then left the room.

Joe would need help to get dressed; he'd been unable to get to the bathroom earlier and much to his disgust had to use a bedpan. He didn't know how he'd manage at home but was determined to leave the hospital as quickly as possible. Just as Joe was considering the logistics of getting dressed, the sister appeared and pulled the curtains around his bed. She held a bundle of leaflets in her hand and sat down on the only chair.

'I know it's going to be difficult for you but there is help out there if you want to take it.' The leaflets she spread on the bed told Joe she wasn't just referring to the practicalities of his injuries. 'These are contact details for a bereavement counselling service. They're excellent and you can self-refer at any time just by ringing this number.' She tapped the reverse of the leaflet with a well-manicured short fingernail. 'We can also get in touch with social services to have someone come to the house for a week or two to help you with getting a shower or making meals if you'd like?'

Joe shuddered. The thought of a stranger coming in to help him shower was abhorrent. He'd manage somehow – he wasn't ancient and incapable – yet. He politely declined and was given a number for if he changed his mind.

'Right, I'll get your discharge letter and prescription ready and a nurse will help you dress. Is there anyone I can phone to come and pick you up?' The sister pulled back the curtains. Joe thought for a minute, not fully hearing what she'd said, his mind on other things.

'What about Alison, my wife? I mean, I know her body's here and I'll have to arrange a funeral, but is there a death certificate or something I need?'

A look of sadness crossed the sister's face. 'I'm sorry, Joe, but Alison will have to stay here for the time being.' The sister sat on the edge of the bed next to him and explained. 'After a fatal accident, the coroner becomes involved to determine precisely what happened and then there'll be an inquest. The death can't be registered until then and so Alison's body won't be released for a funeral until the coroner's made his decision. What we can do is to give you the medical certificate of death for you to take to the coroner who'll then issue an *interim* death certificate so you'll be able to notify the bank.'

Joe was stunned; he'd assumed it would be a simple matter of arranging the funeral yet now it looked as if it could be a long-drawn-out process. He gathered his thoughts and remembered the sister's earlier question.

'Sorry, that's come as a bit of a surprise. It's not what I was expecting. Anyway, could you ring my neighbour for me? If there's no answer I'll get a taxi.' He recited the number.

Sister nodded and smiled as she left him. They must see all sorts, he thought, surely he wasn't the only one who was ignorant of procedure ... or had no family to take him home?

Joe's clothes were filthy, but unless he went home in a hospital gown there was no option but to wear them. His wallet was still in the inside pocket of his jacket so at least he'd have money to pay for a taxi if necessary and someone had had the forethought to put his keys in the pocket too.

There were dark stains on his left-hand jacket sleeve. In the deepest recesses of his mind, Joe knew it was Alison's blood yet he refused to think about it, except to decide to burn all the clothes he'd been wearing the previous day – the events seemed embedded into their very fabric – each fibre held the smell of burning rubber and crushed metal, reminding him of Ali's death when he wanted his memories of her to be only good ones. There was no bag for Joe to pack; all he had was what he stood up in and he resembled a vagrant.

Sister popped her head around the door again to tell him his neighbour, Phil, would be at the hospital within the hour.

6

Phil and Diane Roper had moved into the house next door to the Parkers ten years previously and the two couples had hit it off from day one. They were of a similar age and without living in each other's pockets, both couples more than filled the role of 'good neighbours'. When Alison and Joe acquired Liffey, the friendship extended to dog sitting and the dog was as comfortable in their home as her own, for which Joe was grateful.

True to his word, Phil walked into the ward forty minutes after receiving the call. Joe was waiting, staring at the blank wall and trying to control his emotions. His discharge letter, pain medication and Alison's medical certificate were clutched to his chest. Joe looked at Phil whose expression reflected his sadness.

'Joe, I don't know what to say! We couldn't believe it and I'm so very sorry. Alison was the best – it seems so bloody unfair.'

Joe was to hear similar sentiments over the weeks to come but he knew Phil was sincere.

'Come on, let's get you home.' His neighbour helped Joe to

his feet and, conforming to hospital policy, steered him into a wheelchair and pushed him to the main exit. The car was parked in a pick-up zone nearby and as Phil settled Joe into the passenger seat he said, 'Diane says you'd be very welcome to join us for a meal later, it's going to be a bit difficult for you with your arm in a sling.'

'Thanks, Phil, I appreciate the offer but I think I'd just like to be at home today, another time maybe? How's Liffey? Has she been behaving herself?'

'Yes, she's no trouble, never is – and we'll walk her for you until you're up to it if you like. Diane's the early bird, so she'll take her each morning and I'll take her at night.'

'That's brilliant, thanks. I won't be up to much more than letting her in the garden for a while but I wouldn't like her to miss her exercise.'

'Good, that's settled then. And it goes without saying that if there's anything at all we can do for you just say the word. You and Ali have been good neighbours and we're happy to return the favour.'

'Thanks, I might have to take you up on it too. I'll have to sort out all of Ali's affairs and to be honest it scares the hell out of me!' Joe was close to tears but didn't want to break down in front of his friend.

'We mean it, anything at all, mate.'

Within twenty minutes the car pulled up in front of Joe's house. Phil ran round to open the door, then, taking the keys from Joe's hand, walked ahead to open the front door. He would never know what that little gesture meant to his neighbour. Joe was dreading going into an empty house, knowing how cold and unwelcoming it would feel without Alison there waiting for him.

As soon as they were inside, Diane appeared with Liffey, who almost knocked her master down in her enthusiasm at seeing him. Joe sat on the sofa and stroked the dog with his good hand, trying to contain her excitement lest she bumped his injured side.

Diane, who would usually have hugged her neighbour, squeezed his hand gently. 'I'm so sorry, Joe, really I am. We'll miss Alison terribly; she was such a lovely person.' There were tears in her eyes and Joe had to swallow hard to stop himself from breaking down and sobbing openly.

'Thanks, Diane, and for having Liffey, I knew she'd be fine with you.'

'Any time, and I mean it. Not just having Liffey, who's a delight to look after, but if there's anything you need we're here for you. Now would you like to come and eat with us later? It's just a casserole but you're very welcome.'

'If you don't mind I'm really tired. I think I'll just have a quiet evening and get an early night. The doctor said I needed as much rest as possible, although tomorrow I'll have to start making arrangements ...' His voice trailed off as he thought of the bureaucracy to be dealt with, something he had no inclination to do.

'Ah, well,' Phil interrupted, 'I hope you don't think it presumptuous of me but I've taken a day off work tomorrow to be at your disposal. We know you have no family to speak of, so I thought perhaps I could run you about a bit, you know, the bank or wherever?'

'Oh, Phil, that's so good of you. I was awake most of last night trying to think of everything there is to do, so your support will be appreciated. Unfortunately, I can't arrange the funeral until after the inquest, but I need to get an interim death certificate from the coroner's office. Other than that I'm unsure what else I can do.'

Diane added her assurance of their intention to help. 'Phil's auntie died last year and he was executor of her estate, so he has some idea of what needs to be done.'

Joe's eyes filled up again. 'Thank you, both. You've already made things so much easier.'

'No problem, look I'll put the kettle on and make you a cup of tea and then we'll leave you in peace. Phil will come back at about six to walk Liffey and I'll send a bit of casserole round in case you're hungry.' Diane was only a couple of minutes in the kitchen and then they left Joe with a mug of hot tea, his dog by his side and instructions to call on them if he needed anything.

Once alone, Joe reflected on what exceptional people his neighbours were – they'd stepped up to the mark and proved to be sensitive and thoughtful.

It was 3pm. Liffey settled down beside Joe on the sofa while he sipped his tea. The house felt strange, empty and hollow. Alison's presence, looking out for her husband's comfort, keeping the conversation bright and generally making their house a home, would never be there again and a void as solid as her presence had been was almost suffocating.

Ali was gone and Joe wondered if he'd ever adjust, or even if he wanted to. Liffey snuggled closer to him, a timely comfort, yet she'd soon wonder where Alison was and would also grieve.

Joe dropped his head into Liffey's warm fur and wept bitterly, finally letting go of his emotions while the dog stayed close, sensing his need of her.

7

Hannah slowly wakened, aware of lying in a strange place and unsure if she was still dreaming. Her head pounded, her arms felt stiff and a searing pain shot through her body as she struggled to open her eyes. Someone was holding her hand, squeezing it gently and talking to her – repeating her name.

'Hannah … Hannah can you hear me?' It was Mike. She tried to smile but her mouth was sore, her lips felt crusted and cracked painfully with the movement. An awful metallic taste of blood filled her mouth. What was going on? She tried again to open her eyes. Mike was sitting on a chair beside a hospital bed.

Why was she in a hospital?

Attempting to turn her head and ask what was happening, Hannah's body was stubbornly uncooperative. 'Mike.' Her voice was hoarse, raspy. 'What's going on?'

'It's all right, love. You were in a car accident. Don't worry, you're okay – and I'm here.' Her husband's face swam in and out of focus before her, and Hannah could see the anguish in his watery red eyes.

'But I can't remember.' Panic almost choked the words. How could she have been in an accident and not know?

'It's okay. The doctor said you've possibly banged your head so you may not remember the accident for a while, but it'll come back in time, it's not important.' He stroked her forehead, pushing a lock of hair behind her ears.

'What happened, where was I going? Were the children with me?' The sudden thought of Sam and Kate alarmed her – if the twins had been with her …

'They're both fine and no they weren't in the car, you were alone. Don't worry about it, we can fill you in on the details later.' Mike's smile was forced. Hannah could always tell when he was worried by the slight twitch at the corner of his mouth – he would make a terrible poker player.

Hannah asked nothing more. It was enough to concentrate on breathing and keeping her eyes open, she was exhausted and even these simple tasks were an effort and the pain was horrendous. The skin on her face felt tight – it must be swollen and her eyes wouldn't open fully. Mike reached over the bed and pressed the call button for the nurse.

'I'm all right,' Hannah said, 'just tired.' Aware of tubes in her arms and one of those cages over her legs, she asked, 'Have I broken my leg?'

'No, love … here's the nurse, she'll want to see how you are.' He took a step back from the bed and a rather too cheery nurse approached and took hold of Hannah's hand.

'Hello, Hannah, how are you feeling?'

'Groggy. My head's pounding and my neck's stiff. I'm in a lot of pain too.'

'That's to be expected, when the doctor's seen you we can look at increasing the pain meds. You took quite a battering in the accident, there are a few cuts and bruises on your face and head but they'll heal.' As she spoke the nurse took Hannah's blood pressure and placed something like a bulldog clip onto her finger.

'All good.' The nurse smiled. 'Doctor will be round soon but try to rest. We can always wake you again when he comes.' As she moved away from the bed Mike followed, and when they were out of Hannah's earshot they exchanged a few whispered words.

'What was all that about?' Hannah asked when Mike returned to her side.

'Nothing. Look, I'll ring the kids to let them know you're awake. Rest if you can, I won't be long.'

'Why do they need to know I'm awake – how long have I been asleep?' She studied Mike's anxious expression, trying to read what was in his mind.

'You've been in an induced coma, love, for three days.'

'Three days! What day is it now – and why an induced coma?' Hannah's mind reeled – why did they keep people in an induced coma? She couldn't think straight and certainly didn't remember an accident.

'Shh, don't get yourself upset. I'll ring the kids and they can come in to see you this evening. They've been in a couple of times already, but now you're awake they'll be keen to come again.'

Before there was a chance to protest Mike had gone. Hannah closed her eyes and drifted back into sleep, exhausted.

'Do you want to tell her?' A man's quiet voice interrupted the sanctuary of slumber.

'I'd rather you did.' It was Mike. Hannah opened her eyes wondering if the children were with him. They weren't and the curtains were drawn around her bed.

'Tell me what?' She looked at the solemn faces of her husband and the man beside him, presumably a doctor, and panic gripped her.

'Hello, Hannah.' The doctor smiled. 'I'm Dr Singh. I think

your husband explained that you've been in an accident?' She nodded, willing him to get to the point. 'Well, your car was pretty badly damaged and the firemen had no alternative but to cut you out of the wreckage. When you arrived here, you'd lost a lot of blood and the damage to your right leg was severe. Surgery was the only option and I'm afraid there was no way we could save your leg.'

Hannah's chest tightened as if someone was pressing down on her and hysteria threatened to take over. Struggling to sit up and look down at her legs, she lacked the strength to lift her head and pain shot through her body. The doctor put his hand on her shoulder and Mike held her arm.

'No!' She pushed against them. Hannah couldn't believe it, she wanted to shout that they must be wrong but her voice wouldn't come, the words were strangled in sobs. Was this doctor really telling her they'd cut off her leg?

'We amputated below your knee which is the best possible outcome we could manage, so in time you'll be able to have a prosthetic limb fitted which will mean you'll be able to walk.' The man said the words as if it was good news, as if she should be grateful.

'I want to see it,' Hannah managed to say.

'Perhaps it's best not to–' Mike began but she cut him off.

'I want to see!' She was emphatic, the panic turning rapidly to anger. The doctor motioned to the nurse hovering in the background who came to the top of the bed and helped Hannah to lift her head and shoulders.

'It's dressed, of course,' said the doctor, as he calmly pulled the covers back. Hannah stared down at the huge mass of bandages where her right leg should have been. A plastic tube protruded from the bandages, draining into a bag beside the bed and a catheter was between her legs; it was so ugly – so final.

A sound escaped from somewhere deep inside her, a

muffled sob or gasp, when she really wanted to shout and scream. Hannah struggled to breathe and tears blurred her vision as the nurse gently laid her back down.

'I know it's a shock,' the doctor continued, 'but in time your body will adjust and prosthetic limbs are amazing these days. I'll leave you to talk with your husband and if you have any questions I'll be back later this afternoon.' He turned and left, followed by the nurse, as if they couldn't wait to get out of there. Having imparted their awful news, completed their difficult task, only Mike remained. He looked bewildered and awkward.

'My leg!' Hannah cried bitterly. The reality of what she'd seen for herself was almost too painful to bear. Her husband's arms were suddenly around her and she clung to him, sobbing, feeling Mike's own tears warm against her face.

'I know, I know, it'll be all right …' he repeated.

Hollow words, Hannah thought, how could it be all right ever again?

A few minutes later a nurse peered through the curtains. 'I thought you might like this.' She carried a cup of tea and placed it on the table beside the bed, a cure for all ills. 'Do you need anything else?'

Hannah sniffed and shook her head and as Mike stepped back the nurse checked the drips, touching and adjusting them very deliberately. 'This is the pain medication which you can self-administer, see?' She showed Hannah the button to press which would release the morphine into her arm. 'How bad is the pain, on a scale of one to ten?'

'Nine, ten, I don't know …' Hannah sobbed.

The nurse pressed the button for her and almost instantly Hannah felt the medication flowing through her body.

'It works pretty fast so don't use it too much. It's quite safe, you can't overdose on it, although too much might make you feel nauseous.' The nurse smiled; she looked so young, not much older than Kate. 'If you need anything just press the buzzer.' Her calm efficiency had the effect of settling Hannah down, or was it the morphine? The sobs eased and she gulped in a few deep breaths. Feeling quite light-headed she lay back on the pillows but a wave of nausea swept over her and she tried to reach for the bowl at the bottom of the bed. Mike grabbed it for her just in time and she retched, but there was nothing in her stomach. When the feeling passed, Hannah studied Mike. His face was pale; he'd never been any good around illness and she was surprised to find herself thinking how he would cope with her disability, rather than how *she* would.

'Do the children know?' she asked.

'Yes.' Mike didn't add anything to his answer, as if lost for words but the conversation was interrupted as the twins entered the hospital ward. Hannah forced a smile, pleased to see them yet numb from learning the extent of her injuries. She'd had less than an hour to get used to her loss.

Kate almost threw herself on top of her mother, tears flowing unchecked. 'Oh, Mum, I'm so glad you're all right – we thought we'd lost you!'

Hannah was grateful for the cage protecting her legs – or what was left of them. Sam stood quietly then bent to kiss his mother on the cheek when his sister moved away. He said nothing but reached for her hand and squeezed it briefly.

'How've you been coping without me?' Hannah asked, acting as if everything was normal while fearing it never would be again.

'Okay,' Sam offered unconvincingly.

'We've missed you, but we managed, and Dad says he's not going to be going away again for a while, so we'll all be around to help when you come home.' Kate smiled. Her words, meant as reassurance, brought a chill to Hannah's heart. How much help would she need from her family and how readily could she accept it? The caring role had always been hers, a role she loved. It was so wrong, so unfair, that her husband and children would have to look after her.

'I don't know how long I'll be in here,' Hannah explained, 'but the doctor talked about a prosthetic leg. Maybe I'll have it fitted when I come home?' She hadn't even considered the timescale of her recovery. Hannah desperately wanted to reassure her family, and possibly herself, that she wouldn't be a burden.

The conversation was strained and Hannah was visibly tiring. Finally, Mike decided it was time to go home. Almost as a second thought, he asked, 'Unless you'd like me to stay a little longer?'

'No, I think I need to sleep, but you'll all come again tomorrow won't you?'

'Count on it, Mum.' Kate spoke for them all before they kissed Hannah goodbye, leaving her alone with a legion of troubled thoughts running through her mind.

8

The amber liquid swirled around the glass in his hand. Enhanced by the winter sunshine its translucent colour mesmerised Joe as he studied the whisky. *'No alcohol with the painkillers,'* the doctor had emphasised, but what was the worst that could happen – it already had. He put the glass down on the coffee table where he could see it while deliberating whether or not to drink it.

After his neighbours had left the previous afternoon, Joe dragged himself wearily upstairs to remove his dirty clothes. It was such an effort and he could only manage to tug on his pyjamas rather than a fresh set of clothes; could he live in their comfort until he felt better? There was no longer a reason to get dressed.

Phil returned promptly at 6pm to take Liffey for a walk as promised. He carried a generous portion of Diane's casserole. Joe was sitting in the dark so Phil closed the curtains and turned on the light without comment then he put Liffey's harness on her and left.

Out of politeness, Joe attempted to eat the casserole while

Phil was out but ended up putting most of it into Liffey's bowl; she would enjoy it at least. Phil returned Liffey after half an hour and left his neighbour to rest. The remainder of the day dragged for Joe, one of many to be faced alone.

The following morning Diane arrived early to walk the dog again, and on her return made a pot of tea and toasted some bread for Joe. He noticed the concerned look on her face and although he appreciated her help, even making the effort to thank her was too much – how long would he feel so bereft?

By mid-morning, the tea and toast were cold and the whisky looked so much more inviting. The doorbell rang before Joe took the first sip and Phil called out to him, 'Are you ready, Joe?'

Ready for what? Joe wondered – then remembered – they were going to the coroner's office and the bank.

'Not dressed yet, mate?' Phil stated the obvious as he stood in the lounge doorway. 'Do you need a hand? I'm not as pretty as those hospital nurses but I'm happy to help.'

'Yes, thanks.' Joe stood and trudged upstairs, followed by his friend who was doing his best to pretend things were normal and tactfully didn't mention the cold tea or the far-too-early glass of whisky.

Outside, the cold air stung Joe's face. Strangely it made him feel somewhat better, and having a purpose took his mind off the horror of the accident and its distressing consequences. Their first stop was the coroner's office, where he presented the medical certificate from the hospital and after a reasonable wait received an interim death certificate. Next, they moved on to the bank where Alison's personal account was frozen until probate was granted on the will.

Phil appeared to understand what needed to be done and took the lead, for which Joe was grateful. There was so much to think about when all he wanted to do was to get back home, see his dog, and feel the weight of the glass of whisky in his hand. He imagined the feeling of the liquid in his throat, warm and comforting.

'We wondered if you wanted us to take you to see Alison's mother this afternoon, or is it too soon?' Phil asked.

'I suppose I should, but she's the last person I want to see. You must think me awful but we never really hit it off and I don't think I can face her grief on top of mine.'

'Yeah, I understand. Let us know when you feel up to it and we'll come with you. It might make the visit easier.'

'Thanks, another day perhaps. I'll ring her later this afternoon although I can't tell her a date for the funeral yet, who knows what she'll have to say on that score.' It wasn't a conversation he was looking forward to.

Liffey greeted Joe with her usual enthusiasm on his return which was more than welcome in his present state of mind. He let her out into the garden and then fed her before returning to the kitchen where he picked up a slice of the cold toast and ate it, all the while glancing at the glass of whisky where he'd left it.

In his heart Joe knew that if he gave in and drank the golden liquid, it would bring only temporary relief, so with great determination, he picked up the cold tea instead and put it in the microwave to reheat. Drinking it with the other slice of toast at least took away the light-headedness he was beginning to feel.

Joe was aware he needed to be sensible – Alison wouldn't want him to go to pieces and would be the first one to tell him he must go on living. Finishing the tea and toast he went back into the lounge and lay down on the sofa where he closed his eyes and soon fell into a deep sleep.

Joe didn't know how long he slept until the sound of the doorbell woke him. Opening the door he found a young police constable shivering on the porch.

'Mr Parker? I'd like to ask you some questions about the road traffic accident you were involved in recently.'

Joe invited the constable inside out of the bitter wind, which was blowing more snow into drifts at the side of the road.

The young officer shuffled his feet on the doormat and coughed. 'I'm sorry for your loss and I know this is a difficult time for you, but I'm sure you understand that we need to move ahead quickly with our investigation.'

Joe led the way to the lounge thinking that the constable probably didn't want to be there any more than Joe wanted to be in this position.

When they were seated, the officer took out a notebook and asked if Joe could describe everything he remembered.

'It's still a bit of a blur. The weather was bloody awful, rather like today but even colder with rain pelting down and almost freezing as it touched the road.' He squeezed his eyes shut for a moment as he recalled the worst day of his life. 'We were on the motorway with the traffic moving steadily as we approached a junction, then suddenly a Ford Focus appeared from the slip road, spun 180 degrees and its rear end crashed into a lorry on the motorway.'

Joe wracked his brain to think of something else to say but could remember very little else. 'I tried to brake but the brakes couldn't grip the icy road and my car skidded too. There was no way I could avoid crashing straight into the front of her car. Is she one of those who died?'

'No, the driver of the Ford Focus is still in hospital. And what happened once you were stationary?' The constable was scribbling everything down.

'We felt something crash into us from behind but with the windscreen shattered and the airbag I couldn't see what was happening outside the car ... and my wife, she was unconscious, I was focussed on her.' For an instant Joe was back in the car calling Alison's name with no response. His eyes became moist as he swallowed hard to prevent himself from breaking down.

'I'm sorry, Mr Parker; I understand how distressing this must be. Did you feel the impact from any other vehicles at all?'

'Yes, we seemed to be jolted several times, but I don't remember exactly how many.'

'Well, if you think of anything else, would you give me a ring?' The officer handed him a card.

'It wasn't anyone's fault, was it? I mean, it was the ice that caused the accident, surely?'

'It appears so, but as with all RTAs, we have to investigate and there'll be a coroner's hearing too when you'll probably be called as a witness. We'll keep you updated with the investigation and thanks for your help.'

When the constable left, Joe thought of several things he should have asked, like how many cars were involved and how many people were injured, but he'd have to wait, probably until the inquest. *One more thing to endure alone*, he thought.

Joe was in somewhat of a daze but could put it off no longer; he picked up the telephone and tapped in his mother-in-law's number.

'About time too!' was the angry greeting. 'My only daughter dies and you don't phone me until three days later!'

'Ethel, I've been in hospital myself with a broken collarbone – and she wasn't only your daughter, she was my wife.' Joe was tempted to slam the phone down but tried to exercise a degree of patience, if only for Ali's sake.

'Well, how do you think I've felt not knowing what had happened to her, and you not answering the phone?' His mother-in-law always looked at everything from her perspective, how it would affect her, never mind anyone else.

'I did ask the chaplain in the hospital to let you know. Didn't he send a policeman round to tell you?'

'He did, and what an awful way to hear such news.' Ethel sniffed, clearly disappointed with Joe, a sentiment which was pretty much par for the course. 'So who's going to look after me now? I'm nearly out of milk – can you fetch some round?'

'Ethel, I've just told you, I have a broken collarbone. The car's off the road, too, although I won't be able to drive for a few weeks anyway. One of the reasons I rang was to let you know that I can't arrange a funeral until after the coroner's inquest. I don't know how long it will be but I'll let you know as soon as I do.'

'Perhaps you should insist they get on with it! It's not right, my poor girl not even getting laid to rest. Who do they think they are?'

Joe had expected this reaction and sighed. 'There's nothing we can do to hurry the process and it's only right that they investigate the accident. Two others lost their lives that day as well as Alison, we'll just have to be patient.'

'And what do I do in the meantime?' Ethel was back to thinking of herself again.

'You'll have to ring social services and ask about getting some help, I know Alison talked to you about it before.'

'But I'll have to pay them!'

Impatience simmered inside him – it wasn't as if the old lady couldn't afford to pay for her care – money was no problem, except that she didn't like to spend it. 'I can't see any other way for now,' he said. Joe had always suspected the old lady was more competent than she appeared, but Ethel Forester liked to be waited on – Alison was a saint to have put up with her mother's demands for so many years.

He ended the call quickly; if he stayed on the line much longer he'd almost certainly have said something he would later regret. Ethel was hardly reacting like a grieving mother but he'd try to be civil for Alison's sake. Ethel could make her own care arrangements; she was more than capable of doing so.

9

Ten days in the hospital seemed like an eternity to Hannah even though she'd been in a coma for three of them. Each day dragged by with nothing to look forward to other than visits from her family and, if she was honest, even they were something of a strain. Yet the idea of going home simultaneously delighted and terrified her; at least in the hospital there was help on hand, embarrassing though it was, but the thought of having to ask Mike or Kate to help her onto the toilet was awful.

Hannah hadn't yet had a proper shower – something else for which she'd require help, as with dressing and other mundane tasks normally taken for granted.

A physiotherapist came to see her each day, encouraging Hannah to exercise her good leg and what was left of her right at least three times a day.

'It's important to keep the muscles supple,' the physio explained. 'When you're fitted with a prosthetic leg you'll need to be able to move your thigh as normal so we can't let the muscles atrophy; it'll cause problems later on.' The girl was good at her job and Hannah liked her although each movement proved exhausting. The physiotherapist was always ready to answer questions and seemed to understand the emotional side of the injury as well as the physical.

The first time Hannah's dressing was changed and she saw the full extent of her loss, she was horrified and felt quite nauseous. The angry wound was like nothing she'd ever seen and was made all the more shocking because the swollen ugly mass of flesh she was confronted with was her own body.

After the nurse re-dressed the leg and Hannah was once more alone, she'd cried softly for almost an hour, turned towards the wall so the other patients in the room wouldn't see. Even now the shock remained, easing only slightly. One of the nurses explained that what she was experiencing was a process of grieving – she'd lost a vital part of her body and needed time to mourn, to come to terms with it.

Understanding this made things a little easier and Hannah didn't feel so selfish when she was suddenly struck by a bout of defeatism. However, she needed to work through these emotions and often experienced anger as well as an overwhelming sadness and loss. Hannah tried her best not to show how raw these feelings were, particularly to her family. When they visited, she appeared cheerful, but it was an act, a façade. She hadn't yet reached the stage of feeling 'lucky' like many considered she was to still be alive.

During the first police interview Hannah could tell them nothing about the accident and probably learned more from the young police constable than he did from her. Since then and from various other sources, she'd pieced together some of the facts which her brain had blanked out entirely.

It appeared Hannah's car had been the first to lose control on the ice. It skidded down the slip road, spun at an angle of 180 degrees and hit the rear of an articulated lorry on the motorway. With these second-hand accounts Hannah gathered that the carnage of the accident was severe which was puzzling as she was convinced she wouldn't have been going at any great speed especially in such awful weather conditions. Hannah was always a cautious driver.

However, the gradient on the slip road was fairly steep so perhaps it was the domino effect of the collision which made the consequences so devastating. In addition, Hannah learned that when the lorry driver became aware of what was happening, he braked suddenly, a natural reaction, but one which caused his vehicle to skid towards Hannah's car and exacerbate the impact with it.

The first car to hit Hannah's held two passengers and one of them, a woman, died at the scene. Another woman and a teenage boy were killed as their vehicles lost control, slamming into the mangled wreckage, entirely at the mercy of the ice on the roads.

Remembering nothing at all was troubling Hannah. The doctors tried to be encouraging and said her memory may return but worrying about it could give the opposite effect. The niggling doubt in Hannah's mind was whether or not she could have prevented the accident, or worse still, could she have done something to cause this catastrophic event. Such thoughts troubled Hannah's days and nights, doing nothing to lift her mood.

The swelling on Hannah's leg went down considerably during her stay in hospital. To her, it still looked grotesque, yet perversely she was compelled to look each time the dressing was changed. The drain had been removed and the doctor was pleased with the healing process.

Something Hannah found difficult was hearing her leg referred to as a 'stump'. She knew it was only a word yet such an ugly word, and there seemed no alternative, no sanitised medical term to make the reality more acceptable. The physiotherapist referred to her stump when she talked about how the prosthetic leg would fit, and the doctors used the term when they discussed how the wound was healing. It was something she'd have to get used to but Hannah determinedly avoided using it herself, instead saying 'bad leg' when it was necessary to refer to it.

After a week Hannah was coping with much milder painkillers, generally only paracetamol with occasional ibuprofen. One thing she learned was that the phenomenon of 'phantom pains' was an authentic and distressing fact. At times she couldn't sleep because of the 'pain' in her missing limb, or an itch, which was equally frustrating. Tossing and turning at night, Hannah would grasp at the space where her leg should be, exasperated at the irrational but real sensation. When the 'pain' became unbearable, Amitriptyline, a muscle relaxant, or Gabapentin, helped to alleviate the symptoms.

After the first few days, physio was no longer conducted on her bed and Hannah was wheeled to the hospital gym to use the parallel bars to help her stand. She was introduced to crutches and it soon became clear it would take time to master using them. Hannah was afraid of falling and damaging her leg further even though there was always someone close by to help if she toppled.

Going to the gym was at least a change of scenery and she met other amputees, many who were day patients and at different stages of recovery to herself and with whom she could compare notes and amazingly, even laugh.

A man who attended as an outpatient and had already been fitted with a prosthetic leg told Hannah how he'd fallen from his bed. 'When I sat up, I simply forgot I only had one leg and, silly sod that I am, set off on the missing leg and ended up flat on my face!' He was laughing about it and Hannah found herself joining in. The physio said most patients did this at least once. Perhaps Hannah would one day see the funny side of losing her leg. Maybe there was hope – but she'd have to work hard to find it.

One of the most challenging issues for Hannah to accept was her children's reaction. Sam was unusually quiet during their visits, clearly unsure what to say to his mother, which was to be expected for a seventeen-year-old boy. Kate was almost too gushing, probably trying to compensate for her brother's silence by filling the void with endless chatter.

Mike's reaction was somewhere in between. When the children were there, Mike made an effort to talk, but when there was just the two of them, he lapsed into an almost moody silence; it was as if neither of them could think of anything to say. Hannah suspected Mike was worried about how they'd cope when she was discharged.

'The physio said I'll be able to manage the stairs on my bottom,' Hannah attempted to assure him. 'And using crutches and a wheelchair in the house shouldn't be too much of a problem.' It had been disappointing to learn that it would be several weeks before a prosthetic leg could be fitted. In her ignorance of such matters, Hannah assumed it would be a process of getting one to fit – perhaps even before she left the hospital.

Unfortunately, it proved to be a much more complicated process and measurements couldn't be taken until her leg had reduced to its normal size. Nevertheless, Hannah attempted to encourage Mike. 'The time will soon pass until I get fitted with a leg and then, who knows, I'll probably be as good as new!'

Mike simply nodded, which didn't make her feel any better. Hannah wished he'd be more positive; perhaps say how much he was missing her and encourage her in the little achievements she'd already made. Instead, Mike gave the distinct impression that he was dreading Hannah leaving the hospital, which worried her as much as the practical issues with which she'd have to cope.

On day eleven (Hannah counted religiously) the doctor declared she was fit to go home the following morning and her care would be transferred to a district nurse who would call at their home daily. Again, mixed feelings invaded Hannah's mind. On the positive side, there would be more chance to rest at home; the hospital was always busy and often noisy, even at night, and Hannah did get unbelievably tired. But what if she fell when no one was there, or the pain became unbearable? She also hated the thought of being a burden to her family yet she'd clearly need some help.

When the family arrived later, Hannah told them what the doctor had said.

'That's great, Mum!' Kate seemed genuinely happy and Sam smiled broadly.

Mike frowned. 'Isn't it a bit soon?'

'They wouldn't let me go if they thought I wasn't ready and the district nurse will call every day,' Hannah almost snapped back at him, suspecting perhaps Mike didn't actually want her home, but hoping he was simply concerned for her.

'Right.' He switched into practical mode. 'They said I can take some time off work when I need to, so I'll take it from tomorrow and come to get you in the morning.'

Hannah hoped the children didn't pick up on the cool atmosphere between their parents. For many, this kind of situation would strengthen a relationship – but for them it appeared to be working in quite the opposite way – an invisible wedge seemed to be prising them even further apart than they'd been of late.

'I've made a decision, Mum,' Kate announced with a nervous smile. 'I've decided not to go to university but to stay at home to look after you instead!'

'What?' Hannah couldn't believe what she'd just heard. 'You're not serious, are you?'

'Yeah, of course I am! You're far more important than uni and maybe I can get a part-time job and be around the rest of the time to look after you.'

'But I'm not going to be a complete invalid. I'll get a prosthetic leg in a few weeks and if I get away with it, I'll be fine. You won't need to look after me!' Hannah reacted rather too quickly and saw tears welling in her daughter's eyes. For many years, Kate's ambition in life had been to train as a journalist, and now she was prepared to throw it all away to care for her mother. Hannah was touched and proud, yet simultaneously horrified that she might be an obstacle to her daughter's aspirations.

'Oh, Kate love, I'm sorry. I'm grateful for your concern but the last thing I want is for you to give up university. I love you for even thinking about it, but it's not what I want for you, it wouldn't be right.' She reached out to her daughter and Kate fell into her mother's arms and released the tears she'd so far held back. It struck Hannah just how badly this had affected her children.

As she held her daughter, Sam shuffled closer too and put his arms around her and his sister, tears in his eyes. They were all grieving, grief manifested in different ways. The children were barely mature enough to deal with what had happened to their mother and as yet the full implications were unknown.

While Hannah comforted her children, Mike sat to the side, an observer, seemingly unsure of what to do or say, which didn't go unnoticed by Hannah and only added to her worries.

What did the future hold for them, and did she want to know?

10

Hannah struggled from the car into the house on her crutches. She'd mastered the technique in the hospital but the corridors there were straight and smooth, negotiating the garden gate and crazy-paved path to her house was akin to an obstacle course. Concentrating hard on her balance and remembering what she'd been taught in physio, Hannah was still afraid she might fall flat on her face.

The next door's curtains twitched – Rachel was watching – another reason not to fall over or look inept at such a simple task as getting to the front door.

Rachel had visited the hospital on only one occasion, bringing with her a welcome bundle of luxury toiletries, magazines and Hannah's favourite chocolates. She stayed for a short time, seeing how tired her friend was, and left insisting Hannah should let Mike know if she needed anything else. Grateful for Rachel's sensitivity Hannah looked forward to seeing her again now she was home.

Once inside she was greeted enthusiastically by Kate and almost as keenly by Sam. It was Saturday and they were all at home together, an unusual occurrence for the Graham family.

'I'll make tea!' Kate bounded off to the kitchen to perform a task usually undertaken by her mother. Hannah was again struck by how different life would be, certainly until her prosthetic leg was fitted. Wearily she sat on the sofa with her legs up; it was essential to keep her stump elevated and move it as much as possible.

Mike sat facing her on an armchair and Sam hovered, looking unsure of his role.

'Come here.' Hannah smiled at her son who dutifully perched on the sofa beside her. She took his hand. 'I know it's difficult for you, love, but we'll get through this, I promise!' Sam leaned on his mother's shoulder and allowed her to hold him for a few brief moments. She could tell he was close to tears but knowing Sam he wouldn't give way easily.

Suddenly he sat up. 'Rachel's coming up the path.' He'd spotted their neighbour over his mother's shoulder and pulled away from her.

'Huh, she hasn't wasted any time!' Mike moaned.

'Why shouldn't she come round?'

'She's hardly given you a chance to settle in.'

'Rachel's my friend, Mike, and I'd like to see her. Could you open the door, please?'

With a scowl, Mike rose to let their neighbour in and then made an excuse to go out, mumbling something about getting a takeaway and leaving his wife wondering at his rudeness.

'How are you, Hannah?' Rachel asked, bending carefully to hug her. Kate brought in a tray of tea and then she and Sam tactfully left the two women alone.

'If I'm honest, awful!' Hannah's eyes welled with tears. 'I've been feeling sorry for myself but at the same time trying to make Mike and the kids feel better about this whole thing. It's so hard on the kids and Mike avoids any serious conversation – and don't pretend you hadn't noticed his mood. I want to help them cope but it's a two-way street, surely?'

'Damn right it is! And you have every justification for indulging in a bloody pity party if you want to. It's been a nightmare and it'll take more than just a few days to adjust. Mike will come round and as for Kate and Sam, well they're young and resilient, they'll cope.'

'Kate's talking about not going to university – but I can't let her do that – this is my problem. I don't want it to affect her future!'

'Then tell her. Look, none of you know how this is going to impact your family life – it's early days but there's no reason why you can't resume a normal life when your leg's healed and you get a prosthetic one, which I presume is the aim?'

'Yes, although I don't know how I'll cope.' Hannah noticed Rachel's eyes straying to where her right leg should be. Others had done the same when she was in the hospital, sitting in a chair – an almost morbid curiosity as if they wanted to make sure her leg really was gone.

'It's ugly, isn't it? And such an ugly name too, a "stump". I wake up every morning thinking I'm whole, and then I remember I no longer have a leg, just a *stump*.' Hannah bit her bottom lip, not wanting to break down.

'But you're still Hannah, the same woman, wife and mother and my friend. Nothing can change that.' Rachel's eyes glistened.

'Thanks, Rachel, you're a brick.'

'Now listen, I don't want to become a nuisance, always popping in and suchlike, but I want you to promise me you'll ring if I can do anything, or if you simply need a shoulder to cry on, okay?'

Hannah nodded and smiled. Rachel was so easy to talk to and her earthy common sense was precisely what she needed now. Although there was almost ten years' age difference between the two women, they'd been friends for years, opposites in many ways but always there for each other.

Rachel was the younger of the two, a fiery, opinionated woman, married to Frank, a quiet, unassuming man who adored her. Their relationship often puzzled Hannah who rarely managed to get an entire sentence of conversation from Frank whereas his wife offered an opinion on every subject, whether it was asked for or not. Still, they appeared to get on well, each doing their own thing yet utterly devoted to each other.

Hannah knew that Rachel's long-term plan for her life was well defined and almost set in stone. It consisted of promotion at work by the time she was thirty, her first child at thirty-two and their second and final child at thirty-five. Frank was content to let her make the decisions, nor did he appear to mind the time she devoted to her wide circle of friends, including Hannah, for which she was extremely grateful, especially now.

Frank had his football, a season ticket holder at Manchester City, he never missed a match, home or away and still played in a local Sunday league. Rachel often said she would never dare ask her husband to choose between her and football, and Hannah hoped she was joking.

The sound of Mike's car in the drive prompted Rachel to say goodbye. 'Remember, any time,' she repeated as she left.

11

Mike carried a bundle of fish and chips under his arm and called the children downstairs to help set a tray. They ate on their knees; it was easier than attempting to get Hannah to the table. After they'd eaten, while the twins cleared away, she tried to talk to Mike.

'I'm going to have to make some effort to move around the house. If you could bring the wheelchair in from the car, perhaps I could sit in it and get from here into the kitchen and the downstairs toilet, but I might need some help when I'm in there, all right?'

Mike frowned. 'Do you want me to help with that sort of thing – won't Kate do it?'

'If you don't want to …' Hannah was horrified. Did she disgust her husband so much? If he couldn't bear the thought of helping her with such a basic task, how on earth would she manage? 'It won't be forever, you know! When I'm fitted with a new leg I'll be almost fully independent again.' Mike's expression was unreadable, a mixture of disgust and pity, but whether for himself or his wife, Hannah couldn't tell. 'What is it, Mike, what's wrong?'

'Oh, nothing's wrong, everything's bloody hunky-dory!'
His sarcasm shocked her. He waved his hand towards her leg.
'It's all this, everything! Damn it, Hannah – why did it have to
happen?'

'How should I know? I didn't ask to lose my leg, you
know, and I like it even less than you do!' Their voices were
raised. Hannah couldn't understand why her husband was so
angry with her. Did he blame her for the accident?

Mike looked at her for a moment and then grabbed his
jacket. 'I'm going out!' he shouted and headed for the door.

'Yes, go on then. Run away while you can be sure I can't
run after you!' As she heard the door slam, Hannah regretted
her last comment. She'd barely been home two hours and they
were arguing already. Perhaps it was to be expected. Things
hadn't been right between them for a while, a situation she'd
ignored. Typical ostrich syndrome, head in the sand as usual.

Now it would be twice as bad with the extra pressure of her
injury and Hannah was disappointed, she'd at least hoped for a
bit of compassion from her husband. If he couldn't show any
now, what did that tell her about the state of their marriage and
their long-term future?

Kate appeared in the doorway. 'What's going on, Mum?'

'Nothing for you to worry about. Your dad and I are both a
bit stressed, love, that's all. It's going to take some getting used
to, I'm afraid.'

'Dad shouldn't be shouting at you. It's the last thing you
need!'

'Please don't worry about it; he's just letting off steam. It'll
blow over soon.' Hannah was reassuring herself as much as
Kate. Mike's attitude was concerning – was there something
else going on with him, she wondered.

Hannah was exhausted – a permanent state of affairs at the
moment – but she needed to use the toilet and had no option
other than to ask Kate for help. Her daughter was less

embarrassed than she'd expected and soon Hannah was back on the sofa with her eyes closed, hoping Mike would return shortly with an apology which she'd gladly reciprocate. They'd have to address the tension between them, and soon too, but perhaps if she slept now she'd be better able to cope when he did arrive home.

The next thing Hannah was aware of was the car pulling into the drive. Mike was home. Kate and Sam were both in their rooms, which would allow her to talk with her husband in privacy. She was almost holding her breath as he opened the front door.

'There's a policeman just arriving.' Mike scowled. Any discussion would have to wait until later.

The same young constable who'd interviewed Hannah in the hospital stepped into the lounge. 'Hello, Mrs Graham, how are you?'

'Better for being home, thank you.' She shuffled into a more upright position.

'Good, well, er, I'm sorry to trouble you again and especially over the weekend but it's just to find out if you've remembered anything about the accident yet?'

'No, I'm afraid it's still a blank. I've been trying not to worry about it in the hope my memory will return soon. Is it a problem?'

'Only because you're not going to be in a position to be a witness to what happened, and your vehicle seems to be key to the whole accident. If you're unable to help us we'll have to rely on the evidence of the others involved, although we'd rather have the complete picture. The coroner's hearing has been set for Tuesday 20th February. You'll be getting written confirmation of the date and will be expected to attend. Is that possible?' The young man looked automatically at Hannah's leg and quickly away again, clearly embarrassed by the lapse.

Hannah turned to Mike for an answer; she was in his hands as far as being able to get anywhere was concerned.

'Yes, we'll be able to attend. It seems very soon, is that usual?' he asked.

'The coroner tries to hold the inquest as soon as possible, as the, er, the families of the victims aren't able to arrange the funerals until it's over.'

'Of course, how terribly difficult for them.' Hannah's heart went out to those grieving. Waiting for the funeral must only serve to compound their grief.

'Can you give us an idea of what will happen? It's all very new to us. Is it similar to a trial?' Mike asked.

'No, it's much less formal and without a jury or anything. The purpose is to look at all the evidence and hear from the witnesses. Then the coroner can decide the cause of the accident and subsequent deaths, and rule on his findings.'

Mike then asked the question to which both he and Hannah dreaded the answer. 'Have you any idea what the ruling might be?'

'Well, he'll be looking for possible culpability – what, or possibly who, caused the accident – and depending on his verdict, charges might follow.' The constable looked down to his feet, clearly uncomfortable but his feelings weren't anything like as raw as Hannah's. She listened in silence, each one of the constable's words reverberating in her mind, fear and uncertainty growing unchecked. If only she could remember!

Mike pushed the young officer a little further. 'What kind of charges?'

'At the very worst, manslaughter, or possibly causing death by reckless driving, or driving without due care and attention. Look, I wouldn't worry about it. Everyone's agreed that the conditions were appalling and the coroner may decide on a no-fault verdict. But if you do remember anything which could help us, please get in touch as soon as possible. Otherwise, I'll see you at the hearing.'

The officer couldn't get out of the house quickly enough. His words offered very little in the way of comfort to Hannah, who was quite pale, her head spinning with the implications of what she'd just heard. Wriggling uncomfortably in her seat she waited for Mike to return from seeing their visitor out, wondering how he would react to the news.

'Are you sure you don't remember anything about the accident?' His scowl was almost frightening and his words shocked Hannah.

She was horrified that he needed to ask such a question. 'Of course not. Do you think I'm lying?'

'No … but perhaps you don't want to remember?'

'Mike! You think I caused the accident, don't you? How could you?'

'If you can't remember, how can you be sure you didn't cause it? I don't mean intentionally, but perhaps you tried to speed up a little to get onto the motorway, you know you're always last minute for work, always in a hurry?'

'Mike! I wouldn't do such a thing! I've never taken risks while driving and you know it.' She stared at her husband with wide disbelieving eyes. 'You don't think I could be charged with anything, do you?'

Hannah was scared. Remembering suddenly took on a whole new importance, and her head ached with the fear that she might somehow be to blame for the accident. To have had a hand in the deaths of three innocent people was an unbearable thought and tears rolled down her face as her mind raced ahead to the worst possible scenario.

Hannah might be facing a manslaughter charge!

Could things possibly get any worse?

12

Liffey barked as the letters plopped through the letter box and landed on the doormat. Joe collected them, sorting them into two piles, one for recycling and the other to be opened. Mostly they were the usual bills and circulars and a few more sympathy cards. One envelope which looked somewhat official, he opened first. Staring at the heading he read the words 'Coroner's Inquest' and quickly scanned the page for the date, 20th February 2018. It was another phase in the process and one he'd be glad to get over, not least because then he would be able to arrange Alison's funeral. The last thing he could do for her.

Previously Joe hadn't had cause to consider what was associated with death. Ironically, it was also the worst possible time to absorb and understand everything that needed to be done. Having his arm in a sling and the constant pain of his injury didn't help either – it came as a surprise how difficult it was to manage even the simplest task with one arm incapacitated. Propping the letter on the mantelshelf behind the clock, Joe sighed. Whatever the coroner's findings, they wouldn't bring Alison back.

Joe was due at the hospital for an X-ray. If his bones were not healing he faced the prospect of surgery and a metal plate being fitted, an unpleasant thought which went some way to ensuring he looked after himself and didn't attempt to use his injured arm. Phil again volunteered a lift. He and Diane were a true godsend and Joe didn't know how he'd have coped without their practical help and support.

As Phil drove through the early morning traffic, Joe found himself flinching each time another car approached, unnecessarily so, as Phil was an excellent driver. Joe supposed it was a natural reaction to having been in a serious accident and only hoped it wouldn't affect his confidence when he could get back behind the wheel. At one point, Joe suddenly braced himself, convinced they were about to collide with another car.

Phil glanced at his passenger. 'You all right, mate?'

'Yes, sorry. I'm a bit of a nervous passenger these days.'

Phil nodded in understanding.

The appointment was early and Joe didn't have long to wait. He was quickly seen in the X-ray department and then directed to a waiting room. After only fifteen minutes, Joe was called in and received the good news that the X-ray confirmed the bone was knitting together well and the doctor was pleased with his progress.

'We'll do another X-ray in two weeks and if things are still improving you can start physio and begin to use the arm again. Keep resting it until then and if it's still looking good, I think we can forget about surgery.' The doctor smiled, delighted to be offering good news. It was such a relief to Joe – the last thing he wanted was for his injury to need further treatment – his caution over the last couple of weeks had paid off.

After the appointment, he insisted on buying Phil a coffee in the hospital café, it was the least he could do to repay his friend.

'I got a letter this morning about the inquest, it's on the 20th of this month,' he told Phil.

'Do you want me to come with you or is it just for family?'

'If you can, that would be great, I don't have much in the way of family, only a brother who I haven't had contact with for years and the mother-in-law from hell – doesn't that just describe what a sad life I have?'

'Ah, but you have friends.' Phil grinned.

'Yes I have, and you've proved to be the best, Phil. I'm so grateful to you and Diane. I don't know how I'd have coped without you.'

'We've done no more than anyone else would do. You know we were fond of Alison and we miss her too. I still can't believe what happened sometimes and I think you're coping remarkably well. If it were Diane who'd gone, I'd be a complete wreck.'

'Most of the time I function on autopilot,' Joe admitted. 'Night-times are the worst, it's almost unbearable and I don't sleep too well and dread the early hours, but daylight comes eventually and I've got Liffey to keep me going. Sounds silly, doesn't it, she's just a dog but sometimes I think she understands what I'm going through.'

'Sure she does! Dogs are sensitive creatures – she'll pick up on your feelings. And Liffey must miss Alison too.'

'Yes, I think she does.'

They were silent for a few moments until Phil asked when Joe would be returning to work.

'I'd like to get back as soon as possible but it's not an option yet with this collarbone. Perhaps after the inquest and the next visit here. I'll discuss it with the doctor then, see what he thinks.'

Phil nodded. 'It might be good to focus on something else and I know you enjoy your work. The company seems to have been quite flexible with you.'

'Yes they have. One of the directors rang almost as soon as

I got home from the hospital and told me to take as much time as I needed. They sent a lovely bouquet too – Ali would have loved them.' Joe's voice cracked – he was in danger of breaking down – a definite no-no in public. Sniffing, Joe raised his eyes and forced himself to smile. 'You're right. It'll do me good to get back to work, a routine, you know.'

'Diane and I have been discussing it and we want you to know that we'll be happy to keep on helping with Liffey's care. We can see to her during the day, or at least Diane will when I'm at work and she can come to us any time you're not at home if you like. We love having her, so it could be a kind of dog-share?'

Joe hadn't even considered such practicalities, but Liffey, although happy to be left alone sometimes, was used to Ali being around most days. Phil was right, it wouldn't be fair to leave her alone all day each weekday.

Joe's eyes misted with tears. 'You're so kind and it'll be perfect for Liffey. I've not given much thought to the logistics of returning to work apart from wondering when I'll be able to drive again. It's going to take some getting used to not having Ali around to think of all these practicalities for me.'

Once back home and after an enthusiastic welcome from his dog, Joe sat down, rubbing Liffey's ears thoughtfully as he considered his future. The house was still full of Alison; he hadn't even thought about sorting through her possessions, although he knew he'd have to at some point.

After feeding Liffey, Joe ventured upstairs, turning automatically towards the spare bedroom his wife had used as her sewing room. He'd purposely not entered this room since the accident and almost as soon as he opened the door, he wished he hadn't.

It was a good-sized, bright room, full of natural light from windows on two elevations, but the room was saturated with Alison's presence, as if she'd left it only a moment earlier to return anytime soon. Her sewing machine, perched on the work table, still held fabric under the presser foot where she'd left it the night before she died, too tired to put it away and assuming she'd pick up her task the following evening.

Joe touched the fabric cushion covers, her latest project, a change from the endless soft toys she made to sell at fundraising events for the hospice.

The faint smell of one of Alison's scented candles lingered in the air. She knew Joe disliked them, so used them only in her own space – sweet pea, mimosa, lilac and tea rose – her favourite fragrances. On the shelves were her most loved books – all eight of the Brontë sisters' novels, the complete works of Jane Austen and Daphne du Maurier, together with some of her favourite contemporary authors, Kate Morton and Victoria Hislop.

Alison's trinkets crowded the windowsill, she loved small decorative boxes and tiny milk jugs. Joe picked one of them up, an enamelled silver box with a filigree lid she'd bought in Madeira a few years earlier. He remembered the look of delight on her face at her find and the excitement of securing it at a bargain price.

Photographs decorated almost the whole of one wall, mostly pictures of Liffey, others of the fantastic holidays they'd shared. The sudden ache in Joe's heart made him realise again how much he missed his wife and how she would love to have had children's photographs in her room – images of their children – who had never been born.

Joe was suddenly aware of Liffey in the room with him, sniffing in every corner and giving a little whine. How could a dog comprehend the finality of death, but then how could he?

Man and dog sat together in the small room, surrounded by memories and Alison's simple treasures until dusk wrapped itself around them and Liffey whined, this time for something as basic as a need to go into the garden.

13

February 20th was a wild blustery morning. Hannah hadn't slept the night before; she hadn't slept well since the visit from the police constable signalled the possibility of charges relating to the accident. Until then it wasn't something she'd even considered, assuming it was the atrocious weather conditions which were to blame.

Now her thought processes had changed. The possibility of being somehow culpable haunted her waking hours and prevented restful sleep. Mike refused to discuss it, arguing the stupidity of anticipating something which might never happen. As she hadn't told the children of her fears, it was almost impossible to get Mike alone to talk about anything serious, a situation which Hannah found increasingly frustrating.

Rachel was the only one she could confide in. Rachel, who felt angry on her behalf at the very suggestion that Hannah had caused the accident and who could conceivably stand up and give the coroner a piece of her unique wisdom if he should conclude Hannah was in any way to blame. Grateful for her friend's loyal and fierce support, Hannah wished Mike was equally protective.

Hannah asked Kate and Sam not to attend the inquest, afraid of what they might hear. The ban didn't go down well and eventually she'd almost pleaded with them not to go, getting so upset that they felt obliged to agree. If they'd known Rachel was attending, they might have protested louder.

Hannah set off with Mike to discover her fate with echoes of the constable's words playing on a loop through her mind. *Manslaughter – driving without due care and attention.* A wheelchair had become her usual aid to mobility for any distance, as crutches still proved clumsy unless on even ground. She'd had the first measurements taken for a prosthetic leg and dearly hoped to be upright and walking again soon.

Still embarrassed by her missing limb, Hannah chose to cover herself with a blanket whenever they went out – something Mike was quick to assist with when he lifted her from the car. She was glad of the blanket's warmth today as she shivered with cold and nerves. If she'd still had two legs, Hannah didn't think they would have held her up that morning; she was trembling and felt sick, anticipating the worst possible outcome.

The coroner's court was in a wing of the town hall which they entered through the disabled entrance at the side of the impressive Victorian building. The entrance hall they found themselves in was vast, its high ceiling throwing back echoes of visitors' shoes, or in Hannah's case, the squeaking of wheels. Rachel met them inside. She'd taken a couple of hours off work to attend and squeezed her friend's hand in greeting, comfort Hannah badly needed. An usher showed them the way, holding doors open for Mike to circumnavigate the obstacles of such an old building.

As they entered the room, which was smaller and more comfortable than Hannah expected, people turned to look at her. Some smiled weakly, sympathetically even, and others turned away either from apathy or embarrassment, although they couldn't possibly know who she was. Hannah didn't know them, or whether they'd been involved in the accident or were relatives of those who had. The inquest was an open meeting.

Gazing around the room, Hannah noticed most of the faces were grim with red eyes – from weeping or lack of sleep it was impossible to tell but Hannah felt the weight of each person's sorrow as if she was guilty, the one who'd caused such far-reaching tragedy. Mike sat beside her, his face reflecting the solemnity of everyone else, while Rachel sat on his other side and leaned over to whisper encouragement.

'Well, it's not going to be easy but it'll soon be over!' She smiled, hopeful.

Or will it be just beginning? Hannah thought, blinking back the tears welling in her eyes.

The first surprise was when the coroner introduced herself as a doctor; Hannah expected a judge, or perhaps a magistrate. Dr Eloise Phillips sat at a small table with several files in front of her and started by acknowledging the tragedy of the accident and offering her condolences. She moved swiftly on to state the purpose of the hearing – to rule on the cause of death of the three people who'd lost their lives. Everyone seemed to appreciate her clarity as she outlined the procedure and what was expected of each witness. The second surprise for Hannah was that anyone in the assembly could ask questions.

The first witness to be called was the police traffic officer who'd had the misfortune to arrive first on the scene. Hannah thought he looked so young, not much older than Sam, as he stood nervously at a small podium beside the coroner's table and spoke from his notes.

He informed the gathering that eleven vehicles had been involved in the collision, one of the worst he'd personally ever attended. This was the first of many facts the assembled group would hear, most of them detailed and distressing. It wasn't long before muffled sobs could be heard throughout the room. Hannah's face was wet with silent tears as she listened to the full horrors of the event of which she still had no recollection.

Clearly, the inquest would not be over quickly, and due to the upsetting nature of much of the evidence, the coroner halted the proceedings frequently for short breaks. Some left the room to compose themselves, while others stayed in their seats and whispered together with grim faces.

A distraught Hannah turned to Mike. 'I don't think I can do this.'

'You don't have a choice, but your evidence will be short, seeing as how you can't remember anything.' Hannah couldn't believe his words. Mike sounded as if he didn't fully believe her and his attitude was almost one of annoyance or even sarcasm.

Rachel was more encouraging. 'You'll be fine, the coroner's sympathetic.' But Hannah still wanted to get up and flee from the room – if only she could walk.

Some of the most harrowing evidence to listen to was from those who'd lost loved ones in the accident. The father of the teenage boy who died was driving him to the orthodontist. Tears rolled down the man's cheeks as he relived the horror of that morning.

Joe Parker, whose wife also died on that fateful day, gave evidence next. He described how his Range Rover had crashed into Hannah's car, the brakes ineffective on the packed ice. His evidence was perhaps the most compelling and comforting to Hannah, who thought there was something familiar about his face. When the coroner asked his opinion of the speed her Ford Focus was travelling at the time, his reply was probably the most crucial of all the witness statements.

'It can't have been more than ten miles an hour, probably much less. She was on the slip road – the ice on the roads caused the accident, not anyone speeding. The poor woman didn't stand a chance when her car skidded. The conditions were atrocious, we were all at the weather's mercy.'

After hearing all the other evidence, this man's seemed the most powerful. Joe Parker's vehicle was the second to collide and his wife was killed instantly, yet he spoke fairly and with compassion for Hannah's helplessness, which went a long way to relieving some of the anxiety she felt.

When Hannah was eventually called to give evidence, Mike pushed her to the podium and left the chair at its side. The coroner asked for her name and address and to confirm her car make and registration number. Hannah trembled as she answered, her voice barely a whisper, but the coroner was sympathetic and went on to ask if she had any recollection of the accident. The negative answer was expected and Dr Phillips thanked Hannah for attending and said she could return to her seat. Rachel offered a huge 'told you so' smile as Mike pushed her back and all three felt an enormous sense of relief that this had been all which was required of her.

The hearing broke late for lunch with all the evidence having been presented and only a few questions asked by individuals in the gathering, which Dr Phillips, or the police officer, answered capably and to the apparent satisfaction of the enquirers. The coroner explained that she would sum up and present her findings when they returned from lunch. It appeared the main business of the day was finished.

Rachel and Mike spent the lunch break offering each other reassurance that the inquest went much better than they'd hoped, but Hannah still nursed a sickening knot of unease in her stomach. She desperately needed to hear the coroner say the words that she had not been at fault.

Her wish was granted after the lunch break. Dr Phillips again offered condolences to those who'd lost loved ones and went on to announce that after consultation with the police, she was satisfied the incident was a no-fault accident and therefore those who lost their lives – Mary Simpson, Alison Jane Parker and Keiron Gary Lang – would be recorded as victims of accidental death.

As a low murmur of whispers swept around the room, the coroner thanked everyone for giving their time in attending and wished them well as she stood to leave the room. Mike was the next one to jump up, steering Hannah to the door they'd entered as if in a hurry to get out, but his wife wasn't complaining. On the contrary, she felt emotionally drained, exhausted by the whole experience and although she'd have liked to thank the man who'd spoken on her behalf, Hannah was happy to leave. Rachel was dashing back to work, having been away much longer than anticipated.

'I'll pop in to see how you are this evening.' She hugged her friend. 'I'm so glad they've seen reason!'

Hannah smiled her thanks and allowed Mike to lift her into the car. As yet he hadn't offered an opinion and his expression was impassive as he started to drive home.

Unable to bear the heavy silence, Hannah asked, 'What do you think, Mike?'

'Yes, a good result; it seems to have been just an unfortunate accident.' His reply wasn't what she'd hoped to hear and lacked something, although she didn't quite know what. Conviction perhaps?

The journey home continued in silence and once inside, Hannah asked Mike to help her upstairs to bed where she pulled the quilt up to her chin and fell into a deep dreamless sleep.

14

To have no memory of the accident – was it a blessing or a curse? Joe wondered when he arrived home from the coroner's inquest. Hannah Graham seemed to be in another world, fearful and possibly still in shock at the loss of her leg. It had been a gruelling day for everyone involved. The father of Keiron Lang was clearly a broken man. Most of those in attendance had paid a high price for that fateful day, for venturing out in weather conditions which were atrocious at best.

Joe was content with the verdict even if Ethel was not. As he helped his mother-in-law into a taxi after the hearing she was still grumbling, muttering how someone should be held accountable for the death of her daughter. The black look she gave him suggested Joe was that 'someone' and he instinctively wanted to counter her argument by suggesting that if Ethel hadn't been so demanding and insistent on her daughter attending her, Alison would not have been with him in the car.

You could argue the toss about it all day; if the motorway had been closed, if the slip road had been gritted, if the Ford

Focus had set off two minutes later, if he hadn't had toast for breakfast. *If* was such a sad, lonely word and a senseless one too. No one could have foreseen what would happen or they would all have stayed safely cocooned at home.

Joe's next hurdle was to get through the funeral. Having to wait until after the inquest to arrange Alison's funeral only added to his distress. He'd made an appointment with the undertaker for the following morning – the event was permanently on his mind – one he dreaded. The final goodbye to his beloved wife was drawing closer.

A few well-meaning people suggested that Joe would feel better after the funeral and life would return to some semblance of normality, but did he really want it to? It would be a relief to get rid of the terrible pain he felt at his loss, but not at the expense of forgetting his wife – Joe would never want to do that – there must be a compromise somewhere. Other people managed grief every day, why did he find it so hard?

The undertaker arrived promptly at 9.30am the next day. He was a thin, wiry man with a large hooked nose and a black suit which was shiny in places and had seen better days. However, the man's manner was an improvement on his appearance and more condolences were offered before he talked Joe through the logistics of a funeral. An hour later the undertaker left after a date was tentatively fixed in ten days.

Joe was happy to leave most of the details to the undertaker. It was grim enough to think about your wife in a coffin without deciding what kind of wood it would be made of and if there should be decorative brass handles. Perhaps he'd pay more in the end, but he agreed to the undertaker taking over – arranging the flowers, the notification in the paper and other minor details which were too painful for Joe to even think of. The man oozed efficiency and when he left his client he promised to be in touch with confirmation of the date, or an alternative, the following day.

As it happened, Joe didn't have to wait until the following day as the undertaker rang later in the afternoon to confirm the date and time. So what next, Joe wondered? Perhaps he should ring Ethel and maybe visit Phil and Diane after tea; they'd know what he should be doing.

'Hello, Ethel. I've just had a visit from the undertaker and I'm ringing to let you know the funeral details – it's a week on Thursday at 10am at the crematorium but the funeral car will pick you up and bring you here first.'

Ethel tutted her disapproval. '10am is far too early for me. You'll have to change it.'

'I can't. It was the only time available; the crematorium's a busy place and the next slot would have been in another week.' Joe was amazed that his mother-in-law should expect the funeral to be arranged around her needs when she was more than capable of being up and ready in good time.

'How many cars have you booked?' she snapped.

'Just one and the hearse, there's only you and me, Ethel.'

'Well, I hope it's their best. I don't want to be seen doing things on the cheap.'

Joe took a deep breath to contain his anger. 'You aren't *doing things,* Ethel, I am and it's more than adequate. Alison would have hated extravagance; she'd rather give the money away.'

'And flowers, you've ordered flowers?'

'I have. It will all be tasteful, Ethel, I promise.' Joe was tired and ended the call telling his mother-in-law he'd let her know the exact arrangements nearer the time.

15

Alison's funeral was every bit as dire as Joe expected it would be. The weather at least had improved, with rising temperatures melting the snow almost as swiftly as it had arrived; just too late to spare Alison's life. The large turnout was something of a surprise to Joe, although it shouldn't have been, his wife was loved by everyone she knew. Neighbours and friends mingled with a few distant relatives, mainly Alison's cousins, whom he hardly knew.

There were many other faces Joe didn't recognise – staff from the local hospice where she volunteered each week, and a group from Ali's Pilates class all shook his hand offering the customary platitudes. Joe went through the motions, his aching sorrow clamped down somewhere deep inside as he thanked people for coming, playing the host for as long as he must.

Alison's mother clung to his arm throughout the service and committal, her grief well aired for all to see. If it hadn't been for his neighbour, Diane, taking her from him at the hotel afterwards, Joe would probably have told her to stop snivelling, or worse. Diane was a saint and made sure the old lady received the attention she desired and plenty to eat, leaving Joe free to accept condolences from the other mourners.

To Joe's surprise his brother, David, made the journey to the funeral with his wife, Pam, a woman he'd met on only a few occasions and never quite taken to. They were staying at a Travelodge nearby for a couple of days and expressed a desire to see Joe the next day, 'to catch up,' they said. He could have done without the bother, yet as they'd made an effort to come, he felt obliged to invite them round to the house the following morning.

The hotel provided a pretty standard finger buffet – sandwiches with the crusts cut off, sausage rolls, quiche, pork pies and assorted nuts and crisps. Joe watched as people talked and laughed as at any other social occasion. He felt remote – an outsider looking in on something which didn't concern him at all. His head felt as if it would burst from the cocktail of emotions he experienced – sorrow, regret, anger and frustration – but there was nothing he could do; his wife was gone and he was left behind to carry on alone.

Joe longed for the hands of the clock to move more swiftly so he could get home to be alone, just him and his dog. But the time ticked by unhurriedly, not caring what he wanted. He couldn't, didn't want to believe these people were assembled because Alison was dead, his beautiful Ali, who no longer walked, breathed and laughed on this earth. How he wished he'd died with her. Joe wanted no part of a world without his wife but he knew he must speak to these people and listen to their anecdotes of times spent with Alison. He continued to play the part. You can still exist without living, can't you?

Although much slower than Joe wished, the time did pass and finally he found himself at home, driven by Phil and Diane who had kindly already taken Ethel home. Joe had had a whisky and a pint at the hotel and was tired, bone-weary, so after letting Liffey out into the garden he lay down on the sofa, careful not to jar his arm, and fell into a deep sleep.

The sound of the doorbell broke into his rest, it had turned dark outside whilst he slept and Phil stood on the doorstep waiting to take the dog out for her evening walk.

'Bearing up, mate?' he asked.

'Yes, glad it's all over to be honest and you've been brilliant, Phil. Thanks for looking after Ethel. I honestly couldn't take her misery and complaints today.'

'No problem. Diane was the one to see to her mostly. It was good to see your brother. I managed to have a brief word with him. Will he be staying on?'

'Apparently yes – they've booked in at the Travelodge and are coming round tomorrow. We've never been close, I'm amazed they came.'

'Family can surprise you and rally round at difficult times. The company might be just what you need.' Phil meant well but Joe wasn't looking forward to seeing David and Pam. It was something else to make an effort for.

After Phil walked and returned Liffey, Joe made a token gesture at tidying up, difficult with only one arm, and then mindlessly watched a programme on television about shrinking ice masses before deciding on an early night.

The tears flowed again in the darkness of his bedroom, the bed so vast and empty without Ali. Was it better to think about her or to try not to? Joe was at a loss to know. Liffey, sensing his distress, jumped up on the bed beside him and licked his good arm. He spoke to her, confiding how much he missed Alison and how he dreaded each new day without her.

The dog nuzzled into his side, understanding that all was not well, and eventually, they both slept.

16

David and Pam arrived on the doorstep at 10am with broad smiles as they marched into the lounge.

David slapped Joe on the back. 'How are you today, brother? It's such a lovely morning after all the snow.' His question and apparent upbeat mood was so totally incongruent to the whole situation that it sparked anger in Joe who replied sharply,

'How do you think I bloody feel? I buried my wife yesterday!'

Pam's mouth dropped open and David replied, 'There's no need to snap. I was only trying to cheer you up.'

'Sorry, but please don't expect me to be "cheered up" so easily. I can't do it.' Joe sat down and his visitors followed suit. 'It's too soon, David, and yesterday was a strain, a nightmare. I feel washed out today.'

'Right, well, how about a cup of tea and we can have a chat then?'

Joe wished his brother would go away and take his grinning wife with him but he dutifully rose and went into the kitchen to make tea. Pam followed a minute or two later, asking if she could help, although by the way she gazed around, Joe thought she was simply keen to see more of the house.

'Yes, please, if you could carry the tray for me?' Clearly with his sling, he couldn't perform even such a simple task.

'Oh, yes of course!' Pam picked up the tray and carried it into the lounge where she placed it on the glass coffee table. David had occupied himself by scrutinising the group of photographs Ali had arranged on an occasional table at the window. They were mainly of the couple in various holiday destinations, the usual tourist backgrounds.

'Seems you had some pretty good holidays?' David remarked, a brittle note of envy in his voice.

Joe could think of nothing to say. Was his brother trying to emphasise that he would have no more holidays with Alison?

'Well, that's the advantage of not having kids, I suppose,' David continued. 'Mind you, even without them we could never afford anything other than a caravan at Margate.' He chuckled as if he'd made a hilarious joke.

Advantage! Joe could have screamed at his brother. He'd almost forgotten how insensitive David could be and how jealous he always was of their lifestyle. As Joe handed out tea and biscuits, he bit his tongue to stop being rude and desperately hoped they wouldn't stay long.

Pam continued her appraisal of the house until she noticed Joe watching her. 'So will you be selling this place?' she asked bluntly. 'It's far too big for one, surely? How many bedrooms is it, three or four?'

'I've no plans for doing any such thing. This is where I feel closest to Ali. All my memories are here.'

'Yes, but you have to be sensible and think of the future,' David chipped in.

'Good grief, man. The funeral was only yesterday! I'm getting by one day at a time, never mind thinking of the future!' Even though this was his brother, Joe thought they had some nerve to turn up, after previously showing no interest, and start advising him on what he should and shouldn't be doing.

'But you must have thought about it and there'll be a hefty insurance payment due, no doubt. Then, afterwards, you'll be able to buy a nice little bungalow somewhere, or perhaps one of those new executive apartments – they're perfect for single people.'

Joe was stunned. 'I haven't thought about anything of the sort and why the sudden interest, David? Why turn up after never even returning our Christmas cards for the past few years? What is it you want?'

'We don't want anything!' Outrage echoed in David's voice. 'We're family and just want to comfort you, to help if we can. Alison was a lovely woman but she's gone now – you've got to be practical.'

'Perhaps we are family, David, but you clearly don't know me so why should you think you can advise me now?' Joe was furious with his insensitive meddling brother and was almost on the point of asking him to leave when David saved him the trouble and stood up.

'There's no need to be so rude. I can see we've caught you on a bad day so we'll go now and give you a little space. I'll be in touch when you've had time to get used to your new situation. Goodbye, Joe.' The pair hurried from the lounge and let themselves out of the front door.

Joe was both angry and bemused. It was clear that his brother felt no genuine concern for him. Even as children they were never close. He remembered David as a greedy, sly boy who liked nothing more than to get Joe into trouble with their parents, a more than frequent occurrence. Why then did he suddenly decide to play the concerned elder brother now, unless there was something in it for himself? Joe shuddered as he began to clear away the half-drunk cups of tea.

17

E ach time Joe thought about his brother over the next few
days, he did so with incredulity, a feeling which was to
be heightened when Joe picked up the post from the mat one
morning – a handwritten envelope. He let Liffey into the
garden then sat down and tore open the envelope. It was from
David.

Dear Joe,
I know we didn't part on the best of terms after Alison's
funeral and we would like to remedy this situation if possible.

Joe shuffled uncomfortably in the chair; his brother's letter
sounded like something from a civil servant.

We considered another visit to see you but the truth of the
matter is that we cannot afford the petrol; things are so bad
at the moment we may even have to sell the car. I didn't want
to trouble you with my problems while you have so many of
your own, but we are family and I hope you can see your way
to helping us out of a difficult situation.

It's not as if we've been extravagant but were badly advised regarding recent investments and all our savings have been lost. Pam's been quite unwell with the stress and we find ourselves with credit card debts in excess of our modest income.

As your situation has changed and with compensation and possibly life insurance coming your way, we wondered if you would consider a loan to enable us to pay off the credit company. £15,000 should cover it. It's not as if your needs will be significant now you're alone, and as I say, we are family and should stick together in times of trouble.

Needless to say, if there is anything we can do for you, we will be happy to help.

Your brother,

David

Joe stared again at the words he'd just read. David's letter, incredible though it was, went some way to explaining his brother's interest in any plans Joe might have regarding selling the house and any possible insurance payouts. To casually suggest a figure of £15,000 as if it was nothing was unbelievable and Joe didn't know what to think. His immediate response was to say a resounding 'no' but perhaps it would be better to wait until he calmed down before making any decision. He knew only too well that would have been Alison's sage advice.

Joe remembered a time shortly after he and Alison were married when David asked for a loan of £500, quite a substantial sum in those days. His initial response was to refuse, they didn't have much spare cash themselves after buying their first home but his new young wife persuaded him to give David the money – their happiness was overflowing and she was only too ready to share it. Joe did as she asked but the money was never repaid, contributing to the somewhat cool relationship between the brothers over the years. Joe had little doubt the loan David was currently asking for would also not be repaid.

Putting the letter aside and in an attempt to take his mind off it, Joe set about making a meal. Slowly he'd been increasing his efforts at domesticity, knowing he couldn't rely on Phil and Diane's generosity forever and anticipating becoming more capable as his shoulder healed. His arm was moving without much pain now, although he was still cautious, not wishing to hamper recovery but impatient to drive again and get back to work. The following day Joe was again to attend the hospital for another X-ray which he hoped would confirm the improvement he felt.

By 10.30 the following morning, Joe was in the X-ray department waiting his turn. As Phil was working, Joe had travelled by taxi and would ring for another one to take him home after his appointment.

The radiologist worked quickly and efficiently until soon Joe was in another waiting area, in line to see the consultant.

'Excellent,' was the verdict and both men smiled.

'Can I leave the sling off?' Joe asked.

'Yes but don't overdo things. It might be a good idea to wear the sling for an hour or two at some point during the day to give your arm a rest but if you're sensible and guided by how you feel, I think we can discharge you today.'

'Am I okay to drive?'

'Again, if you feel comfortable and don't drive for lengthy periods you should be fine. Will you be going back to work?'

'Yes, I've not been under any pressure but I think I'm ready to return.'

The doctor frowned. 'Is it heavy work?'

'No, I work for an engineering company as a manager in the finance department, nothing physically strenuous.'

'Good. If you do experience any problems don't hesitate to

come back. You needn't go to your GP for a referral, just ring my secretary and I'll be happy to see you again.' The doctor smiled and offered his hand to Joe who shook it and thanked him before leaving the room.

Walking down the corridor Joe's first thought was a strange, reflex notion – he'd ring Alison to tell her he'd been discharged. As the idea flashed through his mind the absurdity of it hit him hard. How long would it take to accept that she was gone?

Reaching the main outpatient reception, Joe pulled out his phone to ring for a taxi but looking across the waiting area he noticed a familiar face – the woman from the inquest, Hannah Graham. She smiled in recognition.

Joe put his phone away and walked over to speak to her. 'Hello. I suppose it's not a surprise to be seeing you here.' He smiled.

'No, it isn't, is it? And you've lost your sling.'

'Yes. I've had the okay and an honourable discharge!'

'Was it your arm which was broken?' Hannah asked.

'No, my collarbone.'

'Right, it's not my arm either.' Hannah smiled.

'I thought not.' He returned her smile. There was no embarrassment between them and as Joe asked if he could sit down beside her, Hannah nodded.

'Actually, I'm glad to see you as I wanted to thank you for what you said on my behalf at the inquest.'

'I only related what happened.' Joe was surprised by her thanks. 'I told the police the same beforehand. There's no doubt in my mind – the accident couldn't have been avoided.'

'That's such a generous thing to say, especially as you came off so much worse than me.' Hannah lowered her eyes, seemingly embarrassed by the honesty of their conversation.

'My wife would have been the first to say that these things happen, 'ifs' and 'buts' don't alter anything. I don't know if you would call it fate, but whatever, it happened and can't be undone.'

'I did feel there were others there who were looking for someone to blame.' Hannah spoke softly.

'Yes, there always are – it's a sad fact of life.' Joe immediately thought of Ethel. 'It must be difficult for you, not being able to remember, but I do, and there was nothing you could have done to avoid the collision.' Joe spoke emphatically and with meaning – it was important to him that this woman believed him.

'Thank you.' Hannah blinked away the tears welling in her eyes.

'So, are you here for a check-up?' Joe asked to change the subject.

'Actually I'm here for a fitting for a prosthetic leg. I'm hoping I might be able to walk out of here today.'

'How wonderful. I hope it goes well. Are you on your own?'

'My husband brought me and I said I'd ring for him to come and get me when I'm finished. You never know how long these appointments are going to take.'

Joe nodded.

'How are you managing, Mr Parker?' Her question was direct but strangely not intrusive.

'Not too good at times, but they tell me it will get better, and my name's Joe.'

'And I'm Hannah. Do you have family to help you?'

Joe thought this woman was quite blunt, but he rather appreciated it. Most people pussyfooted around him.

'No, we didn't have children but I have great neighbours – and a dog!'

'Oh, a dog can be a wonderful comfort! I always wanted a dog but my husband said the twins were enough.' Hannah and Joe smiled.

'Look, I'll be going in soon.' A porter was looking in Hannah's direction. 'But I'm glad we've met and I've had a chance to thank you properly.'

'That's okay,' he said, 'And I hope the fitting goes well.'

The porter wheeled her away.

What a strange encounter, Joe thought, as he rang for a taxi. Hannah was refreshingly open and honest; perhaps their shared experience removed the necessity for polite conversation and small talk. He was glad they'd met.

18

With the passing weeks, Hannah slowly began to accept her 'stump', although the very word itself still didn't sit well with her and she continued to avoid using it. Her choice of clothing was now invariably trousers and even at home she kept her legs covered. Mike seemed to prefer her to do so and on the odd occasion he'd walked into the bathroom and found her in some degree of undress, he'd turned abruptly and left the room leaving Hannah disheartened. Evidently her husband was repulsed by her appearance and at a time when the comfort of physical contact would be more than welcome, it seemed it was to be denied.

Hannah expected a period of adjustment but Mike clearly had no inclination to make the slightest attempt to improve their relationship or give his wife the comfort and encouragement she craved. Perhaps he still blamed her. If only she could remember what had happened the morning of the accident.

On the day of the fitting for her prosthetic leg the chance meeting with Joe Parker was a welcome bright spot. Their conversation was surprisingly candid and he reiterated the words he'd spoken at the coroner's inquest, emphasising his opinion that no one was responsible for the accident. Those words went a long way to lifting Hannah's mood. If Joe thought she wasn't to blame, and he was there and could remember what happened, then maybe Hannah was tormenting herself for nothing.

Yet the only thing which could offer her the absolute certainty she yearned for would be to remember for herself. Until then there would always be a doubt in her mind, a nagging worry that she'd been responsible for the wretched event which ruined so many lives. Hannah prayed silently each day for her memory to return, terrified it might not, but almost equally afraid that it might.

Tanya Wainwright was the specialist nurse practitioner who Hannah was due to see that morning. At her last visit after confirming that the swelling had gone down sufficiently to measure for the prosthetic leg, Tanya had wrapped Hannah's stump in cling film and applied a plaster cast after taking numerous measurements and carefully marking out the area around the patella. The nurse had been meticulous in her duties and now smiled at her patient as she entered the room.

'Hi, how are you today, Hannah?'

'Fine thanks – a little apprehensive perhaps.'

'About anything in particular?'

'I'm just scared I might not get used to wearing the leg,' Hannah admitted.

'That's quite natural, most people feel the same but I can assure you it won't be long before it seems as if the leg's wearing you!' Tanya manoeuvred her patient to where she wanted her to be and then took out the new leg. 'Want to have a look?' She placed it in Hannah's hands. Hannah was initially surprised at how heavy it felt although she'd been told it would weigh approximately the same as her other leg, for balance.

She'd had the choice of a solid, natural design or a metal

rod with a foot on the bottom, the sort of thing athletes seemed to favour these days, a robotic-looking device which some people thought of as 'cool'. Hannah's choice was the natural option and now as she examined it a thrill ran through her at the thought of being able to walk again.

'This is your first prosthesis, one you can wear in the shower if you like and once you feel confident on it we'll make another with a softer covering to appear more like flesh. We can make the next one with an articulated ankle too, if you'd prefer, which will make wearing heels possible, although not stilettos I'm afraid. So, let's see how this fits.'

Tanya gave Hannah a cotton sock to pull over her stump then placed the specially fitted 'liner' inside the leg and asked her patient to place the stump into the prosthesis. It felt strange, though not uncomfortable and as Hannah moved her legs around, still seated, she grinned at the nurse who returned her smile. 'Great, now let's try standing up.'

They were only a few steps from the parallel bars and Tanya supported her arm while she tried to move the prosthesis.

'It feels like it's going to drop off.' Hannah frowned.

'If it's loose you can try putting another sock on. I've had patients who've worn six or seven socks to get the fit right and some days you'll need more than others.'

Hannah grabbed the bars, positioned herself in between them and walked. Balancing rather shakily on her prosthesis, she put her good leg forward then dragged the prosthesis up to meet it.

'Try to relax into the leg and you'll move more naturally. Stand still for a moment and bend your knees a few times to get used to the feel of it.' Tanya watched as Hannah tried to do as she suggested.

'I thought it would feel more like a real leg,' she moaned.

'Try walking to the end of the bars and then we'll sit down again.'

Once they were both seated, Tanya looked directly at Hannah and said, 'It's never going to feel like your real leg, Hannah, that's gone, but this will feel good in a surprisingly short time. First, your leg muscles need to get used to wearing it and then you'll have the confidence you need to relax and walk normally, which is one of the reasons we nagged you about exercising your stump in hospital. Once the muscles get used to wearing the leg they'll move automatically and you'll walk more naturally.'

'And I thought I'd be walking out of here today.' Hannah didn't know whether to laugh or cry.

'Goodness, no. You need to limit your time on the prosthesis initially, probably only a few minutes for the first few days to get used to wearing it. Even when it's more comfortable, don't overdo it. You'll probably be only too glad to get it off after wearing it for any length of time. Everyone's different and all I can say is to be guided by how you feel. If there's any soreness or chafing, don't persevere, let your stump recover and if you're worried about anything give me a ring. If I'm not available there's always someone here who can advise you or see you if need be. Now, let's have another try, shall we?'

This time knowing what to expect, Hannah stood and moved to the parallel bars unaided. After bending her knees a few more times, she walked the length of the bars with greater ease and finished the short distance with a smile on her face.

'Well done, you're getting used to it already!' Tanya grinned. The nurse then advised Hannah on other aids to help her around the home. Grip bars on doorways and the shower seemed sensible but Hannah was unsure whether she wanted her home to be 'adapted' in this way. It was more outward signs of her disability and she was almost certain Mike wouldn't like the idea.

With the prosthesis in its bag, Hannah again needed to rely on a porter to get to reception where she rang Mike to come and pick her up.

After half an hour he walked in, grimacing. 'What's gone wrong?'

'Nothing, I just need time to practise using it. Can we go home now please? I'm tired.'

Her husband offered no affection or encouragement and Hannah's mood sank. Would things ever get back to normal?

Kate and Sam were far more enthusiastic for their mother when they arrived home from college later in the afternoon. They examined the leg in turn and Hannah explained that this was just her first basic prosthesis and she'd eventually get another, possibly with an articulated ankle joint.

'Wow, so you'll be dancing again before we know it!' Kate joked.

'As if I ever could, you know I've never had a sense of rhythm.'

Kate was keen to see how the leg would fit, and even Sam wanted to stay around to watch. Hannah rolled up her trouser leg and pulled on one of the socks she'd been given to bring home and showed them how the liner fitted inside the leg and her stump dropped into it. She then stood up with Sam holding her lightly for balance and took a few tentative steps.

'Brilliant, Mum! Will you be able to wear it all day?'

'Not at first. I'll need to take it slowly to get used to it but I should be able to build up the time I can wear it and take it from there. You know, walk before I can run sort of thing? Maybe I can think about going back to work too.'

Hannah was delighted that her children showed an interest in her recovery. They accepted the situation far better than Mike; he'd barely looked at the prosthesis when she offered to show him, saying he needed to get back to work. Maybe when she was walking around he'd find it easier to cope.

This accident had significantly impacted all her family.

It was bound to take time for Mike to adjust, she reminded herself.

19

The death of a child is never easy. It's not the natural order of the world and leaves a void which can never be filled. Keiron Lang was just fifteen and an only child when he left behind his devastated parents, three grandparents and other extended family – all of whom loved Keiron dearly and would always feel the gaping hole left by his premature death. He was a young man so full of life and love, and touched the hearts of everyone he came into contact with, but it seemed he was only on loan to his family and for such a short time, far too short.

When Keiron was conceived in 2003, an extra chromosome in the baby's cells caused him to develop Down's syndrome – one of almost 800 babies born with Down's in England and Wales each year. It isn't an inherited condition, simply the result of a one-off genetic change in the sperm or egg at conception and can affect any pregnancy, although the older the mother, the greater the risk.

Cassie Lang was only twenty-eight when the test results in

early pregnancy flagged up the potential risk of giving birth to a baby with Down's and she was advised to have an amniocentesis test. Her response was immediate and negative. Cassie knew it was an invasive procedure involving risk to the baby as fluid was taken from the womb to be tested, but the risk wasn't Cassie's primary reason for refusing the test.

If her baby had Down's, it would make no difference to her and Alan, her husband. They'd planned this baby; he was made up of a small part of each of them and therefore loved and wanted from the moment of conception – even before. There was no way they would even consider an abortion therefore the test was unnecessary.

As their baby grew in Cassie's womb, so did his parents' love – unwavering, unshakable and strong. The birth was as exciting and memorable as every other birth and when Keiron was placed into his mother's arms for the first time her body flooded with love as she gazed into the tiny crumpled features of her perfect son. Down's syndrome would not define Keiron any more than having brown eyes would. His parents looked upon him as a gift from God.

There were whispers on the maternity ward and sympathetic looks. Cassie felt sorry for those other mothers. Was their perception of perfection the only criteria for a healthy child, for a happy, fulfilled family? The difficulties the Langs faced as parents in the years to come might not be so different or more challenging than those other parents faced. Who could predict what lay ahead or define a 'normal' child?

Keiron brought his parents fifteen years of joy. Fifteen years of laughter and sunshine, tears too, of course, but how can you appreciate the light without the darkness? Yet it wasn't nearly long enough – it wasn't what they expected or wanted and when Keiron Lang died in 2018, aged fifteen in a motorway car crash, Cassie and Alan Lang were devastated. A bright light in their home was snuffed out and they knew life would never be the same again.

Keiron's school had been closed for the third consecutive day due to the awful weather and the boy was bored. He loved school and grew frustrated and antsy when he couldn't attend. His parents had fought hard for his place at their local mainstream school where their son's achievements surpassed all expectations and Keiron became a popular hard-working pupil.

It was also the morning of his orthodontist appointment. Alan Lang considered cancelling this due to the atrocious weather, but relented to his son's pleadings and decided to go ahead with the appointment, to provide Keiron with some relief from yet another day confined to home.

Alan, a veterinary surgeon, had an evening surgery at his practice so being free that morning he elected to take his son to the appointment rather than letting Cassie drive in the snow. Alan would always regret his decision to attend the orthodontist, one which changed their lives and robbed them of their precious only child.

'If only' is a short vicious phrase which haunted Alan in the following weeks and months. Fatal motorway crashes happened to other people, didn't they? It was other people's children who died in such violent ways, wasn't it? *If only.*

The toughest thing for Alan to deal with was that he'd walked away from the accident with only slight grazing and a sprained wrist. Why couldn't he have sustained the more significant injuries and his son be spared? Surely Alan didn't deserve to come out of it with barely a scratch when Keiron had lost his life?

The emotional pain simply wasn't enough. Alan wanted to

feel physical pain too – he thought he deserved to feel it – he needed to feel it. He knew that Cassie, too, was haunted by *if only*. She'd told him over and over how she wished she'd stopped him and Keiron from going, or that she'd been with them, then it would have been her in the front seat and she might have survived the impact. Instead, she opted to stay at home and catch up with the ironing.

Alan knew Cassie regretted the decision, one which would haunt her forever. The couple comforted each other in the best way they could, but Keiron's laughing, loving, huge presence left an ache, an enormous vacuum in their lives, one which they had no idea how to fill.

The inquest was torture. Alan sat stiffly beside his wife, squeezing her hand while lost in thought and unable to offer her much in the way of comfort. Cassie's parents sat on her other side and Alan's widowed mother beside him. Not only were the family forced to confront their grief again and relive the accident, but they were also unwilling witnesses to the grief and pain of the others who'd been involved too. So many lives were brutally affected that day – the ice a savage instrument of destruction to many.

One witness told how he'd lost his wife of forty years – a mother of four and a grandmother to six. Another man sat stiffly, his face ashen, eyes dull and lifeless. Alan heard how he, too, had lost his wife that morning, and although appearing composed and speaking with clarity when it was his turn to give evidence, his face was taut and anxious.

The woman in the wheelchair had lost part of her leg and still had no memory of the accident itself. Alan was touched by an overwhelming empathy for all the victims and prayed silently that out of something so brutal and far-reaching, lessons might be learned and compassion would somehow blossom out of such incomprehensible tragedy.

After Alan gave evidence, he returned to his seat where his

vision blurred as images of his son filled his mind. Keiron had taught his parents so much in his short life. He loved unconditionally, cared for other people's feelings and possessed an all-consuming passion for animals.

Having grown up being fascinated by his father's work, Keiron attended the clinic with his dad whenever allowed. Then, from the age of seven, he 'collected' animals to care for on the family's small farm. Keiron had grown up with dogs and cats but wanted more, so when he found an injured owl, he nursed it back to health under his father's guidance.

The chickens came next, then an orphaned pygmy goat he named Biscuit, all extra work for Cassie but she was amazed at how hard Keiron was prepared to work too, even at such a young age. The farm outbuildings became home to any animals in need, and over the years even Keiron lost count of the number and variety of animals they'd fostered.

Alan was relieved to get outside when the inquest concluded. He and Cassie had talked much as the passing days took the accident further into the past, wedging unwelcome distance between them and Keiron. The couple wanted to do something significant to honour the memory of their son, something he'd approve of and which would make him proud. The last few weeks had been a period of painful, unproductive mourning and now they asked themselves what Keiron would have wanted. In the end the answer became clear, but the execution of their plan was to involve much hard work.

20

It was a difficult letter to write, yet Joe didn't want to ring and decided to reply in the same manner his brother had approached him. Initially he experienced anger at David's banal letter and insensitive request for a loan so soon after Alison's death. However, on reflection he felt a degree of sympathy for his elder brother. Joe's life must have seemed charmed compared to David's – until now. And he knew his brother had never achieved the success he felt he deserved.

In the past, Joe had perhaps shown little sympathy for the difficult situations he felt were of David's own making. Now he could almost hear Ali's voice urging compassion and reminding him that this was his brother, his only living relative. Joe intended refusing the loan and pointing out that there was no compensation, or life insurance as they assumed – but for Ali's sake he would let them down gently and leave the way open to maintain contact now they were again in touch. Perhaps when things were more settled he would send them a few thousand as a gift, but he'd not mention it for the time being.

After scrapping the first two attempts, Joe was happy with

his third reply and sealing the envelope he intended to post it straight away. The reason for venturing out on Saturday morning was to fulfil yet another difficult task, a duty he did not relish – visiting Ethel, Alison's mother. Now his arm was free of the sling, Joe could drive again and therefore had no valid reason to stay away, although he knew his mother-in-law would have plenty to say about his absence, most of which would be unpalatable. They'd spoken on the telephone on a few occasions and it was clear Ethel held expectations of her son-in-law which Joe was not able or willing to meet.

The insurance company hadn't quibbled about his claim and paid the full value of his written-off car promptly, enabling Joe to buy another. The purchase of a new car had always been a time of excitement but not this one, as with most other tasks there was little pleasure for him without Ali to share it.

The drive to his mother-in-law's was the first time he'd taken the same route as the morning of the crash, but Joe steeled himself to do it, reasoning that avoiding those roads would remind him every bit as much as taking them. The weather was thankfully unlike the last time, giving the route an entirely different quality.

Ethel Forester lived in a neat semi-detached bungalow, large enough for one and small enough to be easily maintained. Yet Ethel took no responsibility for any maintenance, having expected her daughter to run the home for her, which Alison had felt obliged to do. Joe chipped in with everyday practical jobs when necessary to take the burden off his wife but generally, Ali had been running two homes, typically without complaint.

Ethel's words of greeting didn't surprise Joe when he rang the bell and walked through the door. 'You're late.'

Glancing at his watch he retorted that it was only ten minutes after the time he'd agreed to be there. Ethel then launched into a list of grumbles she'd been storing up to get off her chest, finishing by presenting her son-in-law with a lengthy shopping list, assuming he would see to it immediately.

'Have you done anything about getting some regular help, Ethel?' Joe ignored the list she'd pushed at him with her bony gnarled fingers.

'And have you any idea how much they charge for the kind of help I need?' the old lady retorted.

'But what else do you spend your money on? You're always saying you never go out anywhere, so why not get someone in if you can't manage?'

'Well, now you're driving again you can come over to help me.' It was a statement rather than a request, one Joe anticipated and for which he'd prepared an answer.

'I'm going back to work on Monday and won't have the time to come over as Alison did. Keeping my own place will be more than enough for me, so I won't be driving over here regularly.' Joe might have felt a twinge of guilt if Ethel's sour expression hadn't grown even darker.

'A fine son-in-law you've turned out to be. I've just lost my only daughter and you say you don't want to help me!'

'I'm not saying I don't want to help and I will still visit you but with work and keeping up my home there simply won't be time for me to look after you.' He was trying to be fair but also firm. 'I can help with finding a suitable care company if you like. They can do almost anything, from shopping to cleaning and cooking.'

Ethel stared at him, a look of contempt on her face. Her eyes narrowed. 'If you'd been able to give Alison children then I'd have grandchildren to look after me!'

Joe was speechless; her words were like a slap in the face. When he composed himself, he tried to form a reply without getting angry.

'It was our dearest wish to have children as you well know

but it's hardly fair to say I couldn't give Ali children. We never went down the route of finding out whose *fault* it was.'

'Of course it was your fault – Alison was just too gracious to tell you!' The old woman spat the words at Joe.

'I told you, we never found out why we couldn't have children, and it's none of your business either.'

'Then how come she had a baby before she met you? So you see it *was* your fault. You're impotent; my Alison was perfectly capable of having a baby.'

Joe sat down, completely stunned and trembling with shock. He looked at the triumphant smirk on Ethel's face and any sympathy he'd ever felt for her deserted him.

'That's a vicious lie,' he said through clenched teeth. 'She would have told me …' Joe's eyes filled with tears, a weakness he didn't want his mother-in-law to witness.

She has to be lying; Alison wouldn't have kept something like that from me!

His mind swam with questions; he wanted to know if it was true yet didn't want this woman to say any more. Joe desperately needed to get out of her house but the desire to know won through.

'What happened to the baby?' he eventually asked, hoping it was all a cruel fabrication and he would catch her out in the lie.

'It only lived a few hours, a little girl. She had a weak heart.' Ethel appeared amused at Joe's discomfort. He stared at her in disbelief. How could she be so calculatingly cruel?

'Goodbye, Ethel.' Joe stood and walked to the door, his legs barely carrying him but his determination to get out of the woman's presence supplying the strength he needed.

'But what about my shopping?' he heard her calling after him as he slammed the door.

The drive home seemed interminable. Joe longed for the comfort of his own home, but most of all he longed for Alison to tell him her mother's words were nothing more than bitter vitriolic lies.

Parking in the drive, Joe went inside and straight to the kitchen where he poured himself a large whisky, took it into the lounge and sat down to drink it. Liffey jumped up on the sofa beside him, sensing his mood and they sat together in silence. Joe's mind raced through the past, searching for clues he might have missed – trying to decide if it was possible that Alison had had a baby she'd not told him about.

Ali was twenty-four when they married and Joe twenty-five. He'd only known her for three years so it was feasible that she could have had a baby before they met, but they didn't have secrets from each other, or so he thought until Ethel's hateful words shook his confidence. It was out of character for Alison not to tell him something so monumental; surely she'd have known he'd understand, whatever the circumstances.

For the rest of the day Joe was unsettled, his mind roiling with speculation as to why Alison would keep such a secret. The idea that Ethel was lying still hovered at the back of his mind, yet surely even she couldn't be so callous as to make something up to punish him for whatever sins she imagined he'd committed. Would the old woman stoop so low? Joe wondered if there was anyone he could ask, a friend of Ali's perhaps, someone who'd been close to her in the years before they'd met.

There was Carolyn, her old university friend who'd also been her bridesmaid, but she lived in Canada now; he could hardly contact her to ask about Alison's past. Remembering Carolyn brought a pang of guilt as he'd not thought to write and let her know of Ali's death and he should do so. Joe knew the two women occasionally communicated, usually by email so he'd have to search Ali's laptop for her address, but not now.

A long walk with Liffey was what he needed to clear his

mind and the dog certainly needed no persuasion. He'd send an email to Carolyn later when he was thinking straight and could form the right words, for now he needed the fresh air and exercise to empty his head of his mother-in-law's malicious revelation.

21

Eastleigh in Hampshire was voted number nine on the list of 'best places to live' in the UK in 2006 but as far as David and Pamela Parker were concerned it may as well have been the worst. A pretty town with a population of nearly 30,000, it held many attractions, not least being its situation in such a beautiful area of south-east England, on the river Itchen. But sadly, like all towns, there were areas which were run-down and where the housing was not so desirable.

In one such area, David and Pam rented a damp, pokey flat, the decor most probably the original from when the flat was built in the 1950s. The proximity of the railway lines ensured their sleep was broken with regularity and their relationship became strained as the couple constantly snapped at each other over the slightest little thing.

Life hadn't always been so unkind to David and Pam whose marriage had been punctuated with fluctuating fortunes. For several years until this most recent move, they'd lived in comfort in an exclusive apartment with a sea view, thirty miles away in Bournemouth. At the time, David held down a reasonably good job as a sales rep, with generous commission, a company car and other perks the couple enjoyed yet took for granted.

When the economy slowed and the company squeezed their employees to produce more sales for less reward, David stood his ground, demanding his salary be reinstated – such was his inflated opinion of his worth. He was fired on the spot, the company glad to be rid of even one employee.

For a while Pam sympathised, massaging his wounded ego until the weeks turned into months and the horizon remained empty of another job. Pam nagged, grumbling about their lack of money for the luxuries she'd come to expect in life and goading David for being an inadequate provider. When she eventually discovered that David had failed to pay the rent on their apartment and gambled away their meagre savings, Pam took control of their finances and the decision was made to leave the expensive area of Bournemouth and move to Eastleigh.

The move was hastened by the increasingly frequent visits of heavies from the loan company David had unwisely borrowed from, and the fact that the landlord was threatening eviction for non-payment of rent. Their new address was in reality a hiding place where they hoped not to be discovered.

David and Pam's reduced status and living conditions were far from desirable. They were safe but inconvenienced by being unable to take with them anything which wouldn't fit into their car. Most of the trappings of their former life were abandoned in their hasty departure.

When David received the letter from his brother telling him Alison had died in an accident, they both thought this could be the opportunity they'd been waiting for.

'There's bound to be compensation and Joe's always been the prudent one, so probably life insurance too.' David's thoughts were far from empathy for his brother.

Pam's permanently acerbic expression lifted and her

features grew quite animated as she pondered her husband's words. This was probably the moment their plan took root – initially nothing more sinister than an attempt to ingratiate themselves into Joe's favour in his time of need. They decided to attend the funeral.

His brother's reaction wasn't what David and Pam had expected. Instead of being welcomed they appeared to be an intrusion into Joe's grief rather than the antidote they assumed they'd be.

Pam expressed herself openly to David regarding his younger brother's behaviour after the debacle of a visit to Joe the day after the funeral. 'I can't believe how rude your brother was! After all the effort and expense we went to in trying to support him at this sad time.'

'He's always had a superior attitude even when we were kids. Being the youngest he was spoiled which has clearly affected his character – given him a sense of entitlement. He'll come round. I suppose it's a bit of a bad time for him so we'll give him a few days and get in touch again when he's over it all. There's still hope.'

'Yes, you're probably right. He'll soon realise how much he needs his family now he's alone. How much compensation do you think he'll get?'

'Quite a few thousand, I should think, as well as the life insurance. Joe's house must be worth a packet too and it's far too big for him. Surely he'll see sense and put it on the market?' Their disappointment at getting off to a bad start with Joe lifted as they looked forward to the possibilities his windfall could bring them.

Within a couple of days, David's patience ran out and he decided to act. 'It's time my little brother realised that he's not the only one in the world with problems,' David told Pam. 'I'll test the water and ask for a loan, see how he reacts.'

The letter was written and sent but when Joe's reply

eventually landed on the doormat the couple were again frustrated.

'I don't believe him!' Pam declared after reading the letter twice through. 'There's always compensation for these accidents; someone must be to blame and they should pay up.'

David frowned. 'Well, we can hardly confront him and tell him we think he's lying. On the other hand, his letter's not entirely dismissive. He seems to have some sympathy for our plight so all's not lost yet.'

'It's a pity they didn't both die in the crash – they'd still be together then and Joe wouldn't be such a miserable sod – and you'd be the only surviving relative.' Pam looked at her husband, a question dancing in her eyes. They were both silent for a while, each with their thoughts.

Pam's eyes wandered around the room, taking in the damp patches on the walls, the ugly second-hand furniture they'd been forced to buy when their hasty exit obliged them to leave their possessions in Bournemouth. The dark brown furniture had been cheap – no one else appeared to want it – and the green three-piece suite was almost a replica of the one her grandmother had owned decades earlier.

Pam recalled the deep pile carpet in Joe's comfortable home, the cream leather sofas and expensive stripped pine designer furniture, the modern bespoke kitchen. Her resentment grew. Why should he have such a beautiful home with more space than he'd ever need while they were cramped in this bloody slum? His possessions didn't even make him happy, hadn't his neighbour expressed concern at how *down* Joe was? Yes, Pam thought, it certainly was a pity they both hadn't died in the crash.

Pam's thoughts were interrupted by David's voice.

'Perhaps if my little brother were to have an accident himself, it would be a kindness – like putting a dog out of its misery.' The couple had been drinking most of the day and emboldened by alcohol, they gave voice to thoughts which seemed to them entirely rational.

'Are you serious, David?' Pam's eyes sparkled at the prospect but she was unsure her husband could find the nerve to make something like this happen. 'I mean, it would be a kindness – a mercy killing you could say.' Her mind was exploring the feasibility of going through with such a thing. 'It would have to look like an accident, wouldn't it?'

'Difficult to arrange from a distance.' David appeared to be on board with the idea. 'A fall down the stairs might work, but how would we be in a position to do it?'

'Perhaps a hit-and-run while he's out with that dog of his? You could drive up there and straight back and I could say you'd been with me all the time.'

'Might work. I'd have to know where he walks the dog, his neighbours were looking after it when we were there, but I suppose Joe will be fully recovered now. How much do you think his house is worth?'

'£300,000 at the very least.' Pam grinned at her husband, more animated than she'd been in months. They were seriously considering ending his brother's life and she found the thought exhilarating.

22

It felt incredibly good for Hannah to be walking unaided although it took time and patience to adjust to her prosthesis and she still needed regular breaks from wearing it. Yet Hannah felt human again and was beginning to regain some of her confidence. The twins were a great encouragement and applauded her efforts to walk. More importantly, Kate seemed to have forgotten the crazy notion of giving up going to university to care for her mum. They were in the middle of A levels now and Hannah was glad she'd recovered some of her independence, not wanting her children to worry about her at such a stressful time.

Mike, too, appeared relieved that she no longer needed as much help in everyday matters, but his relief manifested itself in slipping back into his old ways, working too many hours and staying away from home more often than his wife would have liked. However, a semblance of normality descended on their home and although still grieving for her missing leg, Hannah woke up each morning with a determined, if at times forced, positivity.

A week after being fitted with her prosthetic leg, Hannah

walked into the estate agents' office where she worked with a smile to be greeted by a round of applause from her colleagues. It was great to be back, although the senior partner insisted she initially worked only part-time, an arrangement Hannah welcomed for the chance to ease in gradually.

The office was in the throes of a merger with another local estate agent, an exciting time, most of which she'd missed due to the accident. They were shortly moving into larger premises and Hannah, authorised with a generous budget, was given the task of deciding which office equipment and furniture to take and which should be replaced in keeping with their move up in the world. It was a desk-based duty and one she tackled with relish, pitching herself back into the work she loved.

At times she was so absorbed that Hannah forgot she had only one leg until she moved without thinking and her prosthesis dragged her back, necessitating a conscious effort to walk with it. *How much we take for granted*, Hannah thought, *until it's cruelly snatched away from us.*

Arriving home after lunch on a Tuesday afternoon in late May, Hannah was surprised to find Mike waiting for her in the living room. 'Hello, love, I wasn't expecting you until tomorrow. Plans changed, have they?' She dared to anticipate a quiet afternoon and evening at home with her husband and mentally wondered what she could make for tea.

'You could say so. Sit down, Hannah. I need to talk to you.' Mike's expression was grave.

'What is it? What's wrong? Has something happened to one of the children?' She searched his face but couldn't read his thoughts and he appeared to be avoiding eye contact.

'The kids are fine, Hannah, it's not that.' Again he didn't meet her eyes. 'I can't do this anymore.'

'Do what, what are you talking about?'

'You must know. Us, the happy family bit – it's all wrong, Hannah, and I want out.'

'Is this a joke of some kind, Mike, because if it is it's not very funny!'

'It's not a joke. Surely you can see things haven't been right between us for months.'

'Is it because of this?' She laid her hand on her thigh. 'I know it's been difficult for you but I'm managing so much better now ...'

'No, it's not your leg. Things were going wrong before the accident. I was on the point of leaving before it happened – and then – I tried, Hannah, but I just don't love you anymore. I'm sorry.'

Hannah couldn't believe this was happening. Of course, things weren't as they'd been in the early years of their marriage. Life changes, relationships change.

'But what about the children? Are you telling me you want to leave us all?'

'Yes, that's exactly what I'm saying. The kids are grown up and don't need me, and they're off to uni soon. I've not been happy for a long time and I think it's better for us to split up now while we're young enough to make a fresh start.'

'A fresh start! Mike, is there someone else?' The thought hit Hannah like an avalanche. Of course there was someone else – the staying away from home all those nights, not wanting to have sex with her, it added up and she felt suddenly very foolish, naive. How could she not have worked this one out for herself?

Mike didn't answer and looked away.

'Is there, Mike? Tell me. I want to know.'

'Yes.'

'How long?'

'We don't need to do this, Hannah, all the sordid details. It doesn't matter how long. I'm leaving and I think the sooner the better.' He turned from her and went upstairs.

Tears were streaming down Hannah's cheeks as she hauled

herself up after him. The stairs were still a challenge, but she was determined to know exactly what had been going on, how big a fool she'd been.

Mike's suitcase lay open on the bed in their room, almost full. A holdall was on the floor already packed. He was going, her husband was leaving her!

'It's probably just an infatuation, Mike!' She hated the note of pleading in her voice but twenty years of marriage was worth trying to save. 'If you've only just met her it might not last, please let's talk about it?'

'I haven't only just met her. It's been two years and I love her. I want a divorce so I can marry her.' Mike kept his face turned away.

'So you don't love me anymore, is that what you're saying, and the kids?' She heard the desperation in her voice – but two years! How had she not guessed?

'Of course I still love the kids and I'll always be fond of you, but I love Sarah and …' He stopped suddenly and turned to Hannah. 'Look, I'm leaving tonight. I'll stay and see the kids. You shouldn't have to tell them alone, but my mind's made up. I'm sorry.'

Hannah had an impulse to whip off her prosthesis and whack Mike over the head with it – an idiotic thought – she would only fall over and look pathetic. But didn't he think she'd been through enough lately? Couldn't he see how much she needed him? So instead, she watched in silence as her husband emptied the last of his drawers. *One suitcase and a holdall*, she thought, *it's not much*.

'Where's the rest of your stuff?' she asked.

Mike hung his head. 'I've been taking a bit at a time.'

'But why do you have to marry her, Mike? What if it doesn't work out? Please stay and we'll talk about it. We can get over this.'

'I don't want to stay! I've tried, Hannah, honestly,

especially after the accident, but I know it's Sarah I love and besides … she's having a baby.'

Hannah slumped on the bed, stunned. A baby? Mike had professed he didn't want any more children! When the twins were two, she desperately wanted another baby – her body was crying out to procreate again, but he refused absolutely – arguing that they already had a boy and a girl and should be content. Reluctantly she'd agreed, pouring all her maternal instincts into the twins. They'd always been her world, with Mike too, of course.

A sudden thought popped into Hannah's mind. 'This woman's tricked you, hasn't she? She's got pregnant to trap you into marrying her! You don't have to do it, Mike, we'll work through it. You can still support the child. It's only fair, I understand that.'

'No, Hannah, you've got it wrong. We want a baby together. Sarah's thirty-six and has never had children. We planned it. When we knew she was pregnant, I was going to tell you and leave then, but the accident happened. I tried to stay, to make it work, but now you're back on your feet and Sarah needs me – and it's where I want to be.'

Hannah couldn't believe this was happening. Mike willingly making a baby with another woman? No, it couldn't be true! But he'd just told her it was and he was leaving. A deep feeling of humiliation washed over her. She begged him to stay, even if it was only out of pity, she wanted him to stay. How degrading; did she really want a man who didn't love her, who had planned a baby with another woman? Finally, Hannah stood, mortified at her pathetic behaviour, and went downstairs.

Mike made no move to follow, for which she was grateful; Hannah needed to gather her thoughts, to recoup some dignity before the children came home. At least he was staying to tell them himself. He could have taken the cowardly way out and left it to her.

Hannah made coffee and when Mike eventually came downstairs, she handed him a cup and sat in the lounge.

'We have to decide how to tell Kate and Sam,' she said calmly, in control, more rational. 'But it can't be now. They're in the middle of their A levels and need stability.' Clearly, Mike hadn't considered the implications for their children, he'd had other things on his mind, like his lover and their baby. Hannah's thoughts were uncharitable yet it was how she was feeling.

Her husband took the coffee she offered and stared into it as if it was a crystal ball.

'So what do you want me to do?' he asked.

'Kate's last exam is tomorrow and Sam's on Friday. If you must go I'll tell them you're working away, but I want you to come back on Friday night to see them and explain this yourself.'

Mike looked suitably humbled. 'Okay, that seems only fair. Will you be all right for the rest of the week?'

'And what do you care if I'm not?' she snapped.

'I'd hoped we could be civilised about this, for the children's sake if nothing else.'

Hannah looked away. 'I'll be fine,' she said, knowing she'd be anything but.

Less than a minute after her husband walked out of the door, Hannah gave way to the tears she'd been biting back, angry tears for herself and her children. Her feelings about Mike's revelation were a jumble; she was stunned, humiliated and angry. Had she known somewhere in the back of her mind that this was coming? Perhaps she should have done.

Hannah had to agree with Mike – things hadn't been right between them for quite some time. Yet she'd chosen to ignore it, making excuses and hoping their relationship would improve. But now what would happen? Should she simply shrug off her marriage like a wet overcoat, or fight for it? Did she want to fight for it, or was it the failure which hurt more than Mike's leaving?

Mike having carried on the affair for such a long time without her suspecting was mortifying and now he'd gone, leaving Hannah with the messy job of applying the glue to fix her family. Then there were their friends and neighbours, she'd need to tell them and face their pitying looks, the speculation and inevitable gossip.

Putting her feelings aside, Hannah knew Kate and Sam must be her priority. They'd feel deserted, let down and hurt by the very parent who should protect them, but then, hadn't she been the one protecting them throughout their childhood? Mike was never truly comfortable in the role of a father, which was why it was so incredible that he'd chosen to have a baby with this new love of his.

Hannah's head whirled with conflicting thoughts, vacillating between blaming herself and blaming Mike, hating him and longing for him to come running back and tell her it was all a huge mistake and it was her he really loved.

Realistically it wasn't going to happen and somehow Hannah needed to get through the next few days pretending everything was fine, that her heart was not broken into a thousand pieces and she was not the utter wreck she felt inside. It would be painfully hard but Hannah would do it for her children.

23

J oe climbed the stairs and entered Alison's sewing room
once again with Liffey close at his heels as if she knew her
master would need her comforting presence. He carried
three empty cardboard boxes and a roll of black plastic sacks;
it was time to sort out some of his wife's belongings but first
he fired up her laptop to find Carolyn's email address.

Over seventy unopened emails confronted him, mostly
notifications from book groups, or friend requests from
Goodreads, nothing important. They could wait or be deleted.
Joe rarely used social media but Alison had a profile on
Facebook which she'd claimed helped her keep in touch with
friends. Joe had teased her and called it 'virtual curtain
twitching'. He'd never considered the necessity to delete
someone's presence from the internet before and now he
wondered if he should attempt to remove Ali's profiles from
these sites, but would it feel like erasing her life? He scribbled
down Carolyn's email address and turned the laptop off. Social
media could wait for another day.

Joe started his task in the sewing room rather than their
bedroom. As yet he had no desire to remove Alison's clothes

from the room they'd shared, so they still hung in the wardrobe and her toiletries remained untouched in the bathroom. Joe wanted the closeness and comfort of his wife's possessions, often touching her clothes, breathing in her scent, but he knew things couldn't stay this way forever.

Looking around the room, the very essence of Alison layered every surface, like fine dust. Joe sighed, where to begin? Liffey flopped down heavily on the rug, her huge brown eyes watching his every move as if she somehow understood that her mistress was not coming back and Joe was doing his best to carry on.

'It's not easy for you either is it, girl?' Joe bent to stroke her ears, receiving a lick on his hand for his trouble. Straightening up, he turned to Alison's books and began packing them neatly into the largest box, ready for the charity shop. There was a degree of comfort in touching the things Alison had loved and as he worked, Joe found himself talking to her about each item. 'Someone will appreciate this, love,' he whispered. It made the task easier, knowing his wife would approve, and the ethereal comfort of her presence filled the room.

After a couple of hours and some reasonable progress, Joe experienced a sense of satisfaction and decided to finish for the day. His shoulder ached and he didn't want to undo the progress he'd made. He would ask Diane if she wanted Alison's sewing machine. Di enjoyed making things too and the two women had often exchanged patterns and ideas. It would be a small way of repaying her kindness to him.

Joe went downstairs, made a mug of tea, then fired up his laptop to write the email he'd been putting off for the last few days.

```
Hi Carolyn
    Firstly,  I  am  so  sorry  for  not
```

emailing sooner but sadly my reason for doing so now is to tell you of Alison's death. She died on 2nd February as the result of a car crash. I know how close you and Ali were and this will come as a terrible shock, as it has for me.

It was during that horrendous spell of bad weather we suffered at the end of January and the beginning of February. I've never known anything like it.

We were together in the car and involved in a motorway crash which killed three people and left several others badly injured. My only injury was a broken collarbone, painful but relatively light compared to others. I was assured Alison died instantly at the scene and suffered no pain.

As you can imagine, life's proving difficult and I miss her so much. Friends and neighbours have rallied around, and the funeral was a fitting tribute to the wonderful person she was. I'm sorry for not contacting you sooner but my head's been all over the place and I'm only now remembering people I should have contacted. You were very dear to Alison and I know she missed your friendship when you moved but Ali was happy that you and Ben love Canada so much.

It's tough talking about Alison's death, but my next subject brings even more pain. As you probably know, Ali cared for her mother, visiting two or

three times a week and although Ethel and
I have never been close, I felt obliged
to see her when my collarbone had healed
and I was driving again.

It wasn't a great visit. My intention
was to let her know that I wasn't going
to step into Ali's shoes regarding
running around after her, and she took it
badly. It seemed appropriate to suggest
professional care but Ethel baulked at
the suggestion. She remains intent on
blaming me for the accident and also
because we hadn't managed to give her any
grandchildren. Then, in a fit of what I
can only describe as 'pique', Ethel told
me that Alison had given birth to a baby
before she met me — the connotation being
that it was my inadequacies preventing us
from conceiving.

You can imagine how hurtful this was,
but Ethel refused to reveal any more
facts other than to say the baby was a
girl and died within hours of birth of a
weak heart. Perhaps you can understand my
confusion at learning this information. I
thought Alison and I had no secrets and
knew everything about each other, but
this has shaken me more than I can say
and without Ali to discuss it with, I
feel distraught.

What I need to know is, firstly, is it
true and secondly, why didn't Ali tell me
about it? I would have understood if
she'd explained. Now I find my mind

whirring with all kinds of scenarios, wondering who the father was, how she felt about him and would she have still been with him if the baby had lived?

I know this is a big ask and the news of Alison's death will be a shock, but I'm desperate for answers and you're the only one I can think of who was close to her in those years before we met. So please be honest with me, Carolyn. Whatever you can tell me will in no way change how I remember Alison, but for my peace of mind, I need to know the truth.

Kind regards

Joe

Joe hit the send button before there was time to change his mind and hoped Carolyn would reply soon. But then, would the reply bring him the peace he craved?

Work became Joe's only escape and what was left of his home life centred on his dog. It appeared that those he'd considered friends were actually more Alison's friends than his, or was it simply that a bereaved man was something of a dilemma? Most of their social circle were couples and now Joe was alone he didn't fit into their tidy little group anymore. Not that Joe blamed them, he understood and as he wasn't ready to *move on*, it wasn't a problem.

The exception to this was Phil and Diane who remained steadfast friends offering invaluable practical help and emotional support. Diane was forever bringing food or inviting him for a meal, her way of showing she cared, and when they looked after Liffey they made it appear Joe was doing them a favour. Such remarkable people are rare and Joe grew to value them for the true friends they were.

At times Joe wondered how it would have been if he'd been the one to die and Alison was left alone. Undoubtedly she would have handled it better, probably by widening her circle of friends as a coping mechanism, but it wasn't so easy for a man. He couldn't join the WI or an embroidery group and he'd never taken to golf or bowls in the way some men do, so work became his life and Liffey his love.

He continued functioning and remained sane by taking one day at a time and forbidding his thoughts to stray any further ahead.

Joe felt he'd lost his future when Alison died – he didn't want to dwell on the weeks and months ahead – they were just a painful existence to get through, alone.

24

'But why?' Kate's eyes glistened with tears. 'Other people's parents get divorced – not ours – not you! I thought we were happy.' Sam also looked close to tears, his face tense, closed.

It was proving so much harder than Mike had expected. He spoke honestly to his children, lost for any way to soften the blow and having never been particularly eloquent, especially in stressful situations. 'It's nothing to do with you two, love – it's between your mum and me.'

'Is there someone else?' Kate's eyes bored into her father's. Mike looked away, embarrassed, turning to Hannah for help.

'Yes, your dad's met someone else.'

Suddenly Kate flew at Mike and thumped him on his chest. 'I hate you!' she shouted.

Sam sprang forward to pull her away and she collapsed onto the sofa into her mother's waiting arms.

'Well, I still love you,' Mike's voice cracked, 'and I hope when you get used to the situation, you'll both come and see Sarah and me. You'll always be welcome.'

'Never!' Kate shouted. 'How could you do this to Mum, especially now.'

'It's got nothing to do with the accident, Kate; your dad was seeing Sarah before then,' Hannah intervened, but the look of disgust Kate flashed at Mike was withering and left him in no doubt as to how she felt about him. It was going to take time and patience for her to forgive him.

Sam sniffed. 'When are you leaving?'

'I've moved most of my stuff out already, so I'll not be coming back here to stay.' Mike knew he was handling this badly. Kate's reaction took him completely by surprise and the look of dejection on Sam's face cut deeper than he'd expected. Mike hadn't taken much of an active role in his children's lives over the last few years, but now he was leaving he felt a sudden, unexpected rush of love for his children. 'I'm so sorry, but you're both on the point of becoming independent and your mum and I aren't happy together anymore. I'll still be your dad and I'll always be there for you.'

'But not here. Where will you be living?' Sam whispered.

'Sarah has a flat in Bankford, about ten miles away. You can come and visit anytime you want.' Neither sibling commented on the invitation but Mike could almost see their minds turning. He hoped they didn't ask many more questions. The whole situation felt surreal and he thought it prudent to just go and try to meet his children later, when they'd got used to the idea.

Mike gathered up the last of his bags and said goodbye to his wife, son and daughter, closing the door behind him without the lightness of spirit and sense of relief he'd expected. Instead, guilt and regret weighed heavily on his mind and the notion of being a deserter, or worse, gnawed at his very being. His daughter's reaction cut deeply into an already heavy heart. Mike hadn't expected to feel so bad.

When the car pulled off the drive and Mike was on his way out of the street and out of their lives, Hannah turned to Kate and Sam.

'I'm so sorry, my loves – it must be a dreadful shock.'

Kate's face was streaked with tears. She sniffed. 'And to you, Mum! How long have you known?'

'Just since Tuesday. Dad wanted to tell you then, but I asked him to wait until today with your exams and everything. And you should be out celebrating with your friends tonight, I'm sorry if we've ruined it.'

'It's not you who's ruined it. It's him! Did you have any idea he was seeing someone else?' It was typical of Kate to want to know all the details.

'No, love, I didn't, and I felt pretty stupid when he told me. I did know Dad was unhappy and found it difficult to come to terms with the accident. He said he tried to make it work afterwards, but I'm not sure, and if he loves this Sarah ...'

'He might come back.' Sam's pale face and bright eyes almost broke Hannah's heart. 'If things don't work out with her, he'll realise you're the one he loves.'

'I can't see it happening, Sam, they've been seeing each other for two years. And there's something else he should have told you, Sarah's going to have a baby.' *They're old enough to know the full facts*, Hannah thought, even if Mike had been too cowardly to tell them.

'The bastard, I don't ever want to see him again!' Kate's reaction was typical.

'Don't say that, Kate! He's still your father and this baby will be your half-brother or sister. You might want to make room in your life for it. These things happen and I know your dad still cares for you. I think you should give him a chance and see him again to talk it over.'

Sam put his arms around Hannah in a rare yet welcome display of affection. 'You're too nice, Mum, but you'll always have us.'

'Look, let's order a takeaway for tea and then I want you both to go out and celebrate the end of your exams. You deserve it, you've worked so hard and I'm very proud of you both.'

'We're not leaving you alone and I don't feel like celebrating.' Kate spoke for them both.

'Nonsense, I want you to go. I thought I'd ask Rachel to come over later to help me polish off a bottle of wine or two, so I don't want you around to witness my wicked behaviour!' Hannah's words brought half a smile from the twins. Celebrating with their friends was precisely what they needed to take their mind off the situation between their parents.

Rachel was never one to refuse a half share in a bottle of wine or some girly chatter and as Hannah expected she arrived on the doorstep within ten minutes of her call. Perceptive as ever, Rachel noticed the pallor and drawn expression on Hannah's face and immediately demanded to know what was wrong. It was a relief to pour out the angst of the week to an understanding friend.

Hannah had found it an enormous struggle to carry on as usual after Mike had dropped his bombshell on Tuesday but resisted telling anyone until the children knew.

Rachel listened quietly, her silent empathy both encouraging and soothing. When everything was out in the open, she sat back and sighed. 'Well he's a bloody fool! He doesn't know how lucky he is to have you and the kids; you're a prize for any man.'

'Even with only one leg?' Hannah almost whispered.

'What the hell's that got to do with it? You're an amazing woman, Hannah Graham, and don't you forget it! And as for planning a baby with a woman he's having an affair with, while still married to you – well it's just bloody irresponsible. I hope the baby keeps him awake every night and his floozy gets fat, with swollen ankles and pimples!'

'Oh, Rachel!' Hannah laughed out loud. 'I suppose he couldn't help falling in love with her. These things happen.'

'There you go, making excuses for him already. He doesn't deserve it, Hannah. He'll soon find out which side his bread's buttered and then he'll want to come crawling back. When that happens I hope you'll bloody well tell him where to get off. And what about money? You take him for everything he's got, girl! It won't be cheap sending the kids to uni you know, he'll have to cough up, so get yourself a good lawyer.'

'Oh I'm sure he won't be mean about money, he'll see the kids all right, I know.'

'And what about you? All these years you've devoted to him. Make sure you get half of everything he has, more if you can.' Rachel was in full swing, and after only one glass of wine.

'There's time to sort it all out later but he'll have another baby to support, I can't expect too much from him.'

'Yes you bloody can and you can bet your boots I'll be around to make sure you do!'

The conversation continued in the same vein for most of the evening, Rachel's dramatic outbursts making Hannah laugh when she hadn't thought it possible after a week punctuated by tears and utter despair. Her friend's drunken rendition of Cher's 'Do You Believe in Life after Love?' almost doubled Hannah up, it was precisely the tonic she needed.

When Rachel eventually left, Hannah went upstairs to bed, not wanting the children to see her so drunk. She removed her prosthesis and was asleep almost as soon as her head touched the pillow – for once, not lying awake, trying to remember the accident and details she was unsure she wanted to know.

25

David woke in a cold sweat, his legs tangled in the sheets and a thumping headache. It was several weeks since he and Pam had discussed an *accident* befalling his brother, weeks during which he'd vacillated between anticipation at the prospect and fear of discovery – not to mention doubts as to if he would have the nerve to go through with such an outrageous idea.

His sleep was disturbed and his mind in turmoil with images he couldn't escape, so he crept silently out of bed and headed for the kitchen. When his foot caught in a hole in the carpet, David clattered noisily into the wardrobe.

'What the hell are you doing?' Pam sat upright in bed and turned on the lamp.

'Nothing, go back to sleep.'

Pam climbed out of bed, pulled on her robe and followed him to the kitchen. They sat at the little Formica table. 'What's wrong with you, David?'

'You know what's wrong,' he said miserably. 'We're not the sort of people to kill someone – it was a ridiculous idea.'

'I honestly think you'd be doing him a favour. Joe's a miserable old sod without that little wife of his; he'd probably thank you if he knew you were thinking about it.'

'You know he wouldn't – let's just forget the whole stupid idea.'

'Fine, if you're happy to continue living in this hellhole – which I'm not! And by the way, did I tell you I saw one of that loan shark's heavies yesterday? It's as well he didn't know me, but if you'd been with me I can't imagine what might have happened. We'll probably have to move again if they're onto you, and there's no money left, is there?'

David looked unsure. 'You're lying; they wouldn't still be looking for me after all this time!'

'Suit yourself, but I'm just glad it's you they're after and not me.' An uneasy silence hung between them for a few moments until Pam's mood softened. 'Look, I know you're not too keen on our little plan to get rid of Joe, but it would be the answer to all our problems. He's miserable and we're struggling – it seems the ideal solution – a quick trip up north and we'll be in clover.'

Pam placed a hand on David's arm, smiling at him as she let her robe slip from her shoulders.

Two days later David was on the M40 travelling north. It had been a grey drizzly day and as he set off in the early evening he was almost glad to get out of the house, away from Pam and her constant nagging. Now his thoughts were turned inward – he barely noticed the darkening skies and the heavy rain as he stared at the black ribbon of road directly ahead of him.

As usual, Pam had got her way and David could hardly believe he was actually driving to kill his brother. When they'd first discussed the idea, he'd been angry with Joe and wanted revenge. He was also more than a little drunk. But people like them didn't commit murder – and the more he thought about it the more ludicrous it seemed.

His wife, however, was very persuasive and David was wary of getting on her wrong side; she could make life very difficult for him. If Pam turned against him she possessed information which could land him in a very sticky situation.

David was unsure if Pam was lying about seeing one of the moneylender's thugs but he couldn't take the risk. Yet could he go through with this?

Pam had dithered over whether to go with him or stay at home to provide an alibi. Finally, she cooked up a plan involving the local shopkeeper, telling him David was ill in bed and asking his advice about medication. With it being Sunday, she was sure the man would remember her visit and she'd make a point of telling him the doctor's surgery was closed.

David intended to arrive early on Sunday morning, keep a safe distance from Joe's house and wait for him to take his dog out. Once the deed was done, he'd drive home as quickly as his wreck of a car would allow.

Unfortunately, there were too many assumptions to their plan. They assumed Joe would take the dog out at least a couple of times during the day, and for one of those times he would choose somewhere reasonably quiet to present David with the opportunity he needed.

The prospect of CCTV had been keeping David awake at night too. Did any of the houses on Joe's street have cameras which might pick him up? Would he be caught on video following his brother? Pam laughed it off as David being paranoid and watching too much television, but she wasn't the one taking the risk, nor would she be the one who could end up in prison if it all went horribly wrong.

Thankfully the traffic was light, and shortly after midnight, David pulled into a service station to treat himself to an all-day breakfast. There was plenty of time – his brother was hardly likely to be walking the dog in the middle of the night. As David enjoyed his food, the thought of having the money to eat out as often as he liked strengthened his resolve and he allowed himself to contemplate moving into Joe's house. The rewards were undoubtedly great if only he could hold his nerve and get through the next few hours. If luck smiled on him and his chance materialised, it would be worth all the worry of the last few weeks.

It was 3am when David finally pulled up in his brother's street. The torrential rain was beginning to ease as he parked in a spot which afforded him a good view of Joe's front gate without being too close.

Getting out of the car, David swore as he stepped in a puddle. He shook his trouser leg and set off walking around the immediate area, checking for CCTV cameras. None were visible. David relaxed and decided he could grab a few hours' sleep before there was any chance his quarry would appear.

The car was cold and uncomfortable, his damp clothing adding to the discomfort and sleep eluded him. His mind was wired, alert, and his eyes wide and gritty. David supposed he was high on adrenaline. Time ticked by slowly and nearly four hours dragged until there was any movement on the street. A jogger a couple of houses away from Joe's was the first person to appear and David sank low in his seat to avoid being seen. The man turned in the opposite direction and didn't appear to register the parked car, but David got out his phone to look as if he'd stopped to take a call, in case anyone was watching.

David wished he'd brought a book to read but that might appear suspicious and he didn't dare take his eyes off the street. A couple of cars pulled out of driveways, one of them

Joe's next-door neighbour who passed David but didn't appear to recognise the car or its occupant.

Finally, at 7.10am, Joe came out of the gate with his dog on a lead. David held his breath until he saw Joe turn in the opposite direction, away from the main road. Releasing his breath, David switched on the engine and moved slowly forward.

The street was almost too quiet. David was afraid of being spotted so kept his distance without losing sight of Joe. It wasn't easy but his brother was talking to the dog and had no reason to look back.

The path Joe took led past the end of the estate toward an open field. He walked fast for a few more minutes until the footpath narrowed and hedges grew on either side. No more houses. David allowed himself to smile – it was perfect.

Blood pumped quickly through his veins. Could he do this? David's knuckles were white, his face muscles tense as he gripped the steering wheel and moved the car into third gear.

Joe was about thirty yards ahead, the dog still on the lead. If he put his foot down David could reach his brother in a matter of seconds – then it would be all over.

'Right, you bastard!' He spoke through gritted teeth to psych himself up and pressed the accelerator almost to the floor.

Suddenly Joe was no longer there. He'd turned into a gateway which David hadn't noticed, and as he pressed hard on the brake, the car stopped, just before the entrance into which his brother had escaped. David's breath came in heavy pants as if he'd been punched in the stomach and he remained still, half expecting Joe to have heard the brakes and return to see what was going on. But there was nothing, only the pounding of David's heartbeat.

After calming down he quietly opened the door and stepped out, moving to the front of the car and peering tentatively into the field. His brother was already in the distance, throwing a ball for the dog, apparently unaware of anyone else's presence. Returning to the car, David moved off down the narrowing lane, out of sight to consider his next move.

He turned the car around and stopped in a passing place. Should he wait and try to get Joe when he came back out of the field? No, he couldn't see far enough ahead and it was too risky – he'd be on the wrong side of the road and heading back into the street where he might be seen. If he'd only known the gateway was there he'd have made his move a few seconds earlier – but he'd missed his chance.

Thumping the steering wheel in frustration, David swore. The sensible thing to do now would be to go away quickly before he was seen and try again that evening. If not, he might even have to wait for the following morning. Restarting the engine, he drove out of the area as quickly as possible.

Before ringing Pam, who would be expecting his call, David worked out what to say. He'd tell her his morning had been spent reconnoitring the area and watching Joe's movements. Actually, this was probably something he should have thought to do before going in unprepared, and he'd make it sound as if it was a plan he'd thought up on the journey north.

'What the hell's happened?' Pam shouted down the phone. 'Have you done it yet?'

'No, not yet. I decided to wait and watch Joe's routine today to make sure I find the best possible option.'

'Well, why didn't you ring me sooner? I've been frantic with worry! And if you don't do it today the alibi I've put in place won't be any good.'

'I know, but I followed him this morning and he takes the dog to a field just half a mile or so away from the housing estate. I'll keep watch this evening and if he takes the same route, I'll do it then.'

'Good. Let me know as soon as it's over.'

There was little more to say – both were wrapped up in their thoughts. It was going to be a long day for David. He'd head into town and find somewhere warm to eat then wait until he could safely go back to watching Joe's house.

26

Mike drove for less than a mile before his vision blurred and he pulled out of the traffic and stopped the car.

What the hell have I done? His head dropped onto the steering wheel and he screwed up his eyes to clear his sight. The feeling of lightness Mike expected – the anticipation of a new life with his sexy new girlfriend was strangely absent. He'd assumed leaving Hannah would bring a fresh start, like shrugging off an old woollen jumper which was unravelling at the sleeves. But perhaps that jumper was more comfortable than he'd realised.

Breaking his news was never going to be easy, he'd expected as much, but the look of horror and disgust on his children's faces haunted Mike. Kate's violent reaction and angry words cut deeply, bringing home the realisation of precisely how much he loved his children. His intention wasn't to hurt either them or Hannah, but circumstances backed him into a corner, Mike had made a choice and only hoped it was the right one.

Although Sam was less emotional than his sister, it was typical of the boy and Mike knew it didn't mean his son felt the break-up any less than Kate – he was simply different. The whole thing had proved to be so much more complicated than Mike had assumed and the twins' reaction took him by surprise, as did the strength of his own feelings.

Mike expected more of the apathy they'd exhibited since reaching puberty – the time he started to believe they no longer needed or wanted him. Had he wrongly assumed his children were indifferent as to whether he was around or not? Hannah claimed their attitude was a general teenage thing, yet Mike couldn't remember being the same when he was a teenager and had little experience of other children with which to compare.

Maybe Hannah was right and he'd confused being taken for granted as not caring, but the look on Kate's face shocked him and Sam's quiet expression of dismay at his father's betrayal would stay with him forever. When there was nothing more constructive to be said, Mike had left the house for the final time, feeling like a traitor and the very worst kind of coward.

As always, Hannah would be the one to slot the pieces back together, to rebuild their children's confidence and shape the family unit back to what it should be, except this time it would be without him. She'd always been so much better at that sort of thing than Mike – perhaps it was in a woman's make-up – he knew he was sadly lacking in trying times.

In his reflections Mike silently admitted there'd been occasions when he was jealous of Hannah's closeness to the children and her better understanding of their needs. She possessed the knack of being able to diffuse those frequent, difficult situations in family life. But this was something else and, other than Hannah's accident, perhaps the biggest upset of their lives. Guilt overwhelmed Mike as he walked away, leaving Hannah to once again smooth things over.

The accident undoubtedly complicated things, and for a while afterwards Mike endeavoured to stay with his family, feeling duty-bound to attempt to make the marriage work. But Sarah needed him too – and they were having a baby together. Would leaving have been any easier if the accident hadn't happened? Mike would never know and the situation couldn't be reversed. Hannah had lost her leg and Sarah was having his baby. Surely any man would flounder in such a situation.

To compound the guilt, Mike had been with Sarah on the day of the accident, which was also the day he'd intended to tell Hannah he was leaving. Mike had stolen an extra night with Sarah under the pretext of avoiding the bad weather and atrocious motoring conditions.

After making love under the duvet in the early morning Mike and Sarah had eagerly discussed the future, laughing, confident of the happiness awaiting them. The unexpected phone call had ended their good mood and the news of Hannah's accident caused Mike to think again.

During the days of Hannah's hospitalisation, Mike, wracked with guilt, considered calling it off with Sarah. The accident was certainly an ill-timed event which left him with two needy women and he was torn, unable to decide what to do. His attempts to support Hannah were challenging and coping with her injury was way beyond his comfort zone. When she showed signs of coming to terms with her loss, Mike finally decided that his future lay with Sarah.

Mike hadn't intended to fall in love. He was flattered when she appeared to enjoy his company and he didn't expect things to go any further than a little flirting – but isn't that what everyone says? When they'd first met, Sarah reminded him so much of a young Hannah, which perhaps sparked the initial attraction.

Getting used to spending so much time away from home, Mike enjoyed the freedom from responsibility it offered. Second-rate hotels were bearable, a place to lay his head and get a decent breakfast, and the delight of being his own man, of having only himself to please was an attractive proposition.

Without responsibilities at the end of each working day, no one to ferry about in the car, no grass to mow or other domestic chores, was something of a relief. Mike could find a quiet pub and enjoy a few beers and a bit of banter with the locals – it was the kind of freedom he'd missed during the years when the children were small.

It wasn't as if Hannah hadn't been a good wife, and their marriage was generally happy, but she readily put the children first whereas Mike was more selfish and resented her expectations of him as a husband and father. Twins came as a shock to them both; one baby in the house was demanding enough, but two was a full-time job and totally exhausting. For Hannah's sanity, Mike was obliged to become a hands-on dad, something he wasn't cut out for and grew to resent.

Naturally Mike loved his children and was proud of them, but as they grew older and became more independent, he assumed his role was at an end. It was a chicken and egg situation – they no longer appeared to need him so he withdrew – or did he withdraw first and his children learned to function without him? Whatever – Mike struggled with the adolescent stage equally as much as the baby stage whereas Hannah thrived on motherhood and would have loved more children.

Inevitably Hannah changed over the years too, from the carefree, exciting risk-taker he'd first fallen for to a responsible parent. Meeting Sarah was like stepping back in time, being young again and experiencing all those heady emotions of a carefree youth.

Unoriginally Mike had met Sarah in a pub where she worked as a barmaid. She was young and pretty and her attention ensured Mike returned time and again, even though he was aware of the risks. Initially, Mike told himself it was only a bit of harmless flirtation on both sides. He wore a wedding ring, Sarah must have realised he was married, but she never asked and Mike didn't intend getting out photos of the wife and kids – he was having too much fun. When their relationship reached the stage of meeting outside the pub, Mike knew he was out of his depth. But it had gone too far, Sarah was intoxicating, exciting, and he wanted more.

Within a short time, Mike was staying at Sarah's flat as often as possible, telling Hannah he was working elsewhere. Living two lives, the excitement of forbidden fruit outweighed the guilt which surfaced from time to time when he thought about Hannah and the twins.

Sarah showed little interest in his *other* family and Mike slipped into a routine of living a day at a time which enabled him to hide the reality of what he was doing from himself, as well as others. He became adept at compartmentalising his double life.

After a year of duplicity, Sarah wanted more of Mike than he'd ever intended to give, constantly reminding him he had children and she did not. Sarah longed for a child before it was too late, and when the possibility of having a baby together was raised, it became clear Mike would have to make some tough decisions. This woman was beautiful, exciting and she loved him.

Mike knew that having a child with another woman would end his marriage yet initially he tried to blank it out. Eventually, he agreed to having a baby and for a time he and Sarah were blissfully happy. Would he have made the same choices if he'd known what the future held – if he'd known about Hannah's accident or the way the twins would react?

Mike would never know but what he did know was that he was suffering the loss of his family far more than he'd anticipated and even the thought of a new life with Sarah couldn't ease the pain and sorrow he experienced at the hurt he'd caused.

Switching on the car engine, Mike pulled back out into the traffic and found himself heading to the pub rather than straight to Sarah's as he'd intended. *Sarah's*. He'd have to get used to calling her flat 'home' from now on – all bridges were burned – he had no other.

The flat was cramped and Sarah talked about buying a house for when the baby came, dreaming of gardens and domesticity. Mike had a fleeting feeling of having been there before. Still, he convinced himself that this baby would be different and being older, he'd have more patience to cope.

Mike dreaded the first scan, fearful it may be twins. He knew what hard work twins were, but thankfully there was only one baby and his relief was almost tangible as he watched Sarah's delight at the sight of their child moving within her.

Yes, Mike determined as he sat in the pub cradling his beer, things would be different this time. But neither his resolve nor the beer could take away the feeling of being a disappointment, a traitor – not only to Hannah and the children but to himself. Mike would be a better father to this baby yet would try his best to build bridges with Kate and Sam, to still be a father to them. The new baby would be their half-sister or brother, perhaps it would be a starting point and they could be involved in this new life.

Mike downed the last of his beer and headed off to Sarah's – home.

27

Joe was hit by a sudden stab of guilt when he realised he was smiling. He was in his office at work, checking over some figures when a colleague came in to ask him to sign some papers. The man remarked on the improved weather they were having of late and chatted to Joe about his plans for getting his caravan out of storage and preparing for its first outing of the year.

The conversation turned to their respective dogs, and Joe recalled his morning walk with Liffey when she'd bounded over the meadow like a kangaroo. She loved the long grass, especially when it was cool and wet, and for a brief time she completely forgot her fears of traffic and loud noises. Joe laughingly showed his colleague the pictures he'd taken of Liffey on his phone.

Once alone again, Joe experienced what he could only describe as a sense of disloyalty. It was happening frequently, when normality slipped into his day, and he paid the price with a sudden surge of guilt. But surely it was a good thing to be able to smile, even to laugh again; he wasn't betraying the memory of Alison by doing so, was he?

There would come a time when Joe would have to start living again, not merely working and taking his dog out. It was nearly four months since Alison had died and he spent most of his time alone, grieving, not knowing what else to do or even what else he wanted to do. Joe's conversation with his colleague prompted thoughts of travel. Perhaps he should get a caravan or one of those motorhomes, then he could take Liffey off for long weekends and see a bit more of the country.

Joe had often fancied a motorhome but Alison liked her creature comforts too much, a warm bath and a hotel when they were away, and a break from cooking. He'd be okay roughing it a bit and it would be great for Liffey. The thought gave Joe something to focus on – he might research the idea on the internet when he got home. Alison was never far from his thoughts, and he was sure she'd approve.

Once home, Liffey's enthusiastic welcome was precisely what Joe needed. She brought him one of Alison's slippers, a habit she'd taken up whenever they returned home. Joe supposed it was time to get rid of the slippers to save that spark of heartache the custom inevitably brought, but he hadn't so he thanked Liffey and stroked her silky coat. Perhaps neither was ready to part with such routines and reminders of Alison just yet.

Joe had taken to buying M&S ready meals, and removed one from the freezer each morning to defrost by his return in the evening. Intending to search the internet later, he first let Liffey into the garden while he heated his meal. After eating, he grabbed his jacket to walk the dog before settling down with his laptop.

It was a pleasant, warm evening with the sun low in the sky. Their route would be the same as the morning – the meadow was perfect at this time of year and an acceptable distance for both to enjoy the walk. Alison had loved the meadow and Liffey was comfortable with its familiarity. At this time of year, hawthorn trees scented the air, mingled with the pungent smell of garlic. Wild flowers bloomed in abundance – swathes of buttercups, ox-eye daisies, red campion and so many others with names Joe didn't remember. Alison would have known them all.

Joe smiled at Liffey as she scooted round and round when he picked up her harness, excitement growling softly in her throat. 'Come on, old girl, walk time!' He caught his spinning dog, pulled on the harness, clipped on her lead and they set off briskly from the house.

28

Time had dragged for David Parker. It was without doubt the longest day he could ever remember but then it wasn't every day you were hanging around waiting for an opportunity to kill your only brother.

After the duty call to Pam, David headed into town searching for breakfast and somewhere to pass the time. He bought a newspaper and went into a Costa coffee shop where he ordered a muffin and a latte. The next hour was spent huddled in the corner, eking out his coffee and reading the paper from cover to cover until it occurred to him how unwise it was to stay in the same place for too long; people might remember him or think it suspicious that he was so obviously killing time.

David certainly didn't want that, so he moved on to House of Fraser, where he found their coffee shop on the third floor and ordered a bacon bun and tea. Another hour passed, equally as slowly as the first. David read almost every word in the newspaper but still stared at it, keeping his head down while he mulled over the morning's events and thought about what he must do later.

The lane where his brother exercised the dog was perfect for his plan – quiet, with no CCTV cameras or houses overlooking the path – it couldn't be better. If Joe followed the same route as before David would have another chance and this time with a better feel for the area. He'd have preferred it to be dark but the nights were light now and unless he postponed the plan until the autumn, which Pam certainly wouldn't approve of, he'd have to accept the daylight and trust to luck.

It was pretty surreal to think of what he was planning, but in his mind, he'd turned the event into a *task* – a job of work, necessary for the rewards it would bring. David also reminded himself of how depressed his brother was and how he'd almost certainly prefer to be with Alison. Yes, it was a mercy killing, David assured himself – yet there was a quickening of his heart rate the more he thought about it and a sense of panic which threatened to choke him.

David had warmed up from the cold wet night he'd endured and as the sun was quite warm in the middle of the day, he left the coffee shop and walked around the town centre for a while before sitting in a small garden area near the town hall.

Aware his parking time would soon run out, David bought a ham sandwich and took it back to the car, not wanting to risk a ticket, and all the while watching for CCTV cameras. He'd become quite paranoid about them and found it an impossible challenge to find a car park without any, so he drove back out to the suburbs and stopped a couple of miles from his brother's house. Choosing a quiet street, David thought he could have an hour or two's sleep before it was time to begin his vigil once again.

Sleep, however, wouldn't come, his mind was too active, his legs twitchy. At one point, he almost decided to give up on the whole ridiculous plan and return home. Then he remembered Pam. David would have to ring soon to update her, not that there was anything to tell, but he pulled out his phone to get it over with.

Her voice was hardly the comfort he needed. 'You'd better make sure it's this evening!' she ordered, 'I've told several people you're ill in bed, so your alibi's all set up.'

David stopped himself from reminding Pam that he was the one taking all the risk; yes, his wife would give him an alibi, but that was the easy part. He just hoped when this was all behind them she'd remember it was he who changed their fortunes, although he doubted it.

Their conversation was brief. If possible, Pam made him even more nervous and after saying a quick goodbye he went for a walk around the area to stretch his legs and try to breathe in some fresh air to settle his nerves.

It was 3.30pm. David doubted his brother returned from work anywhere near as early, but it was time to get into position, to be prepared. Choosing the same spot as before, David moved to sit in the back seat of his car where the windows were tinted and he wouldn't be seen by anyone passing by. He berated himself for not thinking of this sooner – an empty parked car was less likely to draw attention than one with someone sitting inside of it.

The waiting began. At least this time it wasn't so cold; the sun warmed the car's interior so he removed his jacket. David peered at his watch at least every fifteen minutes, willing the time to pass and his brother to come home.

The ordeal stretched over two seemingly interminable hours until finally, at 5.45pm, Joe drove into the street from the opposite end to where David waited and pulled into his drive. David hoped his brother would opt to take the dog out before his evening meal, but it seemed not as it was nearly an hour later before Joe eventually appeared at the gate and walked his dog down the lane, heading for the meadow.

'Thank bloody goodness!' David said and deftly slipped between the two front seats. Taking up position behind the driving wheel, he started the engine.

David's car moved slowly down the street, yet not so slowly as to attract attention, until his brother came into sight. Joe was already past the houses and well down the lane, the dog pulling excitedly at the lead and his attention was fixed solely on her.

David slowed to a stop, the engine idling as he watched his target. '*I can do this*,' he whispered. His hands were clammy, his breathing erratic. If he didn't act quickly, Joe would turn in to the meadow and David's chance would again be lost.

Pressing the clutch down with unnecessary force, David rammed the gearstick into first, released the clutch and pressed on the accelerator, his legs trembling. The car obeyed, jerking forward at his less than smooth handling until he determinedly took control and rapidly built up speed. Moving swiftly through the gears, David steered the now-speeding car directly towards his unsuspecting brother.

Joe heard the sound of a car and vaguely registered the inappropriate speed for the road on which it was travelling. He automatically shortened Liffey's lead, tugging her closer to his side, expecting the car to roar past him and perhaps frighten the dog. As the engine noise increased, he turned to look over his shoulder, annoyed with whoever was driving like a madman.

The last thing Joe remembered seeing was the car rising onto the narrow path, only a few feet away from him. His heart flipped with recognition as he saw his brother behind the wheel! There was no time to cry out – a sharp pain in his hip demanded Joe's attention and the world spun violently.

An image of Alison's face smiled at Joe as everything went black.

29

The weeks after Mike's departure were some of the most challenging Hannah had ever experienced and coming while she was still recovering from the loss of her leg compounded her grief. Only the presence of Kate and Sam kept her stable, but she was mindful that their departure for university was looming and she'd have to make the most of this summer before her children flew the nest.

After the initial shock of Mike's leaving and the twins' expressions of anger at what he'd done to them as a family, Kate and Sam appeared to have slipped into an unspoken agreement of not mentioning his name around their mother. But Hannah felt duty-bound to talk about her husband; he would always be their father and she believed he wanted to maintain a relationship with them. Yet her children became quite skilful at steering the conversation in other directions.

Mike was in touch every week, suggesting the children might like to meet up with him to go tenpin bowling or to the cinema, but if either twin answered the phone, they had a ready excuse to decline his invitations. Hannah wondered if they'd colluded to make a list of 'reasons' why they weren't available, as the words rolled off their tongues with such practised ease.

Despite all he'd put them through, Hannah felt sorry for Mike. Did he really expect the children to accept this new situation and his girlfriend quite so readily? And did he think through what effect having a baby would have on his *old* family? Hannah was presented with the opportunity to ask these questions when Mike rang one weekend when the twins were out.

'Perhaps I didn't realise it would have such an impact on them,' he admitted solemnly. 'They never wanted my company when I lived with you. I didn't think it would be such a big deal, not being around, I mean.'

'They don't take much notice of the furniture in the lounge but they'd certainly miss it if it suddenly disappeared,' Hannah replied without thinking.

'Oh thanks, so I mean about as much to them as the bloody sofas, do I?'

'No, sorry, I didn't mean it – it was a stupid analogy. It's just a teenage thing, Mike. Kids take everything and everyone for granted at this age – it's not personal.'

'Well, it seems like it to me! My own kids don't want to see me. How do you think I feel?'

Hannah was suddenly annoyed. 'I hope you're not expecting any sympathy from me? You've made your choices, Mike. Perhaps you should have thought it through more thoroughly before you left us!' Her anger dissipated almost as quickly as it rose and she continued more softly. 'Look, you need to give them time to get over the shock. No child expects their parents to divorce, and for you to have been seeing someone else and a new baby on the way is quite a lot for them to process. I'll do what I can to help but there are limits, Mike. Can't you see?'

'Yes, I know and I'm sorry, Hannah. I've hurt you and I

honestly regret it, but any help you can give with the kids will be appreciated; they listen to you.'

'Oh, I'm not so sure, but they're good kids and I'll talk to them, see what I can do.'

Hannah did try to speak to them, more than once, but it was too soon for Kate and Sam and such a busy time. After their exams finished, the twins began looking for temporary jobs to earn some money for university, wanting to keep their student loans to a minimum. Hannah was proud of their responsible attitude. Kate quickly got a job in one of the large hotels as a chambermaid. It was minimum wage but the tips were good and she regularly picked up extra hours covering for staff absences. She appeared to enjoy the work and typically made a whole new set of friends to socialise with.

Hannah's accident inevitably brought with it far-reaching consequences, a few of which could be seen as positive and Kate's new 'grown-up' persona fitted neatly into this category. Given his plan to study sports science at uni, Sam also managed to secure a job which thoroughly suited him, in the local leisure centre, responsible for various activities, including lifeguard duties. The biggest plus in Sam's eyes was free access to all the sporting facilities, a dream come true for someone so sport obsessed. The downside for Hannah was that she saw less of her children than before, especially at weekends.

Their presence would have been especially welcome when two letters arrived one Saturday morning in the middle of June.

Hannah often removed her prosthesis when she was alone in the house, occasionally using crutches on which she was much more proficient than in the early days. She loved the new independence her prosthetic leg brought her although at times it irritated and it was a relief to sit down and take it off. Hannah picked up the letters from the doormat and did just that. With a cup of tea on the table at the side of the sofa and the new Jodi Picoult novel she'd begun to read the night before, she eased open the first letter.

The letterhead announced a local firm of solicitors. Hannah gasped, Mike had started divorce proceedings. Why it should be such a shock, she didn't understand. She knew her husband wanted a divorce as soon as possible to marry Sarah, but it hit her hard.

As Hannah stared at the letter the wording blurred before her – it suddenly all became real. Mike was going through with leaving her no matter how badly he felt about the children. Hannah swallowed hard – Mike must love Sarah very much.

I wonder if he loves her more than he ever loved me?

Hannah shook her head to rid her overactive mind of such unhelpful thoughts. But the tears trickling down her face betrayed her feelings. Unsure whether she still loved Mike, Hannah's reaction suggested maybe she did, a tad at least, but how do you fall out of love with the person you've shared most of your adult life with?

Reaching for her cup, Hannah swallowed a mouthful of tea. Deciding chocolate was in order too, she stood up to fetch the bar of Toblerone from the fridge. Suddenly Hannah was on the floor. 'How bloody stupid!' she shouted out loud. She'd been warned it happened but never thought it would to her. How can you forget you only have one leg?

With just her pride hurt, Hannah rolled onto her side and reached for her prosthetic leg from the side of the sofa. Pulling it onto her stump, she rolled onto her knees and managed to raise herself to stand before flopping back down on the sofa. *Forget the chocolate*, she thought, *where's the bloody wine*?

The second letter was much better news. When the prosthesis was fitted, Hannah assumed she'd be able to drive an automatic car. When her physio told her otherwise, it was a bitter disappointment. No matter how well the leg fitted, using a prosthetic leg to drive was considered unsafe. However, the good news was that Hannah would qualify for an adapted mobility car and the letter in her hand was to inform her the car was ready and would be arriving at the garage later in the week.

It was just the news she needed to offset the shock of Mike's solicitor's letter. Since going back to work, Hannah had been relying on the generosity of Rachel and a colleague from the office to give her lifts, but this meant she'd regain her independence and be mobile once more.

Almost as soon as the smile spread across her face, another thought raced in behind it. Would she have the nerve to drive? It had been impossible to try since the accident and now Hannah wondered if her courage would fail her. Undoubtedly part of the problem was that the accident was still a mystery. Not a single detail of that day had returned to her conscious mind and a nagging doubt persisted as to whether she was somehow responsible for what happened.

Had Hannah done something wrong?

Was she culpable for that awful event, and could she trust herself to drive safely again?

30

Rachel insisted on a trip to the Trafford Centre, claiming it would take Hannah's mind off the divorce proceedings so hastily set in motion. 'We can celebrate the new car too,' she grinned, 'you'll be able to give me lifts now!'

Hannah wasn't so sure. Perhaps she'd confess her anxieties about driving again to Rachel – there was no one else she could confide in and her friend's down-to-earth common sense was precisely what she needed. Hannah also considered asking Rachel to accompany her to pick up the car and sit in with her until she felt confident enough to drive alone.

The vast shopping mall was always busy on Sundays but they'd planned which shops to visit rather than wander around aimlessly so Hannah wouldn't tire too quickly. A coffee and a lunch stop would punctuate the walking, so it wouldn't be too demanding.

Approaching the central area, Hannah and Rachel noticed a small crowd gathered at what appeared to be a makeshift animal pen, attracting the attention of several children. Rachel, always curious, dragged her friend closer to see what was happening.

A group of excited children petted a lively pygmy goat in the pen, their laughter and enthusiasm making Rachel smile. Other children sat on chairs, nursing rabbits and guinea pigs, fascinated with finding furry living creatures in a boring shopping centre – their faces testimony to the welcome interlude.

'Don't forget to wash your hands before you go,' a woman reminded a brother and sister who, at their mother's insistence, reluctantly passed a couple of rabbits to other children waiting in line.

Rachel moved to a display board to read the information posted on it. 'Look, Hannah! This explains what it's all about.' As she read more her eyes widened and she reached for her friend's arm to pull her closer. 'I think you should read this.'

Our son, Keiron, was tragically killed in a road traffic accident earlier this year. Keiron loved life and had a passion for animals, particularly those in need of care. To celebrate our son's life, we are working towards opening 'Keiron's Farm', a centre to care for injured and abandoned animals and educate children to care for the creatures we, as human beings, have a responsibility for.

Keiron was born nearly sixteen years ago with Down's syndrome but he taught us so much about love and caring for others during his short life. Sadly, our only child left us far too soon when we were not ready to let him go, but we know he would be the first to want to make his life count, to build something positive from such a tragedy.

'Keiron's Farm' is an ambitious project but our son always dreamed 'big' and we're learning to do the same. We've been overwhelmed by the generosity and support of many who wish to assist in setting up and running this venture. In addition, links with the Down's syndrome society and several children's groups have been established and interest expressed in using 'Keiron's Farm' to help their members interact with and learn about our animals.

Initially, we plan to offer four full-time jobs to young people with learning disabilities, and our dream is that this number will grow until we can provide animal therapy sessions to as many disabled children as need them.

We already have several animals, many of which Keiron had 'collected' and cared for himself. Today we have Biscuit, the pygmy goat, and several of Keiron's chickens, rabbits and guinea pigs. We also care for two elderly donkeys and a Shetland pony and receive requests to house other needy animals every week.

Please feel free to talk to us about our plans and any help you can offer will be gratefully appreciated. We intend to hold an open day in the autumn – the date will be announced in the local press and on social media.

Thank you for showing an interest in our plans,

Alan & Cassie Lang

'I thought he looked familiar. I remember him from the inquest. Come on, Hannah, let's go and talk to him.' Rachel turned towards Alan Lang.

'No, I can't!' Hannah pulled away, moving in the opposite direction.

'But why ...?' The look on her friend's face told Rachel she'd been insensitive. She quickly changed direction and they hurried away together.

Ten minutes later, sitting in a coffee shop in the quietest corner Rachel could find, she apologised. 'I'm so sorry, that was crass of me. As usual I stupidly didn't think.'

'No, it's just me being silly. They're doing something so wonderful, but I couldn't face them.'

'Why? Did it bring it all back to you, a flashback or something?'

'I don't have flashbacks – I still can't remember anything about it, it's just …' Hannah generally found expressing her feelings hard, but it all came tumbling out and in halting words she admitted to her friend the constant feelings of guilt, and doubt as to whether she was to blame and had inadvertently caused the accident. Hannah then confessed her fears about driving again, her lack of confidence and concern as to whether she was safe to drive.

Hannah remained dry-eyed but with a pale face, her eyes dull and distant. When the words finally dried up, Rachel reached out and covered her friend's hand with her own, squeezing it gently.

'Hannah, the police investigated the accident thoroughly and the coroner ruled that no one was to blame. I know it's easy to say, but I also know you. You wouldn't have done anything stupid in such appalling conditions. You're too sensible – you're the most sensible person I know! So please don't beat yourself up about this. I'm sure you didn't do anything to have caused the accident; you're such a stickler for rules. I've heard you tell people what you think of using a mobile when driving – and drink driving. I'm sorry for almost dragging you into a situation where you'd be uncomfortable. I thought you might be interested.'

'Actually, I am interested but I couldn't face them, thinking their son might have died because of me.'

'Don't say that! He didn't! He died because of an accident which, by definition, is no one's fault. Anyway, I picked up a leaflet about their plans if you're interested?'

Hannah smiled. She might have felt uncomfortable talking to the boy's parents but she was certainly curious to see what they planned to do in his memory. It sounded a wonderful idea and perhaps she'd send them a donation, anonymously of course.

31

David pulled up outside his home at 2am and could remember nothing of the drive from Greater Manchester to Eastleigh other than the sensation of a heavy weight pressing down on his chest, and a feeling of complete self-disgust and deep regret at what he'd done. It seemed unreal until the car was mounting the narrow footpath just a few yards away from his brother, by which time David's foot was almost frozen to the accelerator pedal and it was too late to avoid the collision.

The impact was nothing like David expected. Joe was solid enough, flesh and blood as the heavy thud of his body confirmed. But in another way he was an apparition, a shadow in a dreamlike event. How David wished it had been a dream. But no; the body bounced on the front of the bonnet then rolled off the car's nearside and ended up in a shallow ditch. For a split second, their eyes met and then Joe was gone. David was sure Joe recognised him; why the hell didn't he think of wearing a ski mask or something?

Panic had set in and David maintained his speed to the bottom of the lane where he turned right at the T-junction half a mile away. He desperately wanted to stop but was too afraid, as if perhaps Joe might be running after him, shouting for him to wait and explain himself. Finally, after twenty minutes, he risked pulling into a lay-by where he switched off the engine and sucked in huge gulps of air.

David's whole body trembled and tears streamed down his face. Wiping his eyes and nose on his sleeve, he looked around to see if anyone was taking notice of him. It was a country road with no pedestrians in sight and only a handful of other cars passing in each direction. He hadn't a clue where he was; reconnoitring his escape route hadn't occurred to him, but all he wanted to do was to get as far away as possible, although not home. Yet there was nowhere else to go and Pam would be waiting.

Remembering his wife, David knew he should ring her, but the last thing he wanted was to hear her voice asking if Joe was dead, so he decided to switch off his phone and face Pam's wrath when he arrived home.

Mentally pulling himself together, David turned the key in the ignition, set the satnav with trembling hands and followed the monotone instructions thrown out at him by the nasal female voice. He was acutely aware that he mustn't draw attention to himself; there would be no speeding, no stopping for a drink, although he badly needed one, and no stopping at service stations where his image might be picked up on CCTV.

His speed was probably too slow but David was in no hurry and his mind was certainly not on the road. Questions rattled through his head; should he have gone back to see if Joe was dead? Should he have run over the body to make sure? David shuddered at the thought. But the question he wished he'd considered more carefully was, *why the hell did I ever agree to do this?* He'd done some pretty shady things in the past and often been on the wrong side of the law. David didn't claim to be a saint, but he wasn't a murderer! Yet now, that's precisely what he was.

Pulling up outside his home, a light was burning in their flat; it would have been too much to hope that Pam might have gone to bed.

The woman was on her feet and in her husband's face as he came through the door. 'Where the hell have you been? Why didn't you ring?' she shouted. At least her first question wasn't 'Is Joe dead?' David didn't know how he'd have reacted to that one.

'You know where I've been – killing my brother!' he spat, as if he could get rid of what he'd done by expelling the words from his mouth. Pam correctly read his mood, so wisely said nothing and silently left the room to put the kettle on. Returning with two mugs of steaming tea, Pam found David flopped on the armchair staring blankly at the wall. She put a mug in his hand and sat down on the opposite sofa.

'I was worried about you.' Her tone was more conciliatory now.

They were both silent for a few minutes until David said, 'We shouldn't have done it.'

'It's too late now, isn't it? Besides, no one will know.'

'I'll know! Joe was my brother!'

'So he is dead then?'

'I should think so. I didn't stop to take his pulse, if that's what you mean!'

'Don't be sarcastic, David, it doesn't suit you. Do you want to talk about it?'

'What is there to talk about? I feel bloody awful. I should never have let you talk me into it.'

'Me – talk you into it? I seem to remember you were the one who first suggested it. So don't lay the blame at my feet!'

'It was just silly talk then – drunken ramblings – you persuaded me to go ahead with all your talk of money and his house. I should never have listened to you.' David rested his head on the chair and momentarily closed his eyes; the image of Joe's body bouncing off the car seemed to be deeply etched into the back of his eyelids. He snapped his eyes open, stood up and announced, 'I'm going to bed!' Spilling the hot tea over the floor beside him, he left an astounded Pam staring after him.

32

Rest was impossible. David rose at 6.30am, leaving Pam snoring peacefully in their bed. His head ached from two nights of very little sleep and his eyes felt heavy and gritty. He made coffee in the kitchen, sat by the cracked window and looked out onto the factory opposite, where workers were arriving to begin their morning shift. A buzz of conversation drifted upwards. David almost envied them their dull little lives and boring routine; to have nothing more to worry about than getting through the next few hours seemed almost desirable but he only had himself to blame for his current predicament.

How, David wondered, had he fallen so low as to kill his brother? Yes, he'd been in some scrapes and several tight spots over the years, but owing money, cheating, and stealing were far from actually killing someone. And what if he was found out? It was apparent from Pam's reaction the night before that she would save her own skin before his; she may have encouraged him but he should have had more sense than to listen.

Talking about killing someone and doing it were poles

apart – he'd been stupid to think he could take such a wild plan to the extreme and not feel remorse about his actions. Joe was his little brother! Maybe they'd never been close but they shared a bond, the same genes. How could David have stooped so low?

What would transpire over the following days was David's chief concern. As Joe's next of kin, he would most likely hear from the police to inform him of the death, and it would probably be today. If his brother survived the impact and, as David suspected, had seen who was driving, he would still hear from the police, but without the tea and sympathy. Whatever was to come, he hoped it would happen quickly; the not knowing was unbearable. David wanted this nightmare to be over – one way or another.

When the phone rang at 7am, he almost spilt his coffee, David instinctively knew it was about Joe.

'Hello, is that David Parker?' a man's voice asked.

'Yes, speaking.'

'My name's Phil Roper, I don't suppose you remember me but we met at your sister-in-law's funeral a few months ago?'

'Yes, I remember. You live next door to Joe, don't you?' David was trying to keep his tone light. 'What can I do for you, Mr Roper?'

'I'm so sorry, David, but I have some bad news about Joe. There was an incident yesterday, a hit-and-run, and I'm afraid your brother's been killed.'

'No! Surely not – not so soon after dear Alison too! A hit-and-run, you say?'

'Yes. Joe was walking Liffey, his dog, and it appears a car mounted the footpath, hit him full-on and then drove away. The dog's barking eventually attracted attention but no one can say how long Joe lay there or whether perhaps he could have been saved if he'd been found sooner. I'm so sorry. This must be an awful shock to you. I've given your name to the police as next of kin but thought it might be better to contact you first, although they still want to speak to you about the investigation. Your brother was a great friend to my wife and me, and we'll miss him terribly. I suppose you'll be coming up soon to, er, see to the arrangements?'

'Yes of course. I'm between jobs at the moment so I can come later today. Do the police have any idea who did this awful thing?'

'Not that I know of, but they're looking for possible witnesses so let's hope they find the bastard.'

'Yes, of course. Do you have a key to the house, Phil?'

'Yes, that's how I found your number, from Joe's address book. We're also looking after Liffey for the time being – she's used to being with us – is that okay with you, David?'

'That's very kind of you, thank you. We'll arrange to have it taken to a shelter or something when we come. Will you be around later today if we call in for the key?'

There was a protracted silence for a few moments before Phil answered quietly, 'Yes, I'll be here.' Then he put the phone down.

Pam was at her husband's side. 'Was it the police? What did they say?'

'I'm sure you gathered Joe's dead. That was his neighbour, he has a key to the house and I told him we'll travel up today. The police want to see me too.'

'It'll be routine in the circumstances.'

'Phil said they're looking for witnesses, investigating …'

'Of course they are, but they won't find any, will they?' Pam grinned.

David felt sick as he turned to go and get dressed. 'You'd better pack a few things,' he almost growled at his wife.

33

Mike was aware that Sarah wanted things to move faster and knew she'd been disappointed he'd taken so long to leave Hannah, but after the accident, she could hardly insist he left his family when things were so tense. Now he'd made the move Mike felt pressure to get the divorce underway.

'How long will the divorce take?' Sarah asked one morning as Mike was getting ready for work.

'I don't know. I've never been divorced before, have you?'

'Don't be flippant, Mike. We need to get things sorted out; this flat's hardly big enough for the two of us, never mind a baby. It's time to decide on a house.'

Mike sighed; they'd been to view a new build that Sarah had set her heart on and wanted to make an offer, but he thought the third bedroom was too small, hardly more than a box room.

'I know you liked the Greenacres house but the spare bedroom would hardly take a bed. It won't be big enough when Kate and Sam come to stay.' He'd said it all before.

'Realistically, Mike, is that ever going to happen? The

twins are still barely speaking to you and they haven't even been to meet me.'

'I'm hoping it will happen – this baby isn't a replacement for my existing children!' As soon as the words were out of his mouth Mike regretted them. Sarah visibly bristled.

'It's not easy for me constantly being the villain in this situation!'

'You're not the villain; I am. It was me who left them and now I'm paying the price.'

Sarah's eyes flashed. Mike knew he wasn't handling the conversation well.

'So, are you regretting leaving Hannah now? Is living with me the price you're paying?' Sarah's voice rose. 'Am I a mistake? Is our baby a mistake?'

'No, Sarah, that's not what I'm saying; the price I'm paying is losing the twins' respect. You know I love you and our baby.' He moved closer to hold her, but she stepped back from his reach. 'Look, I've got to get to work. We'll talk later, okay?'

Sarah shrugged and Mike left before the argument escalated, but his thoughts were a jumble. It wasn't like Sarah to be so unreasonable – he hoped it was just the hormone changes in her body causing her moodiness. He could do with a little more harmony in their relationship; shouldn't they still be in the honeymoon period?

Mike's train of thought turned to financial matters, currently something of a headache. He earned a good salary and Hannah wasn't asking for too much help, but he was sure that would change when her solicitor got to work. Mike sighed; had he made the right decision in leaving his family for Sarah? Some might say the attentions of a younger woman had turned his head, but would they be right? With the baby on the way it was too late – the decision was made.

At 2pm, Mike was outside the City Hotel waiting for his

daughter to finish her shift. The urgency he felt to remedy the situation with his children prompted him to call Hannah at work and she'd reluctantly told him what time Kate finished for the day.

Mike watched his daughter walk out of the back of the hotel with a young man; they were talking animatedly and Kate laughed at something he said. Kate was a lovely girl and Mike felt a swell of pride as he watched her walking gracefully towards him, a sense tinged with the sadness of knowing he was no longer involved in her life. Mike exited the car and called her name. Startled, Kate turned and spoke to her colleague, who walked away in the other direction.

'What are you doing here?' A cool stare accompanied the question.

'I hoped we might be able to have a chat, catch up, you know?'

'I've got an hour.' Kate walked around to the passenger side and climbed into the car. Surprised, Mike jumped in too and switched on the engine, heading towards the Costa on the next block.

'How did you know what time I finished?' she asked.

'Your mum, but in fairness I had to wheedle it out of her.'

Kate nodded and remained silent until they were inside with their coffees.

'So is this the big attempt to get me onside?' she asked.

'Well, I have to do something, don't I? You won't return my calls and shrug me off when you do answer.'

'Why me, why didn't you try to see Sam?' Clearly, Kate didn't intend to make this easy for him.

'Because you're the one who said you hated me and I'm finding that sentiment impossible to live with,' Mike answered honestly. 'And Sam will come round in his own good time. He usually follows your lead, always has done.'

Kate had the good grace to hang her head and look a little

ashamed. 'I don't hate you, Dad. I was just angry and disappointed.'

'That's good to know. You're too much like your mother to hate anyone, but you had me worried. I've missed you, Kate. I know I've not been the greatest dad in the world but not seeing you hurts. Will you come and visit, meet Sarah?'

Kate paused for a moment then drew in a deep breath. 'I suppose so,' she said unenthusiastically, but Mike would take grudging agreement over an outright refusal any time. He was surprised at how well this was going.

'So when's the baby due?' she asked.

'Four weeks.' He smiled.

'So soon!' Kate was a little shocked; a baby due so soon was more of a reality than his girlfriend vaguely 'being pregnant'. 'Do you know if it's a boy or a girl?'

'No, Sarah didn't want to know.'

'What's she like?' It was a reasonable question yet a difficult one for Mike to answer. He started to describe her appearance.

'No, what's she like as a person, Dad? Why did you choose her instead of us?' Kate persisted.

'Oh, Kate, love, it wasn't a simple 'either or' choice; relationships are more complicated. Your mum and I have been drifting apart for years, we just didn't have much in common anymore.'

'Except Sam and me.'

'Yes, you're right and I should have seen it sooner. I was wrong to allow anything to develop with Sarah, but it did, and now we're having a baby together – which doesn't mean I don't want you and your brother anymore. On the contrary, I love you and want to see you both, to continue being your dad. Do you think that can happen?'

'I honestly don't know. Of course, I want you to be my dad, but what if I don't like Sarah?'

'I'm sure you will when you get to know her. What about Saturday, will you come for lunch?'

'I'm working all day, changeover day; it's always busy.'

'Sunday then?' Mike wanted to pin her down while the mood was amicable.

'Okay, Sunday. Are you going to ask Sam?'

'Yes. Do you think he'll come?'

'I'll have a word first. I'm sure he'll be fine about it.'

Mike smiled, a sense of relief washing over him. He was confident that if the twins could only get to know Sarah they'd like her, which would suffice for the present.

'Thanks, Kate. I'll leave it a couple of days and then ring him when you've had a chance to talk to him. Another latte?'

34

David was drained. Driving back to Greater Manchester was the last thing he wanted to do but it would look suspicious if he didn't rush to his brother's home on the news of his death. He'd have appreciated Pam driving, but she didn't like motorways and always preferred to be driven rather than drive herself. She didn't appear to understand the conflicting emotions David was experiencing and kept up an endless stream of cheerful chatter during the drive.

After a few minutes, David tuned out, annoyed at her insensitivity and not wishing to hear her plans of what they could do with Joe's house and money.

To some degree, he shared her excitement at the prospect of a new life, which only compounded the heavy feeling of guilt. Yet David was not motivated by base greed, like his wife, but by a desire to escape the fear of being found by those he owed money to and who would hurt him badly if they discovered where he was living. The thugs would never unearth him in the suburbs of Greater Manchester.

It was the perfect opportunity for a fresh start if he could only forget the awful act he'd been forced into to achieve his freedom. David was also worried about the police. How thorough would their investigation be? Would they assume it was just a random hit-and-run? He certainly hoped so. If they did ask awkward questions, Pam would vouch for him. She'd told several people he was ill in bed at the time Joe was killed. However, before they faced the police, they had to meet Joe's friend – a man he could barely remember from Alison's funeral but who was soon to become their next-door neighbour.

It was almost midday as they pulled up outside Joe's house. The street was quiet, and as they left the car David thought it prudent to remind his wife that his only brother had died and they should act accordingly, a prompt which earned him a murderous look.

David rang the Ropers' doorbell and waited quietly for someone to answer. Eventually, a woman opened the door, introducing herself as Diane and inviting them inside. They reluctantly stepped over the threshold, accepting Diane's condolences while silently willing her to give them the key and allow them to go. Finally, Phil Roper appeared in the hallway, and they again listened to more commiserations while playing the part of grieving relatives.

'I told the police you were coming up today and they asked if you could contact them as soon as possible,' Phil informed them. 'They seemed pretty keen to talk to you.'

David swallowed hard. 'Yes. I'll ring them. Now if I could have the keys?'

'Would you like me to come in with you?' Phil offered.

'No, thank you, it won't be necessary.'

Diane took the keys from the console in the hall and handed them over. 'If we can help in any way …'

'Thank you; we'll let you know.' David took the keys and the couple left, anxious to get out of the house.

As Joe's front door swung open, Pam's smile turned into a frown. 'I think new carpets will be in order – there's a strong dog smell in here.'

'We can't rush in and change things straightaway; it'll look odd.'

'Oh, don't be so cautious. This is the first good thing to have happened to us in years; can't you relax and enjoy it?'

'No, I bloody can't! We've got to get in touch with the police, remember. It's not a Sunday school picnic. We're not out of the woods yet.'

'Come on. I want a better look at the kitchen.' Pam screwed her nose up at her husband's warnings. David silently followed her.

'Wow, look at these units. They must have cost a fortune! And the tiles, I'm going to love pottering in here.' They moved back into the lounge and David sat down on one of the leather sofas, stroking the soft fabric.

'Alison certainly had good taste,' he remarked.

Pam's eyes sparkled with curiosity. 'Upstairs next. I hope they've got an en suite – I've always fancied one!' She pushed open the first door on the landing to reveal a twin-bedded room, presumably a guest room and briefly glanced around, making approving sounds and nodding. The main bathroom was behind the second door and Pam squealed with delight when she saw the huge air bath and separate shower cubicle, all immaculate, the sun bouncing off the gleaming white tiles.

'This is even better than I'd hoped. That must be the master bedroom. Let's have a look.'

The door was ajar and Pam pushed past David to get in first. Suddenly she screamed, making him jump, and turned back towards him, trembling.

'What the hell is it?' He pushed the door fully open and blanched as he saw Joe sitting in the window seat, his solemn face bruised and swollen. David gasped, staggered backwards and stared at his brother.

'No, I'm not a ghost.' Joe spoke in low, even tones. 'Your clumsy attempt to kill me didn't quite go to plan.' He said nothing else, just stared at his elder brother, disappointment rather than hatred in his eyes.

'Now wait a minute, you've got it all wrong! Whatever you think, it wasn't me, I've been ill in bed for the last few days, haven't I, Pam?' David smiled feebly while his wife nodded frantically. 'Surely you can't believe I'd attempt to kill you?' Even as he spoke the words, the look on Joe's face told him his brother knew the truth.

'David, you were as close to me as you are now. I saw you. Please don't take me for a fool.'

Suddenly, Pam threw herself at Joe and wrapped her hands around his neck. 'You bastard! You should be dead!'

David was quick to pull her off. 'Stop it! Haven't you done enough damage, woman? Joe saw me. He knows!'

As Pam shook herself free from her husband's grip, David turned to his brother and said, 'Look, you probably won't believe me but I'm delighted you're not dead. It was a stupid idea and I hate myself for doing something so despicable. There's no excuse. I've been in a lot of trouble and people are looking for me, not very nice people, and the pressure's been building up. I saw this as a way out. But honestly, Joe, it's such a relief to see you alive, and whatever you decide to do, I know I deserve it.'

'Shut up, you fool!' Pam shouted. 'He could have the police in the next room listening, for all we know. He's tricked us into coming here!'

'Enough, Pam, I've had enough. It's over, so just shut up! If Joe wants to bring the police into this, I can't say I blame him. We deserve it.'

'What do you mean "we"? It was your doing, not mine!' Pam screamed.

It was as David had expected, his wife would deny everything, but it didn't matter. He experienced such overwhelming relief at seeing his brother alive and knowing he wasn't a murderer after all. If the police became involved, so be it, he would tell them everything.

Looking at Joe he saw the sadness in his brother's bruised and swollen eyes. There was nothing more he could say. At that moment, David Parker hated himself more than he would ever have thought possible, more than even Joe could hate him. He was tired; he wanted to crawl away and hide, sink into the oblivion of sleep and forget all about how low he'd stooped. David mouthed the words, *I'm sorry,* to his brother and hung his head like a child caught out in some misdemeanour.

The doorbell shattered the silence and Joe limped downstairs to answer it. Pam followed and made to grab him again. 'Is that the police?' she snarled as David held her back.

'No, it's Phil from next door. He's here to check I'm okay. I think you'd be wise to bear in mind that both he and his wife know everything, just in case you have ideas of another attempt.'

'Now what do we do?' Pam hissed through her teeth at her husband. 'He's probably already told the police.'

David shook his head. 'It doesn't matter anymore; can't you see it's over?' But she was agitated, ready to fight for what she wanted, refusing to accept failure.

Phil was in the hallway, the look of disgust on his face as he glanced past his neighbour to David spoke more than any words could have done. 'Do you want me to do anything, Joe?' His eyes remained on David.

'No, thanks, Phil. I think we're done here. My brother and his wife were just leaving.'

David couldn't believe what he heard. Was Joe simply going to let them go, to walk away without calling the police? Pam almost knocked him over in her haste to get to the front door.

'But Joe …'

'Goodbye, David.' Joe turned his back on him and walked through to the kitchen.

35

Seeing his brother deliberately attempting to run him down had, without doubt, been the most distressing event in Joe's life after losing Alison. He heard the speeding car and groaned inwardly at the senseless recklessness of the driver, but then he turned to look over his shoulder.

David's face, clearly visible, was bright red as if he was about to have a heart attack but there was no time to register anything else before the sudden pain of being struck by a car travelling at such speed.

Joe's memory of events was a little hazy. However, he clearly remembered seeing David before bouncing on the bonnet, crashing into a hedge and then rolling into the ditch at the side of the road and losing consciousness.

When he came around, his first thought was for Liffey. Had she been struck too? But he realised his dog was licking his face; she was unhurt. Then the pain registered. It seared through his hip and shoulder when he tried to move and his head felt as if the percussion section of the Hallé Orchestra were rehearsing inside his skull. Helpless, Joe stayed still, not wishing to exacerbate any injuries he may have sustained.

Far more significant than the physical pain was the realisation that his brother had deliberately tried to kill him. Joe wondered what he'd done for his last remaining family member to hate him so much. Trying to think through the fog in his brain, he turned to Liffey for help.

'Liffey, fetch Phil, fetch Diane,' he tried. The dog licked his face and tilted her head to one side.

'Go! Good girl, fetch Phil, fetch Diane,' he repeated.

Liffey barked once and ran in the direction of home. Joe was surprised and fully expected her to bring him back a stick, but she was gone too long. When she did return, it was with both of his neighbours in tow.

'Good girl, good girl, Liffey!' Once again his friends had come to the rescue.

Phil ran back for the car and insisted on taking Joe to the hospital for a check-up. Joe protested but eventually gave in to the ministrations of his friend and then the staff at A & E.

X-rays confirmed only bruising to his hip and shoulder and apart from a slight concussion, swelling and a black eye, Joe was good to go.

'If the hedge hadn't broken your fall, it could have been a different story,' Phil pointed out on the way home. He wanted to take Joe to the police station to report the incident and the only way Joe could explain his reluctance was to tell him the truth – it had been his brother who'd attempted to murder him.

Phil's eyebrows raised. 'The man's evil, pure evil! You should still report him. He might try again.'

'We'll have to think of something to scare him off …' Joe said thoughtfully.

'Count me in,' Phil volunteered. 'Anything to teach him a lesson!'

And so the plan to let David think he'd succeeded took root. Phil and Diane were enthusiastic co-conspirators, although initially, Diane favoured involving the police and allowing them to deal with the situation. But she was talked around and agreed to play her small part.

And now David and Pam were gone. Joe was confident he would never hear from his brother again.

'Thank you both for your help.' He was indebted to his friends again. 'Whatever you said to David on the phone, Phil, you must have been convincing. They didn't doubt your story at all.'

Diane shook her head slowly. 'They certainly fell for it, didn't they? It's rather disturbing that Phil's such a good liar. They believed him without question.'

'Yes, I rather enjoyed the subterfuge until the bastard said he'd be putting Liffey in a shelter! I was so tempted to give him a piece of my mind. I knew then what sort of a man your brother was; he has a complete lack of humanity.'

Diane put her hand on Phil's arm. 'I think Joe knows that, dear.'

'Oh yes, sorry, Joe. I didn't mean that putting Liffey in a shelter was worse than attempting to kill you, of course …'

'Stop digging, Phil,' Diane cautioned.

'It's okay,' Joe assured them. 'I couldn't agree more and Liffey's certainly proved she's anything but a dumb animal.'

'Absolutely!' Diane smiled. 'Hearing her barking outside the house and then her insistence that we follow her was like one of those old episodes of *Lassie Come Home*. Well done, girl!' She reached down to stroke the dog's silky ears. 'Now, will you be okay by yourself tonight, Joe?'

'Yes, thank you. I'm sure David won't be coming back, and you've done far too much for me already. Besides, I've got Liffey, haven't I?'

36

The email popped into Joe's inbox on the evening after his confrontation with David. It had been quite a day. Joe had begun to wonder if Carolyn was ever going to reply and if he'd been wrong to approach her when he barely knew her. Several times he'd been on the point of emailing again but something stopped him; not wanting to learn an unpalatable truth perhaps. Now it had arrived. Joe sat on the sofa to read it with Liffey curled up beside him, her head on his lap.

```
My dear Joe,
    Your email came as such a shock and
I'm  so  terribly  saddened  to  hear  of
Alison's death. My thoughts and prayers
are with you at this difficult time and
I'm only sorry I'm not able to offer my
help in a more tangible way. What I can
do, however, is to tell you what happened
to  Alison  in  the  hope  that  you'll
understand why she never told you about
the baby.
```

As far as I'm aware, she only ever told her mother and myself, and I have to say, Ethel is (and in my opinion always has been) a bitter, twisted old woman who didn't deserve such a caring daughter.

Alison swore me to secrecy, but as she's no longer with us, I feel sure she would want you to know the truth rather than Ethel's distorted version of it, designed no doubt to repay you for whatever wrong she imagines you have done her.

It happened in about the third month of our first year at uni. Alison and I were in rooms next to each other in the halls of residence and we became great friends, enjoying our new-found freedom away from the constraints of home.

Alison had grown up very much under Ethel's thumb and was naïve in many ways, which sadly made her somewhat vulnerable. I don't think she'd ever had a boyfriend, so it seemed exciting and a new adventure to be savoured when a third-year student invited her out. Neither of us knew the boy in question but a date at the cinema seemed innocuous enough. I remember helping her get ready and her excitement anticipating her first date.

The boy concerned owned a car and picked Alison up from the halls as arranged. I almost envied her — he was rather good-looking and confident, quite a catch, but three hours later, a very different Alison was banging on my door.

I was horrified to find her bruised, scratched and in a dreadful state. Her 'date' had taken her to the cinema and then driven out into the country, where it seemed he expected 'favours' for his trouble. When Alison resisted, he raped her — quite violently, then drove her back to the halls and dropped her off outside as if nothing had happened.

As you can imagine, she was distraught, but became almost hysterical when I suggested going to the police. In those days, rape wasn't always taken seriously by the police, especially what's now termed 'date rape'. Alison was terrified she wouldn't be believed and telling the police would be like being violated all over again.

Sadly, she was probably right; society wasn't as enlightened about such things then as it is today, particularly in the case of date rape. It's often a question of consent, which is very difficult to prove one way or another.

I'm sorry, Joe, this must be so hard for you to read and I'm sure you know where it's leading. Alison didn't report the incident and a few weeks later, matters were made so much worse when she discovered she was pregnant.

I tried to persuade her to see a doctor and tell him what had happened, sure she would be offered an abortion, but Alison was horrified at the suggestion and said it wasn't the baby's fault and she couldn't punish an innocent child. It was so typical of her. She must have been torn apart yet bore it stoically.

When the baby started to show, Ali left uni and returned to face Ethel. I don't think she ever really told me the half of what she suffered from her mother, who called her a slut and as you can imagine, much worse.

I find it difficult to believe that Ethel would throw this back at you now after all the trouble she gave her daughter at the time. She's nothing but a selfish old witch! Anyway, the rest you know, Alison had the baby and was quite prepared to devote herself to being a single mother until fate took over and the baby died.

Alison came back to uni to finish her course. I think it was a relief to get away from her mother again. I was in the second year and we shared a house with another girl, so I was able to look after Alison.

Alison was such a gentle soul and never felt sorry for herself — she even grieved over the baby. After a while, we made a pact never to speak of the incident again, and we didn't for a long time — it seemed to be her way of coping.

The only time I brought the subject up again was a few years later, after she'd met you and you were planning your wedding.

As her bridesmaid, I felt it right to suggest she tell you what had happened. I didn't know you well but was sure you'd understand. Alison disagreed, not because she thought you wouldn't understand, but because she didn't want you to be burdened by what she'd suffered. It was a deep sadness to her, but one she didn't want you to feel for her.

I don't know if I'm explaining this well, but please believe her motives were pure. She wished only to protect you from the pain of learning about her ordeal.

You have lost a wonderful woman and I've lost a very dear friend. This will be painful for you to read, I know, and if you want to talk, please feel free to video call me at any time — listening is the least I can do for you and Alison. God bless you, Joe,

Carolyn

In this heartfelt reply, many of Joe's questions were answered. He'd purposefully tried not to dwell on his mother-in-law's hateful words, but they were always there, lurking at the back of his mind, ready to assault him at a low point of which there were many. The story the email told was incredibly sad, and Alison's wish to protect him typified his wife's nature.

The email surprisingly brought Joe comfort. Alison's

memory was once again intact and he felt shame at those niggling, disturbing doubts he'd allowed to creep into his thoughts, the scenarios he'd imagined, which did his wife no credit and now filled him with remorse.

Initially, Joe was tempted to confront Ethel and tell her exactly what he thought of her; she was prepared to let him think ill of his wife, to besmirch her daughter's character to spite him. Her actions spoke volumes about her warped character. But Joe was tired. The last couple of days had been incredibly tough – the events exhausting, both physically and emotionally.

Would he ever come to terms with his brother wanting him dead? Perhaps not, but maybe David was more to be pitied than hated. Joe had witnessed what hatred could do; he determined to let go of bitterness and resentment. He didn't want to be the person with a chip on his shoulder, the man with a distorted image of the world, if only for Alison's sake.

Joe took a few days off work to recover from his injuries. He telephoned in, admitting to an accident, without going into details. His head throbbed constantly and his shoulder and hip were stiffening, causing pain with each movement, so a few days downtime was necessary. Joe would rest and take gentle exercise by walking Liffey over the meadow. There would be time to continue sorting Alison's belongings too, not an easy task but one he was achieving in stages.

Reading Carolyn's email once again, Joe allowed tears to fall for his wife's sufferings, but his image of Alison remained one of a vibrant, loving and warm human being. He knew she would want him to live, not simply to exist. He'd write to Carolyn, thank her for her honesty, and let her know how much it had helped him, but first he needed rest. After letting Liffey into the garden, Joe took a couple of painkillers, went to bed and slept soundly for ten hours.

37

The drive back to Eastleigh was pure hell for David Parker. Pam was wired and barely stopped talking for the whole four hours. The only respite from her whinging voice was a ten-minute break at a service station to use the bathrooms. She slated Joe as if it was his fault he'd survived the attempt on his life, and she criticised David for not doing the job correctly.

David attempted to counter her criticisms, asking why she hadn't mowed his brother down if she could have done a better job. He attempted to explain how emotionally difficult it had been for him, but his pleas were ignored.

Pam's self-pitying whine continued – the whole world was apparently against them and just when a new, prosperous life was within their grasp, it had been cruelly snatched away and was everyone's fault but hers. It appeared to David that Pam had no conscience whatsoever and when he tried to explain how pleased he was that Joe was still alive and to describe his remorse about his actions, she called David feeble and cowardly.

Eventually, he stopped listening. Mentally shutting off

from her nagging, he attempted to think of ways out of his situation, including getting free of Pam's hold on him.

The couple had been together for nearly twenty-three years, some of which had been happy, especially the early years. When David was employed and earning decent money, Pam was quite affable and was a knockout in the looks department then too. Not having children was a choice – they spent money as soon as it was earned, assuming their situation would remain stable.

There was no planning for the future, no wise investments, and no savings, despite what David told Joe in the letter, and therefore when the gambling took hold of David, the couple's troubles multiplied rapidly. Credit cards were taken out to pay off debts on other cards, and they borrowed from anywhere they could until eventually, in fear of violence from some of David's more unsavoury creditors, they ran away.

For them Eastleigh was the pits – the flat the worst place they'd ever lived and the downward spiral began with their move. And now, with no alternative, they were returning. Ugly thoughts wormed around in David's mind filling him with self-loathing and disgust for the things he'd done and for how low he had sunk – he could even add attempted murder to the list. When Joe allowed him to walk away without reporting the attempt on his life to the police, it was a relief yet shamed him even more.

By the time they arrived home, David had reached a decision.

As Pam snored softly beside him, he planned his escape. If he could avoid the thugs who were looking for him, surely he could escape Pam. But it would have to be far away – David couldn't afford for her to learn his whereabouts – she knew too much about his past misdeeds and could get him into a lot of trouble. Stealth was the only way; he'd leave Pam before she suspected his intentions, which meant as soon as possible.

In hindsight, Eastleigh hadn't been far enough away from Bournemouth for David to be confident of not being found. He wouldn't make the same mistake again. The Midlands would be a better place to hide, Birmingham perhaps, somewhere densely populated. He would get a job, try to make his way again and regain a modicum of self-respect.

David knew he'd have to act before Pam realised something was wrong and before he attempted murder again – this time his victim being his wife. Without much to pack, certainly nothing of any value, one suitcase would be enough and David would simply disappear into the blue. With that satisfying thought in mind, he eventually drifted off to sleep.

The following morning Pam appeared subdued and much quieter than usual. David thought she was probably all talked out or in one of her increasingly frequent moods. Neither of them raised the subject of the previous day's debacle and they skirted around each other, not an easy accomplishment in their pokey flat. Both were restless for different reasons.

Finally, when Pam announced she was going into town, her husband decided there was no time like the present. As soon as she left the flat, he ran to the window and watched her walk down the street, heading for the bus stop. He knew she'd be going on a shoplifting spree; this was her way of cheering herself up, Pam's twisted version of retail therapy.

David dragged the large suitcase from the top of the wardrobe and threw it on the bed. It was an expensive case, one of the few decent things they'd rescued from Bournemouth when they'd left in such a hurry, and he started to pile his clothes inside. There was plenty of room; he didn't possess much but thought he'd take a few bits of bedding and towels too, there was room in the car and they were every bit as much his as Pam's.

David's thoughts raced ahead; he would search for a bedsit to rent and find a job. Anything would do, flipping burgers, security work, or even a janitor. Hell, he would clean toilets if it meant he'd be able to live with himself again. It didn't take long to clear the bathroom of his toiletries; his whole life fitted into one suitcase.

David's mood was more optimistic than it had been for weeks, as if life might still hold some meaning for him. He was set on a course and determined to escape and reinvent himself. For the first time in days he smiled as he carried the case to the door, ready to load it in the car.

To his surprise and horror, as he opened the door to step out into his new life, Pam was standing outside, fumbling for her key. She took one look at the case in David's hand, and all hell broke loose.

38

Joe woke early, his head pounding and his body aching. Liffey lay on the bed beside him, her chin resting only inches from his face, looking hopefully at him with those doleful irresistible eyes. With slow, deliberate movements, Joe rolled out of bed, the pain worse than the day before, his limbs stiff, making every movement an effort.

Taking the stairs slowly, he made it to the back door to let Liffey out; she'd have to see to herself until Diane arrived to take her for a run.

Briefly, he wondered how his brother was feeling this morning. David had expressed a modicum of remorse, but Joe was uncertain how genuine the sentiment was; perhaps it was only an act to dissuade him from involving the police? However, his brother was no longer Joe's concern – it was doubtful he'd ever hear from him again.

Leaving the back door open for the dog to come in when she was ready, Joe limped upstairs and stood under the shower for fifteen minutes, allowing the warm jets of water to massage his aching body. Refreshed and somewhat more mobile, he dressed and went about the early morning tasks of feeding himself and Liffey.

As well as thoughts of David and the previous day's events, Carolyn's email was very much still on Joe's mind. It answered so many questions yet presented him with more to think about. Ethel's role in past events was indeed a black one, and anger simmered within him as he thought of how little compassion she'd shown to Alison during her time of need. Ethel had used her daughter as an unpaid carer and was now prepared to besmirch her memory to score points against Joe. What an incredibly selfish woman Ethel was.

Diane arrived to take Liffey for a walk and fussed over Joe as much as he'd allow. She and Phil had been brilliant throughout the last few months and he didn't know how he'd have managed without them. When Liffey was returned and the house in order, Joe sat in the conservatory with a coffee, intending to do nothing more until lunchtime. Instead, he drifted off to sleep, woken by the telephone when he was surprised to see it was after 1pm.

'Good afternoon, is that Mr Joe Parker?' a man's voice enquired.

'It is, yes.'

'Er, hello, I'm Detective Sergeant Ted Armstrong from Hampshire Constabulary in Eastleigh. Could I confirm whether or not you are a relative of Mr David Parker?'

Joe's heart sank. What could have happened now? 'Yes, I'm his younger brother, is anything wrong?'

'I'm very sorry to tell you that your brother is dead, Mr Parker. We found your number in a phone book at his flat and I wonder if I could ask you a few questions? I'm sorry for your loss and for having to inform you on the telephone like this, but circumstances dictate we act swiftly.'

Joe paused for a moment, stunned by the detective's words.

'Are you still there?' DS Armstrong asked.

Joe sat on the nearest chair, took a deep breath then answered, 'Yes, sorry. It's just a shock, that's all. How did he die?'

'It appears to be a domestic incident which got out of hand. Could you tell me the last time you saw your brother, Mr Parker?' The sergeant wasn't unsympathetic yet was choosing his words carefully, probing without giving much away.

'Um, yes, I saw him yesterday.' Joe's mind raced – should he tell the sergeant everything, and what did he mean by a domestic?

'Yesterday?' The sergeant sounded surprised. 'Did you visit him here?'

'No, David and his wife came here to visit me but only for an hour or so ...'

'A four-hour drive for an hour's visit seems a little unusual.'

A rhythmic tapping noise accompanied the detective's words and Joe imagined the man tapping his pen on the desk. 'Yes, I agree. Look, I'm sorry, sergeant, but by a domestic what exactly do you mean?'

'We've arrested Mrs Parker on suspicion of murder, but you don't seem too surprised.' The sergeant appeared to pick up on every nuance of Joe's answers. There wasn't time for Joe to think through what was prudent to tell him. He'd simply have to tell the truth.

'Look, Sergeant Armstrong, the thing is, I'm, er, recovering from a recent accident, well no, it wasn't an accident. There's something you should know about my brother ...'

39

Sarah had been on edge all morning and nothing Mike could say seemed to help. She'd spent most of Saturday cleaning the flat, even though to Mike's eye, it didn't need it.

'Slow down, love, they're teenagers; they won't notice a bit of dust.'

'But I will! What do you think I should wear?'

'What's wrong with what you've got on?'

'Jeans? You're joking!'

'I bet that's what they'll be wearing, well, not maternity jeans obviously. I want them to meet the real you. Look, it's great you're making such an effort, but you're going to wear yourself out. They'll love you just as you are. I do, don't I?'

Sarah shook her head with a look that said *huh, men.*

'I hope the Yorkshire puddings rise. They will like a roast dinner, won't they?'

'Yes, they eat anything, particularly Sam, although you wouldn't think it to look at him.'

'Perhaps you're right. I'll keep the jeans on and change this top.' She headed off into the bedroom to change.

Mike sighed. He wouldn't admit it to Sarah, but he was

also nervous about the twins' visit. It was important to him that they accepted his new partner.

Looking around the flat, he took stock of his new home. It was modern but small, basically just one long living room, a bedroom, bathroom and tiny kitchen, all somewhat girly, with pink carpets in both the lounge and bedroom. The blinds danced with brilliantly painted butterflies and daisies, too many overstuffed cushions crowded the sofa and a small glass table with four tubular steel chairs filled almost a third of the room. It was big enough for a single woman, but not a couple and certainly not a family. Clearly they needed somewhere larger but it wouldn't be before the baby was born now. Sarah owned the flat; she'd never earned much as a barmaid, but her grandmother had left her enough money to buy the flat outright, so at least they'd have a deposit to put down on a house.

It was bizarre for Mike to be starting again, worrying about money and anticipating a new baby, both things he'd thought behind him forever. His mates had teased him about Sarah at first, saying she'd tire of him and he'd never cope with a baby at his age. But Mike was determined to prove them wrong, even though there were times when he felt under pressure, not like it had been with Hannah. Over their years together, they'd grown used to each other, something he'd latterly interpreted as apathy and their marriage as stale. With hindsight, he remembered it as being comfortable, even undemanding. But when his thoughts wandered in that direction, Mike pulled himself up sharply, reminded himself that a marriage shouldn't be like an old pair of slippers. Sarah was younger, exciting, full of life and energy, or at least she had been until this pregnancy; he hoped she'd keep him young and fresh.

Mike watched Sarah waddle out of the bedroom wearing a fresh white gypsy top, looking barely older than Kate. She'd brushed her hair until it shone and applied a little lip gloss.

'I'll put the Yorkshires in now – the veg are boiling – do you think the twins will be on time?' Sarah sounded breathless.

'It'll be a first if they are but carry on, I'm sure it'll be fine.' The doorbell saved Mike from Sarah's sarcastic reply as her eyes widened.

'They're early!' she gasped.

'Must be keen!' Mike grimaced and moved to open the door and greet his children. Introductions were somewhat awkward, but Kate had made an effort and brought a bunch of garage flowers for her hostess. Sarah took the first opportunity to leave the three of them alone while she found a vase and attended to the cooking. The twins were unusually quiet; aware that everything they said could be heard throughout the flat.

'Nice place.' Sam swivelled his head to take it all in.

'It's a bit small for when the baby comes, we're looking for a house,' Mike explained. An awkward silence followed. The usual parent/sulky teenager role was uncomfortably transformed into host/guests as Mike offered his children a drink.

'Thanks, Dad, I'll have a beer.' Sam grinned as Mike raised his eyebrows.

'Just a Diet Coke for me if you have it,' Kate added.

Sarah was spooning batter into the hot fat in the kitchen. She looked flustered so Mike gave her a Coke first. 'Relax.' He smiled but she was absorbed in the cooking and didn't respond.

The meal was good and although conversation was somewhat stilted, the children were polite and complimented Sarah on her cooking. She in turn asked questions about their courses at university and aspirations for the future. It all seemed forced and manufactured but Mike silently reassured himself that it was going well for a first visit.

'Dessert, anyone?' Sarah stood – then groaned and looked down at her feet. She was standing in a pool of water, embarrassed and confused. 'No! There's another three weeks yet!'

Mike looked from his girlfriend to his daughter, unsure what to do. Sam wrinkled his nose.

Kate stood up. 'Have you got a bag packed?'

'No, I thought I had plenty of time.'

'Come on, I'll help you. Dad, we need to get her to hospital.'

Kate looked around the uber-pink bedroom. An unassembled cot was propped against one wall and a plastic box full of unopened baby clothes confirmed they were far from ready for this baby's arrival. 'Night clothes?' Kate asked.

'Top drawer and the holdall's on top of the wardrobe.' Sarah perched on the edge of the bed holding her back.

'You might want to change those jeans,' Kate suggested.

'Oh, yes.'

Mike came into the room, embarrassed at the sight of Kate throwing things into the holdall while his girlfriend changed her clothes. The last thing he'd expected was that the baby would arrive when his children were visiting. With three weeks to go, did it mean something was wrong?

'Is the oven off?' Kate asked in a brisk, matter-of-fact manner. When did she become so practical? he wondered.

Mike turned to Sarah. 'Yes. Are you okay, love?'

'Of course I'm not. I'm having the damn baby!'

Kate picked up the bag and went to join Sam in the lounge.

'Shall we go?' Sam whispered to his sister. 'I think dessert's off the menu.'

'Never mind dessert!' Kate chastised. 'We'll see them off to the hospital and then make our escape. It's certainly livened the visit up, hasn't it?' She grinned.

Mike helped Sarah into the car. She didn't appear to be handling the pain well – but he couldn't stop thinking about Hannah and how brave she'd been.

Kate asked Mike to ring her as soon as there was any news. He nodded but didn't seem to take anything in as he pulled away from the kerb, with Sarah moaning in the passenger seat.

'Do you think she'll be all right?' Sam asked his sister.

'Well, she's only having a baby; it's been done before, you know.'

'Yes, but isn't it rather early? I thought they said another three weeks.'

'Yeah, but I'm sure everything will be fine. It wasn't as if she was bleeding. That would have been something to worry about.'

Sam pulled a face and changed the subject. 'Shall we go back home? Mum'll be wondering how the visit went. It must be strange for her. Dad having a baby with his girlfriend and us off to uni soon. She's going to miss us, isn't she?'

'She's got good friends and her job. I offered to stay and look after her but she wasn't having any of it.'

'I suppose we didn't know how she'd manage then, and it was before Dad left. She's brilliant though, isn't she, always thinking of others.' Sam rarely offered his opinions and Kate was surprised he even thought about such things.

'Let's get ice cream at the mini-market and take it back with us instead of dessert, and we can tell Mum what happened.' Sam nudged his sister.

That's more like it, Kate thought, *thinking of his stomach as usual.*

40

Hannah followed the progress of Keiron's Farm with interest, often turning to the Facebook page to read the regular updates. It was packed with photographs showing the progress to date, a visual diary of how busy Cassie and Alan Lang had been. Hannah was impressed. What they'd achieved in just a few short months was amazing. It was apparent that the Langs' home was ideally suited to the purpose towards which they were working. Kismet, some might say.

Faced with the photographs of Keiron was difficult for Hannah. He was a smiley boy, covered with freckles and a mass of red hair flopping into bright green eyes. With everything to live for he should have had years of happiness ahead of him. Hannah fought back the tears and the now familiar, unwelcome feeling of guilt which she still couldn't shake off.

The decision of the coroner and the opinions of her family and friends all stressed the irrationality of her guilt, but until she could remember the accident for herself, it would remain firmly lodged at the back of her mind. But would she ever remember? Seeing the photos of the boy, so vivacious and animated, it was difficult for Hannah to believe he was dead, and she could only imagine the heartbreak his parents must be battling with each day.

Keiron's love for animals was evident – there were images of him with his chickens – rescued battery hens, the pygmy goat he called Biscuit and various other animals and birds. The Langs had undoubtedly found a fitting project as a memorial to their son, and their hard work and dedication shone from every photograph and post.

Accounts from others who'd helped by donating money or practical means captured Hannah's interest. The pupils at Keiron's school had raised over ten thousand pounds through a sponsored walk, and pledged to hold at least one fundraising event each year to help the continuation of the work. Hannah found the accounts humbling and didn't hesitate to turn to the 'Just Giving' page to make a generous donation; her desire to support this fantastic project was strong. It was a living tribute to a remarkable young man.

Hannah was simultaneously humbled and inspired by the Lang family. It gave her pause for thought about her own life since the accident. True, she'd lost a leg, but not her life – her husband, but not her children. When dark moods and moments of self-pity edged into her mind, Hannah vowed to think of Keiron and his parents and to be grateful for her remaining blessings.

———

True to her word, Rachel accompanied Hannah to collect her mobility car and after a brief lesson from the mechanic at the garage, sat with her friend while she drove for the first time since the accident. The desire to regain her independence spurred Hannah on. Nerves settled in, but her goal was to ferry her children around and be useful again.

Rachel encouraged and applauded Hannah, insisting they drove on the motorway, although not yet to the accident site. Her insistence paid off. After over an hour's practice, Hannah's confidence returned, the car was easy to manage and she enjoyed being in control. Hannah was delighted – it would make life so much easier, especially as she was working full time again.

A car was essential before the accident, but impaired mobility made it crucial – using a bus was impractical as walking to and from bus stops proved difficult and even painful at times. Yes, Hannah would enjoy her regained self-sufficiency; it was another step to living a normal life.

One of the first places she would be visiting in her new car was a solicitor's office. With more than a little reluctance, Hannah engaged the services of a local firm recommended to her, having accepted that her marriage was over for good. As Mike was having a baby with another woman, it was pretty final and there was no reason to contest the divorce. Mike was never coming back and she didn't want to be stubborn out of spite.

Hannah found a parking space with relative ease, just a short walk from the solicitor's office, housed in an old Victorian building. It was once a grand home now carved up into commercial units. Steps led to the front entrance, but thankfully Ms Emily Cowan's office was on the ground floor. The waiting room was stuffy, airless, and as Hannah was early, she perched uncomfortably on one of the plastic bucket seats to await her appointment, listening to the high-pitched sing-song voice of the receptionist repeating the same sentence to every caller.

Eventually Ms Cowan appeared in the doorway and invited Hannah into her office. A plush chair on the visitor's side of a modern glass desk and air conditioning greeted her, a welcome relief on such a hot day. Emily Cowan was younger than

Hannah expected, mid-thirties perhaps, a tiny, slim woman with a severe blonde bob and rather pinched features. Her broad smile softened the overall effect.

The solicitor opened the conversation and got straight to the point. 'Now then, Mrs Graham, I believe your husband has filed for divorce?' Hannah was relieved; Rachel had spent the last evening drumming instructions into her; the most important was to be concise as solicitors charged by the hour. Don't waste time with chit-chat, Rachel warned. Hannah fumbled in her bag for Mike's solicitor's letter and handed it over. Ms Cowan skimmed the page and put it on top of a manila file. Hannah's divorce file.

'It's pretty standard. As your husband admits to an affair, it should be a straightforward case. Have you got your marriage certificate with you?'

'Oh, no, I never thought …'

'Could you drop it into the office soon?'

'Yes, of course, sorry.' Hannah shuffled uncomfortably in the chair, listening to her solicitor outlining the process and wondering how often she'd done this. What a depressingly sad job.

When the issue of joint property and finances arose, Hannah explained her wishes. 'Mike has a new partner and a baby to consider. I've got a good job so I only want Mike to contribute towards our children.'

Emily Cowan looked up from her notes to stare at her new client, one eyebrow raised and a look which suggested Hannah was betraying the whole of womankind. The solicitor commenced a little speech, one she'd probably used several times before, about Mike taking nearly twenty years of her life, how Hannah had cared for him and their children and now he was discarding her, with no more thought than if she was an old newspaper.

Hannah squirmed, feeling like a naughty schoolgirl, yet

becoming increasingly irritated as she listened. This woman didn't know what her marriage had been like – divorces were not 'one size fits all', were they?

'Actually,' Hannah spoke up, 'I know all the clichés, the best years of my life and so forth, but this is how I want it to be, civilised, and I'd rather err on being generous so our children have a good example and don't see their parents fighting over money.' Why did everyone think life was all about money? Hannah earned enough for her needs and considered herself fortunate. Her dignity was more important than grasping for a generous settlement.

'That's fine then.' Ms Cowan's features softened as she abandoned the stock speech. 'You're the client. I'm happy to do whatever you wish.'

The air was cleared and Hannah remained only long enough to answer all the necessary questions to allow her solicitor to respond to the petition. She then left, promising to drop in the marriage certificate the following day. No doubt there would be other questions to answer, but she'd made her wishes clear and was content.

41

D S Ted Armstrong was a tall, wiry man, about forty, and almost entirely bald. His pale blue eyes were hooded by heavy lids and seemed to take in everything he saw, blinking the information away to store for future reference. He arrived late morning on the day after his telephone call, alone, which surprised Joe, and with an easy languid manner he prised out the information he wanted.

Joe had asked Phil and Diane to be with him at the interview. The detective would almost certainly want to know of their involvement in recent events, and being Saturday, it was no problem for them to be there. Joe appreciated the moral support. When he broke the news of David's death, his friends were understandably shocked and Joe was concerned he may somehow have landed them in trouble by involving them in his plans.

Diane made coffee and after the detective once again offered his condolences, they sat in the lounge, awkwardly taking the measure of each other.

DS Armstrong turned his gaze to Joe. 'Mr Parker, from what you told me on the telephone yesterday, your brother attempted to kill you a few days ago, yet you decided not to report this to the police. Can you tell me why?'

Joe had tried to explain on the phone but related the details again. 'I've no doubt it was an attempt to kill me, but David was my brother, and whatever he'd done, I couldn't bring myself to report it and possibly see him sent to prison.'

'And you hatched a plan with your neighbours to teach him a lesson?'

'You could say that, but it was entirely my doing. Phil and Diane agreed to help but only after trying to persuade me to tell the police.' Joe wondered what charges the police could bring against him; surely there'd be something. He didn't care for himself but the last thing he wanted was for his friends to be involved.

'And your brother and his wife left after learning you were still alive?'

'Yes, I assumed they were going home, as it appears they did.'

'When you saw your brother in the car which hit you, was he alone?' Armstrong asked.

'As far as I could see, it all happened so quickly.'

'So his wife wasn't with him that day?'

'That's right, but I've no doubt she was part of his plan, if not the instigator.' Having heard some of their conversations when they were in his house, Joe was convinced David had succumbed to Pam's influence and she was more culpable than his brother.

DS Armstrong turned his attention to Phil. 'And you, Mr Roper, did you witness Mr Parker's brother's attempt on his life?'

'Well no, but Liffey came to fetch us, which was the first we knew about it, and we found Joe in the ditch down by the meadow.'

'And this Liffey is?' DS Armstrong tilted his head almost

to his shoulder. Joe nearly chuckled, wondering if he'd want to interview Liffey next.

'The dog,' Phil replied. 'It may sound a bit far-fetched but it's what happened.'

Armstrong glanced at Liffey who was snoring gently in the corner of the room. 'Right, the dog. So when the dog led you to the scene, what happened?'

'I took Joe to the hospital. He didn't want to go to the police.'

Joe was becoming a little frustrated with the questions and wanted a few of his own answering. 'DS Armstrong, unless you intend to charge me with failing to report a crime, I don't see where your questions are leading. So far you've told me very little about what happened to my brother and I'd like to know how he died.'

The detective shifted his weight in the chair and nodded. 'Right, of course, but I'm afraid it's not pleasant.'

'Death seldom is, my wife died five months ago and now my brother, and I'm feeling as if I'm under suspicion here.'

'I'm sorry to hear it, Mr Parker, and I apologise. I assure you you're in no way under suspicion. Your brother died from stab wounds – several punctures in what appears to have been a frenzied attack. If it's any consolation, death would have been instantaneous; most of the wounds were inflicted post mortem.'

Diane's hand flew to her mouth. Phil wrapped a comforting arm around her, his face pale. Joe felt sick. His brother might have done some terrible things but he didn't deserve this. Pam must be insane.

'And it was Pam who killed him?' Joe asked.

'We've arrested Mrs Parker on suspicion of murder. There was a call from a concerned neighbour about noise from their flat and when our officers arrived they found your brother. Mrs

Parker was picked up almost immediately and there is strong evidence to tie her to the incident.'

'So why all the questions about David's attempt to run me over?'

'Well, if you wish to press charges, obviously not against your brother, but against Pamela Parker, we can add a charge of conspiracy to the one of murder.'

'But surely conspiracy would be impossible to prove, especially now David's dead?'

'It would be difficult, but it's a matter of putting pressure on our suspect. If she thinks other charges are in the offing, she may come clean about the murder.'

'What? You mean the woman's trying to say she didn't do it?'

'Exactly.'

'Bloody hell, she must be mad!'

'And I think insanity will be her line of defence.' It was the most forthcoming thing Armstrong had said.

Reluctantly DS Armstrong agreed to leave Joe to consider pressing charges. 'We'll keep you informed of any progress in the case, Mr Parker, and if you'd like to discuss anything, this is my direct line.' He handed Joe a card and then left, uttering more condolences.

'D'you think they're trained in stock phrases at copper school?' Phil remarked when he'd gone. 'What are you going to do, Joe?'

Joe blinked away tears. 'I haven't a clue. They seem to think I should be sorting out the flat and everything, all the talk about when the 'crime scene' is released. It's the same bloody roundabout all over again, isn't it?'

Phil put his hand on Joe's shoulder. 'Bloody hell, mate; surely no one can force you to take responsibility for their affairs, especially in the circumstances.'

'Don't get in a state about it, Joe,' Diane chipped in. 'I

should think the investigation will take some considerable time. There must be a protocol for these situations, or you could just put the flat in the hands of house clearers or leave the landlord to do it.'

'I'll have to arrange a funeral. It's a hell of a way to die and he was family …'

'You should wait a few days, see what DS Armstrong comes back with. There's no urgency and you're not in any fit state to be arranging anything at the moment.'

'You're right, Phil. How the hell could she do such a thing to her own husband, but then I've never understood how anyone can kill another human being – it's barbaric.'

'Me neither, yet it happens and it's come close to home for you, right when you could have done without it. Now, no arguments, you're coming round to ours for some lunch and Liffey too. It's only cold ham and salad and you don't have to stay if you don't want to – you need to rest,' Diane insisted.

Joe was in no mood to argue and accepted his friends' ministrations, grateful for their presence. He would do as they suggested, think things over and then talk to the detective when he felt better. Nothing he could do would help David now.

42

'She's perfect, isn't she?' Sarah gazed down at the scrunched-up features and red face of her new baby daughter, who lay in her arms, her tiny fists waving angrily at the world.

'Just like her mum!' Mike smiled. Baby Isla's early arrival had given them quite a fright. Sarah was beside herself by the time they reached the hospital and it didn't take the medical staff long to decide on an emergency caesarean. Isla was breached, three weeks premature, and in distress, so an operation was the only safe option.

Mike paced the corridors in traditional style, worried for his girlfriend and the baby. He wished he'd asked Kate to stay with them. She'd been brilliant when Sarah's waters broke, whereas he couldn't get past it happening three weeks early and panic set in, rendering him useless. Kate, however, was calm and practical, packing a bag and then ushering them off to the hospital as if she dealt with such emergencies every day.

While Sarah was in surgery, Mike wondered when his little girl had grown up to be such a caring young woman and why he'd been so stupid as to not to get to know his children better.

Perhaps their relationship would be different now. This new baby might even bring them closer together.

It hadn't been long, although to Mike it seemed so, until the doctor came to tell him they had safely delivered his new baby daughter. Mother and child were fine and now he could see for himself.

Sarah couldn't take her eyes off her new daughter. 'Five pounds, ten ounces is a good weight for a premature baby. I'll probably have to stay in a couple of nights until Isla's strong enough to go home.'

Mike beamed, stunned by a cocktail of unexpected emotions. Sarah appeared to have calmed down with the safe arrival of their baby and was more like her old self, a change he silently welcomed.

'Can I take her?' He reached down for the tiny bundle and carefully lifted her into his arms. He'd been very much hands-on when the twins were born, out of necessity, and the feeling of holding Isla was both new and familiar. Mike experienced a rush of love and wanted to hold this precious baby forever, to protect and cherish her, but he also wanted to dash back to the flat to prepare for his family's homecoming. The cot was to be assembled, the clothes unpacked and a hundred other things crowded his mind. They'd intended to buy a steriliser, bottles and all the other paraphernalia associated with feeding but had left it too late. He'd have to go to the all-night Tesco; they'd probably have everything he needed.

Perhaps tomorrow Mike would go to the estate agents and put an offer on the Greenacres house on which Sarah had set her heart. It wasn't perfect, yet it was apparent that compromise came into play when buying a house. He'd make it work. Sarah and Isla deserved it. As he held his baby daughter, Mike silently vowed never to take this child for granted, never to lose the bond he felt today, and, if it wasn't too late, to make things up with Sam and Kate.

'Kate? It's Dad. You have a new baby sister!' Mike grinned into the phone even though he knew his daughter couldn't see him – he hadn't stopped smiling since Isla's birth.

'Oh, wow! Are they both okay?'

'Yes, fine. The baby was distressed when we arrived at the hospital and they very quickly decided on a caesarean but they're both good now.' There was relief in Mike's voice.

'That's fantastic! What weight is she?'

'Five pounds, ten ounces, good for a premature baby.'

'Give her a kiss from me, will you. Can I come in to see them?'

Kate's interest delighted her father. 'Yes, Sarah would love that. She was quite impressed with how you organised us all this afternoon, and so am I. They'll be in the hospital for a couple of days and I know Sarah's mum is visiting tomorrow afternoon, so will the evening suit you?'

'Great! I'll see if Sam wants to come too, shall I?'

'No, I'll let him know. I was going to ring him next.'

'Okay then, see you tomorrow.'

The conversation ended and Mike immediately rang his son, who didn't perhaps enthuse quite as much as Kate but seemed pleased for his dad and agreed to visit the following evening. Mike wanted to ask Sam to tell his mother, strangely wanting Hannah to know, but he didn't, assuming one of them would tell her anyway.

Isla's birth had a profound effect on Mike, more than he'd anticipated. His mind travelled back to when the twins were born, a magical time. He recalled the milestones as they learned to walk and talk, often only to each other, and the bond they shared as twins.

When did he start to feel they didn't need him, and why? Was it because they had each other, perhaps? They appeared so self-sufficient as they grew, or was he looking for excuses? Hannah hadn't experienced those feelings; she'd adored their children from day one and had been a wonderful mother. So at what point did he begin to fail them, for Mike was sure he had, even though he loved them.

Shaking off his reflective, somewhat melancholy mood, Mike reminded himself the clock couldn't be turned back and amends could only be made in the present and the future. Silently he vowed to make it up to Kate and Sam and to be the best father he could to his new daughter, his second chance.

Mike went back into the ward to see Sarah and Isla, both sleeping. He kissed Sarah on the forehead and she opened her eyes.

'Go back to sleep, darling – it's been a busy day. I've rung everyone and they all send their love. I'm going home now but I'll be back first thing in the morning. Goodnight.' He kissed his new baby daughter and left them to rest.

43

It took almost two weeks for Joe's bruised and swollen face to improve. The colours changed from yellow to black, then yellow again, and his hip and shoulder were still quite sore. Walking Liffey was good exercise, although he slowed his pace accordingly, not wanting to seize up – he'd had enough recuperating after the accident in February.

If he didn't keep busy, Joe's thoughts ran away with him. It would be easy to fall into the trap of self-pity after the dramas which had befallen him of late, yet he steadfastly refused to go there. The year was certainly turning out like no other he'd ever experienced. Losing Alison was more than enough to bear, but David's death hit him hard. It was still an ongoing investigation; Pam had been charged with murder but Joe knew little more.

When a call from DS Armstrong came requesting another interview, Joe could no longer put off a visit to Eastleigh. He'd hoped to keep his involvement to a minimum – arranging the funeral perhaps, but he was aware there was also the matter of the flat and whatever possessions were there.

The drive was uncomfortable as Joe's hip was still painful.

He travelled after work on Friday night, having already taken more time off work than he should, and the traffic was mercifully light. Joe was meeting DS Armstrong at 9am on Saturday – the detective assured him he'd be working through the weekend.

Joe had booked a room in a Premier Inn for the night. It was clean and comfortable and surprisingly he slept soundly, thoroughly exhausted.

After a hearty breakfast in the Inn's restaurant, Joe set off to meet Ted Armstrong. There was no police station in Eastleigh, so he travelled the five miles to Southampton Central, where the detective was based and was greeted cordially and offered coffee, which he accepted gratefully. Armstrong started to update him, getting straight to the point.

'Mrs Parker has confessed to manslaughter. She's pleading a disturbed mind due to her husband's constant abuse.' As ever, he spoke in a monotone.

Joe's jaw dropped. 'Constant abuse? Is she trying to say that David abused her throughout the marriage?'

'Yes. Mrs Parker is citing physical abuse and mental cruelty.' Armstrong observed Joe for any reaction and then asked, 'Do you buy that?'

'No way! I can't claim to have been close to David, especially in later years, but I'm sure he wouldn't have been violent.'

'You think so – even though he tried to kill you?'

'I know it seems incongruent, but if you'd told me it was the other way round and Pam abused him, I'd find it much easier to believe. During our last encounter, David appeared almost remorseful for his actions. Pam was the more hostile of the two. I got the distinct impression she'd been the driving force behind his attempt to kill me.' Joe couldn't be sure, yet that's how he'd read it.

'Sadly, impressions count for nothing in a court of law, Mr

Parker. Her defence will be thorough and the prosecution is currently looking for witnesses to disprove her story, yet rather unsuccessfully, I'm afraid. Your brother and his wife appear to have kept themselves to themselves.'

'But surely there'll need to be witnesses to prove her defence too?' Joe asked.

'Presumably, but the workings of the court are often a mystery to me. However, we're doing all we can to investigate their relationship and precisely what happened. The information you gave me about your brother's attempt on your life will be integral to the case, and in due course, you'll be called to give evidence to the events of that time.'

'What? But what's it got to do with Pam killing David? Surely I don't have to be involved?' Joe was horrified; he hadn't expected this, and to have to go over everything in court was the last thing he wanted. It also occurred to him that if he testified to David running him down, it would only strengthen Pam's claim of David being a violent man. What had he got himself into?

'I'm sorry, Mr Parker, but depending on what charge the CPS pursue, it's a likely possibility that you'll be called to give evidence. Now, I have the address and number for the landlord of the flat your brother rented. He's aware you're here this weekend and need to see the flat.'

Joe took the folded piece of paper Armstrong offered and left the police station in a daze. Having assumed telling the detective the truth and holding nothing back was the best way forward, it seemed as if his honesty would assist Pam in getting away with murder – literally. Joe sat in his car, trying to get his head around the detective's words and the implications for the near future. He had no desire to get involved with any part of David's life. They'd not been close when he was alive, yet it appeared Joe was the one to sort out the mess his brother had left behind.

Eventually, Joe pulled out his phone and dialled the number Armstrong had given him. He spoke briefly to David's landlord and agreed to meet him at the flat later in the afternoon. Joe's next task was to pick up a death certificate from the hospital and register the death at the registrar's office.

Mentally he thanked Phil for the crash course he'd received in the red tape involved with death. Wading through the bureaucracy after Alison's death had been torturous, and he'd certainly not expected to be repeating the process so soon.

George Thompson could have been anywhere between sixty and seventy years old, Joe couldn't tell. A short, stocky man with a head far too large for his body, a ruddy complexion, bulbous nose, and he reeked of cigarettes and beer. Thompson was waiting inside the flat when Joe arrived and he was not in the best of humour.

The man scowled. 'I need this place clearing out, and fast! The police have kept me out too bloody long and I'm losing money on it – and mentioning money, your brother owed seven hundred pounds in back rent and I don't take cheques or cards or nothing.'

'Seven hundred? But I haven't got that much on me in cash.' Joe shook his head. It seemed he'd not only have to pay for a funeral but settle David's debts too. He'd brought around five hundred pounds with him but would clearly need more.

'There's a cash machine on the high street. If you're staying here this afternoon, I can call back in a couple of hours to collect it.'

'I bet you can!'

'Look, you're getting off bloody lightly with only seven hundred quid. They haven't exactly looked after this place, as you can see, and I'll have work to do before I can let it again. Just be bloody grateful I'm not asking for more. And now there's the stigma of having a murder committed here an' all. Who's going to want to live here now, eh?' Joe thought

Thompson was a real bundle of joy, sympathy oozed from him.

'I'll get your money if you'll leave me a key. Two hours is all I need so if you come back, it'll be waiting for you and you can have the key.'

'When're you gonna move the stuff out then?'

'I doubt I'll want to take anything so I'll put it in the hands of a house clearer. Can I give them your name and number to liaise with?' Joe already wanted to be out of this flat, it reeked of misery and his eyes strayed to a dark patch on the worn, dirty carpet, which he thought must be his brother's blood.

'Okay by me, as long as they can do it quickly.' Thompson slammed a key on the table and grunted a farewell.

Joe surveyed his surroundings, appalled that his brother had come to this; the flat was small but the state of it horrified him. He thought about his parents and how they'd raised the brothers. Possessing very little money, they'd lived in a small rented house, with second-hand furniture and nothing in the way of luxuries, but the place was always spotless, the floors scrubbed, the rooms tidy. Their mother would have been horrified to see the filth in which her eldest son ended his days. Unwashed pots filled the kitchen sink, a pedal bin overflowed with rubbish and the odour of rotting food filled the room.

Joe understood the police had been working at the flat as a crime scene, but this was more than a couple of weeks' worth of neglect. Sickened by his surroundings, he decided to walk to the cash machine first to fill his lungs with fresh air before facing the task of looking through his brother's meagre possessions.

Returning to the flat, Joe searched everywhere there might be important documents, yet found very little. The extent of his findings were two out-of-date passports, a couple of empty cheque books, several old bank statements and a post office savings account from thirty years earlier with less than five pounds in.

He put them all in a plastic carrier bag to take home for shredding, then found a roll of bin liners and threw in the worst of the rubbish lying around the flat. Finally, he filled a dustbin at the back of the building and left several bags beside it, hoping the rubbish would be collected soon.

44

Two hours later, Joe was anxious to leave the flat. The only other thing he wanted to do was to take a cursory look inside David's suitcase. The police had initially taken it away but returned it to the flat where it stood in the hallway. It certainly wasn't neat; either David packed in a hurry or the police found nothing of interest and didn't bother to tidy the contents.

The case contained everything necessary for several days or even weeks away, but the item that surprised Joe the most was a letter addressed to him, already stamped and ready to post. It was tucked deep in a side pocket and Joe took it over to the window where he perched cautiously on the arm of a chair and opened it with apprehension.

It was his brother's handwriting, still familiar to Joe from their shared childhood and still with the power to tug at his emotions. Tears blurred his vision as he unfolded the paper and read.

My Dear Joe,
I'm consumed with guilt and have no expectations of

your forgiveness or compassion, but I'm going away and wanted to attempt an explanation of how I reached such deplorable depths.

We were never close as boys and in hindsight I admit it was my fault. I allowed jealousy to make me such an awful brother, you didn't deserve the way I treated you. Sadly, we can never go back and live our past again any more than we can predict our future, but I'm determined to try for a new start. When I'm settled and back on my feet, I'll get in touch, but for the moment, I don't want you to know where I'm going, so you won't think I'm asking for charity.

It would be easy to pass the blame for what happened to Pam but it was me driving the car, and I have to accept responsibility. You never really knew my wife, and I'm hoping that knowing some of my struggles with her will help you understand why I behaved so badly.

At one point I held down a reasonably good job as a sales rep, a job I lost through my own greed. Pam nagged constantly, grumbling about the lack of money for the luxuries she'd come to expect. When she discovered I was gambling and in debt, she was furious. We were forced to leave Bournemouth and move to Eastleigh where Pam seemed intent on making my life hell.

It was what our mother would have called a 'moonlight flit'. In reality, we were in hiding from those I owed money to. The living conditions were far from desirable and unsurprisingly our relationship crumbled. We constantly snapped at each other over the slightest little thing.

After three years of living hand to mouth, we were angry at the world for how we perceived we'd been treated and were forever looking for the golden opportunity we felt one day would come our way.

Oh, Joe, how low we sank! Love and respect for each

other died and I was beginning to loathe Pam almost as much as I loathed myself.

When we received your letter telling us of Alison's death in an accident, I was devastated for you, but Pam saw it as an opportunity. Her permanently sour expression lifted and her features became animated as she snatched the letter from me to read for herself. This was probably the moment the 'plan' began to form, and we decided to attend the funeral.

After that debacle, I felt such shame at how crass and insensitive we'd been, yet Pam, fuelled with anger, couldn't settle, determined to come out on top, at any cost. It was just silly talk at first, drunken ramblings. I didn't think she was seriously considering murder. However, Pam persuaded me with her usual goading and belittling. I should never have listened but I was so low and rose to her challenge to 'be a man for once', and I did it, or so I thought.

You can't imagine my self-disgust and deep regret when I thought you were dead and that I'd murdered my only brother.

My hatred of Pam was building inside, a cancer eating into me. I was pleased when we came back to Greater Manchester and discovered you were alive. Conflicting emotions battled inside of me, but please believe me, the primary one was of relief.

I found it incredible that you allowed us to leave. Your generosity has given me the hope that I might be able to turn my life around, so I'm leaving Pam – on the quiet, of course. She would never willingly let me go. I'm waiting for an opportunity when she'll be out of the flat long enough to allow my escape.

And so, Joe, I don't know what you'll think of this letter, an excuse, an explanation or just the ramblings of a bloody fool? Whatever you decide, I hope we'll meet again someday

*and be able to heal our traumatised souls together. Whatever
happens, I am so very sorry.*
  Your penitent brother,
  David

Joe was exhausted by the time he finished reading the
letter. Conflicting emotions fizzed in his mind, but if anything,
it made him long even more for his brother to be alive so they
could talk things through properly and start again. But it was
too late. Pam had had the last word on David's future. He'd
failed in his attempt to escape. Joe pocketed the letter – he
would read it again when he was at home.

After paying George Thompson off, Joe couldn't wait to
get away. He drove back to the Premier Inn, took a shower to
rid himself of the stench of the flat and then went to the bar
where he ordered a large whisky.

Joe hadn't realised how extreme his brother's
circumstances had become, but would he have behaved
differently if he'd known? Could he have done anything about
it? Joe would never know – David was dead.

In due course Joe would arrange the funeral although as in
Alison's case, an inquest was to be held, meaning a delay in
the body being released. It seemed this, and paying off his
debts was all he could do for his only brother.

45

Hannah couldn't breathe; it was as if all the oxygen had been sucked out of the room. She sat up, her nightdress soaked with perspiration, her jaw stiff and twisted and her fingers clawing at the sheets.

On one level, Hannah knew she was awake and in her bedroom but in the disorientation that often follows sleep, she was inside her little Ford Focus. The room was hot yet she felt as cold as the ice had been on that fateful day. Was it a dream, or was it a memory? Was she finally recalling those events which her mind had so stubbornly blocked from her consciousness, bringing doubt and anguish?

She glanced at the clock. The digits flashed 4.30am and Hannah knew there would be no more sleep. The house was silent; the twins must still be sleeping, so the scream which had been so real to her only moments earlier, had probably just been in her head.

The lethal combination of freezing rain and wind battered the windscreen so hard she feared it might shatter, the violent pounding deafening, frightening. Suddenly the car seemed to shift of its own volition, veering slightly to the left. Hannah tried to counter the shift by turning into the skid. But the car had taken on a mind of its own; she was no longer in control. Fear swelled inside her, cold as the ice outside, as momentum gathered, and Hannah was carried along inside the prison of her car, utterly helpless as it descended the gradient, sliding uncontrollably towards the inevitable.

An articulated lorry approaching from the right came into her vision, and the car suddenly fishtailed like a ride at a fairground. There was an explosive boom, the horrified faces of a man and a woman, and the piercing sound of Hannah's voice, an impotent scream. Then nothing. Dark interminable silence.

When Hannah's breathing slowed and the blood stopped pounding through her temples, she reached for her prosthesis and pulled it on. Making her way downstairs and into the kitchen, she occupied her trembling hands with the mundane task of making coffee. A shiver ran through her body even though the early morning sun warmed the kitchen to a comfortable temperature – it was as if ice was running through her veins.

Wrapping her hands around the hot mug soothed her and Hannah tried to think rationally, analysing what had just happened. Had it been a dream, or was she remembering the accident? How the hell was she supposed to know the difference! Could it be what they call 'false memories' or a dream based on other people's accounts of what occurred that day? Hannah's mind spun – she was unsure what to think or believe. The wall clock ticked loudly. She'd never noticed the sound before – an irritating intrusion – dripping water torture.

As the caffeine reinvigorated her body, her mind cleared.

The dream had been too vivid to be *only* a dream and as it played again through her mind, Hannah grew more and more convinced that it was a memory. In her mind's eye, she saw herself leaving for work, exchanging a few words with Rachel and hurrying to the car out of the bitterly cold weather. These were things no one else could have told her – they must be genuine recollections. Up until now, Hannah hadn't remembered speaking to Rachel, but she recalled their brief exchange and how bad she felt at letting her friend down. A mental picture of herself, down to what she was wearing, lodged in Hannah's mind – she couldn't have learned such details at the inquest.

Yes! She remembered it all, the panic of being thrust towards the motorway, the unresponsive brakes and the sheer terror of being powerless to prevent the inevitable. The movements of Hannah's car seemed like a ballet performed in slow motion – deadly choreography which she was powerless to stop – but the approaching vehicles on the motorway were travelling at speed.

Hannah had braced herself for the collision, her little Ford Focus spun around as it reached the end of the slip road and smashed into the back of an articulated lorry. For a split second, everything was still. Hannah grew suddenly aware of the terrified faces of a man and a woman heading straight towards her, and then everything went black.

It was a memory, a sad, mournful memory, yet also a relief. *It hadn't been her fault!* As Hannah thought about it, the more she could see there was nothing she could have done to prevent the sequence of events that morning. The control of her car was irrevocably taken out of her hands; she was at the mercy of the elements, as was everyone else involved in the collision. Fate took over, remorseless, cruel, harsh and severe. Hannah couldn't have prevented the accident, and there was nothing she had done to cause it either.

It was as if a weight was suddenly lifted from her as she sat at the kitchen table and she smiled. For the first time since the accident, Hannah knew with clarity that she had no culpability in those awful events – she'd longed for this moment and it arrived like an unexpected gift, a tremendous release. The knowledge brought liberty, and Hannah knew she could continue her life without the burden of guilt and shame which had haunted her since the accident. Finally, Hannah was free from such debilitating emotions.

With no idea of how long she sat there, Hannah grinned at Sam when he appeared in the kitchen doorway.

'It's only six o'clock, Mum. What are you doing up?'

'Couldn't sleep; what's your excuse?'

'I'm on early shift at the leisure centre. Any chance of a lift, seeing as how you're up?'

'I can think of nothing I'd like to do more than give my handsome son a lift to work! Grab some breakfast while I get dressed.'

46

David's funeral was the saddest service Joe had ever attended, not just for the expected reasons, but because he and the undertakers were the only ones present. Such a contrast to the packed service for Alison, when people Joe didn't even know had turned up to pay their respects. David hadn't been religious, so a civil celebrant presided over a short service at the Eastleigh crematorium.

When the curtains closed, it seemed as if David's life was not just over but would be forgotten by everyone except his brother. Yet what memories would Joe have? Regrettably, perhaps the most abiding one would be of the day he tried to kill him. Seeing David's face at the wheel of the car was an image which would remain with Joe, but above all else, he was saddened that his brother's life had ended in such a violent way. It would probably be months before Pam's trial, and he'd not heard from DS Armstrong, which presumably meant there was no progress to report.

It was a relief to arrive home, and the welcome Joe received from Liffey went a long way to bringing him comfort. He had good friends and a lovely home. Even though he still missed Alison with every fibre of his being, he was learning to be grateful for the blessings he still had.

Memories of Alison prompted thoughts of her mother. It was over a month since Joe had spoken to Ethel on the phone, a brief conversation as someone knocked on her door only a minute after she answered the phone. The old lady hadn't rung back, so Joe assumed she didn't want to talk, but he felt he should visit again to make sure she was coping, if only for Alison's sake.

Joe embarked upon this duty visit one Saturday morning without forewarning Ethel he was coming. He rang the doorbell and almost immediately heard her voice through the entry intercom. When she buzzed him in and he stood before her in the lounge, she looked him up and down.

'Well, it *is* you. I thought you were dead too!' Ethel's voice held her usual sarcastic note.

Why does she always have to be so bloody snarky, Joe thought but pressed his lips tightly together to stop himself from replying similarly.

'I've been in an accident, Ethel, and laid up for a while,' Joe explained. There was no way he would tell her of David's death; it was still very raw and Ethel was the last person he wanted asking intrusive questions – prying into his affairs.

The old lady squinted at him. 'Huh, another accident, that's a bit careless, isn't it?'

'I'm getting better now, thank you. Anyway, how are you? Did you get any help from Social Services sorted out?'

'Don't talk to me about Social Services; they're useless. A lady came to visit and just about gave me the third degree. If I want any help, I have to tell them everything; they even want to assess my finances and expect me to tell them every penny I have. Then there'll be another visit to assess my care needs. And even after jumping through all of their hoops they want me to pay for the service. It's ridiculous!'

It was no more than Joe expected and he refrained from offering an opinion. 'So what have you decided to do?'

'Well, Mrs Hoskins in the bungalow across the street suggested I put an ad in the newsagent's window, so I did. A nice young girl came round, Tina her name is, from Romania or some such place, and she started almost straight away.'

'And is she good? Are you happy with her?' Joe grew more relaxed and looked around the flat. It did look clean and tidy.

'Oh yes, she'll do anything; shopping, cleaning, laundry and cooking, and she's a lot cheaper than Social Services were going to be.'

'Good. I'm glad you're sorted out.' Joe was relieved help was in place.

'It's no thanks to you, is it? I could have starved to death for all you care.' She had to go and spoil it, to have another dig at him. *Well, two can play at that game*, Joe thought.

'Ethel, you're far more able than you make out. If only you'd get up off your backside and do things for yourself occasionally, you'd probably feel much better!'

Ethel's jaw dropped. 'How dare you talk to me in such a manner!'

'It's time someone did. You think the world revolves around you, but here's the news – it doesn't. And while we have this little heart to heart, I'd like to point out that you maligned the memory of your daughter with your vicious lies. I learned the truth about the baby, and you don't come out of that situation too well either.'

'Don't blame me! She got herself pregnant; she had to suffer the consequences.'

'No, Ethel, your daughter was raped, and she was only eighteen. Don't you have any compassion in that cold heart of yours? It wasn't Alison's fault, she was abused and suffered greatly for it, and you have the gall to throw it at me, telling me half the story and besmirching her memory in the process.

And I'm sure she got little comfort from you at the time, aren't you ashamed of yourself?'

Ethel's mouth dropped open again; she'd never been spoken to in such a manner before, and if Joe hadn't been so angry he'd have laughed at her horrified expression. Had he gone too far, he wondered? No, perhaps he should have spoken out years earlier, and if he'd known about Alison's past, he probably would have.

'I think I'd like you to leave now!' Ethel was red in the face and couldn't look at her son-in-law.

'Yes, I think that's an excellent idea, but if you feel like apologising, you've got my number.'

'Me, apologise? It's you who should apologise. I'm an old woman and I'm ill. How dare you treat me like this.' She glared at him, recovering from the shock of Joe's pertinent words. Her fighting spirit returning.

'You're as ill as it suits, you don't fool me, and you didn't fool Alison either. She knew what you were like but cared for you out of duty because she was that kind of person. You don't know how lucky you were to have had a daughter like her.' Perhaps he'd said too much. 'Yes, I'll go now. I hope you have the decency to think about what I've said.' With those words, Joe turned and walked out of the door, unsure whether he would ever hear from Ethel again.

Travelling home, Joe fleetingly wondered if he should have been so outspoken, a thought quickly replaced by the feeling that perhaps someone should have said this to her years earlier. He hadn't gone there intending to have a showdown but it was up to Ethel now – he'd leave it to her whether or not she contacted him again; she knew where he stood and what he thought, but would it make any difference?

47

The mood was decidedly festive. Bunting fluttered in the breeze and the uncommonly bright September sun bathed the whole scene with kaleidoscopic prisms of light. A party atmosphere buoyed the general mood with children's laughter heard in every corner of the farm.

For Alan and Cassie Lang, this day had been a long time in the making, yet it was nothing short of a miracle in the opinions of the hundreds of visitors who passed through their gates during the day. In the seven months since their son, Keiron, had been so tragically killed, they'd achieved something which most people would never accomplish in a lifetime – their child's goal.

Sadly the dream was born of a nightmare, but Keiron's Farm was the perfect tribute, something their son would have loved wholeheartedly and a living memorial which would continue for many years to come.

Alan and Cassie marvelled at the number of people who rallied around to help, and not only in the setting up of the venture, as several volunteers generously signed up to help with the day-to-day running of the farm, clearly inspired by the couple's hard work and vision. Alan took a three-month sabbatical from his career as a veterinary surgeon to work alongside his wife but planned to return to work to help finance the farm.

The couple greeted the considerable number of visitors, undoubtedly swelled by the exceptionally good weather. Many had known Keiron and wanted to honour him and although there was no charge for entry to the farm, the donation boxes were healthily full.

Alan and Cassie had mingled with visitors for the last two hours, answering questions and accepting compliments while thinking of their son. They observed the activity around them with mixed feelings. There was no question that having Keiron with them, alive and vital as he'd always been, would be preferable – but it could never be – this was perhaps the next best thing.

Keiron would have loved the set-up. Animals were his passion and having a centre to care for old, sick, and abused animals would have been his utopia. The ethos was to never turn away an animal in need – a massive undertaking in both finance and staffing. Partnerships had been formed with several organisations – disability groups who wished to use the facility for their members and local schools that recognised the educational value of Keiron's Farm. A mammoth task, but Alan and Cassie were not afraid of hard work – this was their way of channelling their grief and honouring their son.

Hannah's interest in Keiron's Farm remained strong and when her memory returned there was nothing to prevent her attending the open day. Kate and Sam were keen to go too, which delighted Hannah, who was only too aware her children were leaving for university in a few more weeks, so time with them was precious.

The night before opening day, Hannah's leg had been playing up. Phantom pains woke her throughout the night and she'd risen several times, walking around to ease the surreal feeling until eventually taking a tablet in the hope of sleep. In the morning, she was tired but still keen to visit Keiron's Farm and meet Alan and Cassie Lang, a couple who were elevated to the status of heroes in her mind.

On their arrival, Hannah was delighted to find parking reserved for disabled drivers, which significantly cut down the distance she'd have to walk. She and her children happily dropped donations into the buckets as they passed into the bustling farm. They moved on to learn more about this remarkable project, which touched them perhaps more than most, feeling something of a connection with the Langs' loss.

Kate was delighted with everything she saw. 'Ooh, I could bring Isla here when she's bigger. She'd love the animals!' Hannah smiled; the birth of Mike's latest child had affected the twins, particularly Kate, who was always up for a bit of babysitting and adored her new sister. Hannah had yet to meet the new arrival – it would mean meeting Sarah, and she wasn't quite ready for that.

However, the divorce was proceeding and was thankfully amicable, as she'd wished. Mike and Sarah had recently moved into a new home and Hannah was pleased for them and delighted that Mike's relationship with the twins appeared better than ever – go figure!

Sam picked up an information leaflet with a layout diagram and proceeded to steer his mother and sister in the direction of the animals. Volunteers were on hand to answer questions and tell stories of the farm's residents, many of which were quite harrowing.

Hannah was impressed with the tremendous effort the

Langs had put into making their son's dream a reality. There were only two restricted areas, one a hospital block, the other a quiet space for new or timid animals to settle in. Otherwise, there was much to see. Donkeys, Shetland ponies and goats were enjoying visitors' attentions and the extra food, while cats weaved in and out of the multitude of legs as if they owned the place, which in a way they did.

After an hour, Hannah needed to sit down, so they headed towards a marquee for a welcome cup of tea and a break. It was there she saw Cassie Lang. The woman was heading her way. Hannah was unsure whether to speak but reminded herself there was absolutely no reason she shouldn't. Cassie deserved to be congratulated on such a remarkable achievement. As Cassie neared Hannah's table, Hannah reached up to catch her arm.

'Mrs Lang?' she said.

Cassie smiled and sat down on a seat next to her.

'My name's Hannah Graham. I want to congratulate you on your endeavour – it's remarkable – you've done an amazing job.'

'Thank you, Mrs Graham. I remember you from the inquest, and I think I saw you at the Trafford Centre? How are you doing?'

Hannah was surprised Cassie recognised her. 'I'm fine, thank you, up and about again now.' She gave an embarrassed smile.

'So I see. I'm pleased for you and thank you for coming today. We all lost so much on that awful day; it's good to catch up on how others are getting along. I've just been talking to Joe Parker. I don't know if you remember him. He lost his wife in the accident?'

'Oh yes, I bumped into Joe at the hospital. How is he?'

'He seems to be heading your way, so perhaps he can tell you for himself?' Cassie stood to leave and nodded towards where Joe was approaching. 'It's been lovely to meet you, Mrs Graham. Please keep in touch; it would be good to chat when I've more time.' Cassie left, and Joe Parker slid into her seat.

'I thought it was you!' He sounded pleased to see her and Hannah introduced him to her children.

Joe's eyes swept the busy farm. 'Isn't this wonderful? Alan and Cassie have worked tremendously hard to achieve all this.'

'They certainly have,' Hannah agreed. 'And the weather's perfect. Who'd have thought we'd have one of the best summers for years after such an abysmal winter.'

A very costly winter, Hannah thought but didn't say.

'Mum, will you be okay if we go and explore a bit? Kate wants to get a few more pictures.'

'Of course, take your time, love; I'll probably still be here, drinking the teapot dry.'

Sam and Kate said goodbye to Joe and hurried away to see more of the farm.

'Your daughter's the image of you. You must be very proud of them,' Joe remarked.

'I am; they're great kids, off to uni soon and I'll miss them like crazy, but don't tell them I said so.'

'Your secret's safe with me.'

'So, how are you getting on, Joe?'

'Okay, well … maybe not okay, you know?'

Hannah nodded, a simple heartfelt response.

Joe sighed. 'I almost envy Cassie and Alan for how they've channelled their grief into something positive. They're an extraordinary couple and what they've done here is nothing short of amazing. I didn't know them before, so I never met Keiron, but he must have been a remarkable young man to inspire all this. They've found a reason to keep going – to cope with their grief – I suppose that's what I envy. But they say we all find our own coping mechanisms, eventually.'

'So, how do *you* cope?' Hannah looked directly at him. Joe

appeared surprised at her candidness but smiled as he tried to form an answer.

'Nothing so original for me I'm afraid, simply one day at a time. Time's supposed to heal but lately it seems to bring one problem after another. My brother died a couple of months ago; he was murdered.' Joe's hands were clasped together so tightly that his knuckles were white. Empathy flooded through Hannah as he shared the recent events in his life with her.

'Oh, how terrible for you. I'm so sorry! You must be devastated.'

'I can't claim we were close and it's a bit of a long story – I wouldn't want to bore you with all the details …'

'It wouldn't bore me at all. I've been told I'm a pretty good listener.'

'Another time perhaps?'

'Yes, I'd like that.' Hannah studied the man sitting just a few feet away from her. He had the air of having lived through so much. Lines of sadness and loss covered what must once have been laughter lines, and grief dulled his eyes. She hoped Joe could still find joy, he deserved no less.

'How about you, Hannah, how are you managing?'

'Rather like you – a day at a time. As you see, I'm upright and have become quite a whiz on crutches when the leg gets too much.'

'Good for you. It can't be easy. Is your husband not with you today?' Joe looked around.

'Ah, that's another story. We've split up.'

'Oh, Hannah, I'm sorry, and here's me going on about my woes!'

'Don't worry, at least he hasn't died. Sorry, that's not very tactful, is it?'

Joe smiled rather sadly. 'It wasn't because of the accident, was it? Your leg, I mean?'

'No, apparently there was someone else, a younger woman

with whom he's recently had a baby. Typically I was the last to know, or even suspect.' Hannah's empty laugh couldn't disguise the hurt in her eyes.

'It must be tough for you. Can I be so presumptuous as to say he must be a bloody fool?' Joe looked earnestly at Hannah and her eyes filled with tears.

'Now I've upset you, sorry again. Can I get you another cup of tea; I think I'd like one now?'

'Good idea.' Hannah sniffed. 'Tea is always a good idea.'

As Joe left for a few moments, she blew her nose and took a few deep breaths. Perhaps they should stick to talking about the weather, it was much safer. She liked Joe; they'd both been through so much, which gave them a bond. Hannah wondered if there *would* be 'another time' and found herself hoping there would.

48

Cassie left Hannah's table and headed for the office. An elderly man sat on a bench in the shade of a tree wiping his brow with his handkerchief.

'Are you okay?' Cassie asked and the man smiled.

'I am, Mrs Lang, thank you.'

'Can I get you something? A glass of water perhaps.'

'You've already helped me more than you know.' The man's watery eyes followed Cassie as she sat down beside him.

'We've met before, haven't we?' She knew he was familiar but couldn't place him.

'Yes, at the inquest. My wife, Mary, also died in the accident.'

'I remember. Mr Simpson, isn't it?'

'Bernard, please.'

'And I'm Cassie. But I don't understand how I've helped you.'

'You're busy. I don't want to take up your time.'

'I have time.' Cassie smiled at the man who nodded his thanks.

'Mary shouldn't have gone out in that appalling weather but she wanted to help our daughter. The school was closed and Nicola had to work so she asked Mary to look after the grandchildren. I didn't want her to go but she hated letting the family down, so she went ... and you know the rest.' The handkerchief came out again as Bernard wiped his eyes. Cassie placed her hand over his as he continued. 'We didn't exactly argue but she knew I was displeased with her. Afterwards I regretted speaking harshly. If only I'd known it was the last conversation we'd have.'

'We all have regrets but events can't be changed.'

'The days after the accident were a nightmare. Nicola took me to stay with her family but it wasn't for me. I wanted to go home, to grieve alone with my memories of Mary. But I'm ashamed to say that the grieving turned to wallowing. I let things slip – Nicola tried to help but I pushed her away. And then, one day I decided to end my misery, to join Mary and escape the endless hurt.'

Cassie understood the depth of Bernard's pain, she'd travelled that road herself. 'I'm glad you didn't.' Her voice cracked.

'That's partly to do with you. On the day I'd chosen to be my last I saw an article in the local paper about your venture. It pulled me up rather sharply and I finally saw myself for the pitiful fool I was and felt shame at my selfishness. Mary would have given me a right good ticking off for sure and maybe seeing your story was her way of doing it. You're a wonderful example, Cassie. What you and your husband have achieved is remarkable and a lesson to us all. There I was feeling sorry for myself, yet you channelled your grief into something so tangible and positive. What you've done is incredibly brave and a fitting tribute to your son and if you'll allow me to, I'll do whatever I can to help.'

Cassie sniffed and nodded. She wanted to say so much, to thank Bernard and tell him she understood, but the words wouldn't form in her mouth. A gentle squeeze on his arm was all she could manage but she was sure he'd understand.

49

Hannah understood Rachel's disappointment at not attending the open day, but work had taken priority and now her friend was clearly itching to hear everything. So on a quiet Sunday afternoon they sat in Hannah's lounge, enjoying a glass of wine. Hannah's prosthesis lay on the carpet and she'd swung her legs up onto the sofa – after a morning of cleaning, her leg was playing up. Rachel was probably one of the few people with whom she felt comfortable enough to relax in this way.

'It's amazing, Rachel. They must have worked incredibly hard to achieve everything in just a few months. Their farm lends itself perfectly to such a project, the space is ideal and they've utilised all the outbuildings. So much thought and love has gone into the planning. I chatted briefly with Cassie, but she was busy; everyone wanted to congratulate her. I'd thought about volunteering somehow, but honestly, what could I do with this leg?' Hannah rubbed her aching stump.

'There's plenty you could do! It won't be all mucking out and grooming ponies, there's bound to be paperwork and your organisational skills are second to none. Give Cassie a ring or send an email; you might be just what they're looking for.'

'Do you think so? When the twins go to uni it's going to be so quiet around here, I don't want to give myself time to sit and mope and it's such a worthwhile venture.' Hannah dreaded the day Kate and Sam would leave, a day which was rapidly drawing closer. It would have been bad enough if Mike was still with her, but being alone was scary. Maybe this would help – having regained her memory, Hannah was confident to approach Cassie and Alan, no longer feeling responsible for the accident that killed their son.

'You won't know unless you ask,' Rachel said, stating the obvious. 'Did the kids enjoy it?'

'Oh yes, they were most impressed. Everyone was. But you know, I couldn't have gone if I hadn't remembered the details of the accident. I'd been carrying around an awful dread that I was to blame for the whole thing and it was getting to me. My memory coming back is the best thing that's happened since then!'

'So they didn't treat you like a social pariah then?' Rachel smiled, playfully mocking her friend.

'No, not at all, I felt quite at ease with Cassie, and I met Joe Parker in the tea tent too. I needed to sit down and the twins left me there for a while. We had quite a long chat, which I'd have been uncomfortable with before I remembered everything. I suppose I'm more self-assured now, knowing it wasn't my fault. I'm a victim of a freak accident, the same as they are.'

'Joe Parker? Isn't he the one whose wife died in the accident?'

'Yes. We met briefly at the hospital when I went for my first fitting. I was glad of the opportunity to thank him for his testimony at the inquest, so it was good to see him again. His brother's died since the accident too. It must be awful for him.'

Hannah decided not to mention he'd been murdered, it was Joe's private business.

'Bloody hell! How utterly unfair,' Rachel said, but then her face split with a huge grin as she asked, 'So what's he like, this Joe?'

'Oh, Rachel, don't think that! He's just a nice man who I shared a cup of tea with.'

'Why shouldn't I ask? You're single, he's single, and you're a very attractive woman, Hannah Graham. Is he, you know, fit?'

Hannah laughed but then became serious. 'Typical of you to ask that. Joe's a lovely man who I met by chance. For heaven's sake he's just lost his wife, and besides, he'd never be interested in me!' Hannah scowled.

'Why ever not?' A flicker of amusement danced in Rachel's eyes.

'You know why not.' Hannah absently rubbed her leg. 'It's repulsive.' There – she'd said it – she was convinced no man would ever consider her attractive ever again.

'And you're an expert on what repulses this Joe, are you?'

'This *stump* would repulse any man. It's ugly, hideous …'

'Hannah, listen to me. It does not define you! You are still the same person you were before the accident, a warm caring person and hell, woman, look in the mirror – you're gorgeous. Besides, from what you tell me, Joe sounds a very nice bloke and if having a prosthetic leg puts him off, then he's not worth having. You'd have to give him, or any man for that matter, a chance to prove he's not so shallow.'

Hannah suddenly burst into tears and Rachel moved beside her to wrap a comforting arm around her shoulder.

'Go on then, let it all out,' she whispered as her friend released her pent-up emotions in huge sobs.

After a few minutes, Hannah quietened and apologised.

'I'm sorry, Rachel; I thought I was done with all the tears, the feeling sorry for myself.'

'Don't apologise. Tears are cathartic, and you bottle things up far too much. A good cry does us all good sometimes. You don't always have to be brave; none of us can be strong all the time and you've had a lot going on recently.'

Hannah blew her nose. 'Thanks, maybe you're right. This year's been all losses, first my leg, then Mike, and now the twins. I know all children have to grow up and leave home sometime, but I'm not looking forward to it. The house will be so quiet.'

'I'll do my best to make more noise, shall I?' They laughed together as Rachel refilled their wine glasses. 'Getting back to Joe, did you give him your telephone number?'

Hannah blushed as she admitted, 'Yes, I did. We did seem to hit it off well and I think we could get along as friends, so when he asked if I'd mind him ringing me occasionally to see how I was getting on, I said that would be fine.'

'Good for you. It sounds as if you could both do with some company. You might be good for each other.'

When Rachel went home, having done her best to cheer her friend up, Hannah's mood lapsed into melancholy. Kate and Sam wouldn't be in for another couple of hours but she knew she mustn't rely on them for company – they'd be leaving home very soon. She was proud of them both. Sam was to study sports science at university, while Kate had chosen journalism and media studies. They'd do well and Hannah knew it wasn't just her biased opinion.

Over the last few months, Sam had changed the most. His frame had at last filled out, probably with all the extra exercise he was getting, and his confidence had grown. Working at the leisure centre allowed him to meet so many new people and his social circle increased almost overnight. Sam had grown protective towards his mother, demonstrating a gentle side that Mike always said came from her.

Kate loved her summer job but had also been writing articles covering a wide range of topics and submitting them to magazines hoping for publication. They were delighted when several were accepted, and Kate was so proud to see her name in print beneath an article she'd written. The extra money would come in useful, and her initiative would go down well on the course at university. Kate had even taken her camera and notebook to Keiron's Farm the previous day. With permission from Alan Lang, Kate made notes for a feature on the project she had in mind to send to a couple of magazines, hoping they might be interested.

Yes, Hannah knew she didn't need to worry about her children; she would miss them but perhaps Rachel was right – Hannah needed to work on increasing her social circle.

50

Joe noticed an improvement in his general health of late, which he attributed to giving up smoking. It hadn't been an easy journey and on several occasions he'd been sorely tempted, particularly with the stress of late, but it was over four months since he'd smoked his last cigarette. He'd lost weight, not consciously and not perhaps in the best of ways. Sometimes it was because he forgot to eat, but he felt better for it and knew Alison would have been proud of him.

Attending social events without Alison still felt odd to Joe yet at Keiron's Farm on Saturday the whole project was so fascinating that he soon became absorbed in everything around him. Meeting Hannah Graham again was an unexpected pleasure; she was so easy to talk to, straightforward and honest, qualities he'd always admired in a person. They chatted generally, both in awe of the Langs' hard work, and on a deeper level, as Joe shared the details of his brother's death and Hannah told him she and her husband were separated.

Hannah also reported better news – she'd regained her memory and it was clear to Joe that a weight had been lifted from her. He assured her again of his certainty that there'd been nothing she or anyone else could have done to prevent the accident. Joe understood her relief and would probably have felt much the same himself if the situation was reversed.

Wanting to see Hannah again and sure she felt the same, Joe asked for her phone number, feeling like a tongue-tied schoolboy. Their shared life-changing experience of the accident created a bond between them, and now that they were both on their own, why shouldn't they meet up as friends? He hoped perhaps Hannah would like to go out to dinner with him one night – he missed such simple pleasures – and assumed she would too. With the certainty that Hannah was honest enough to say no if the idea didn't appeal, Joe could only ask and hope she'd say yes.

The open day was a pleasant way to fill Joe's weekend, and he returned to work on Monday morning ready to focus on the growing pile of accounts on his desk. However, before making any significant inroads into the day's work, he was disturbed by a telephone call from DS Armstrong.

Joe's heart sank; he hadn't heard from the detective for several weeks and assumed no news was good news, so what did the man want now?

'Good morning, Mr Parker. I need to update you on Mrs Pamela Parker's circumstances.' Armstrong's speech sounded as if it was straight from a textbook. 'After an incident at the women's facility where she's currently held, moving her to a secure psychiatric hospital has been necessary.'

'Can you tell me what this incident was?' Joe asked.

'The latest one, and there have been a few minor incidents of a similar ilk, was an attack on another detainee. Mrs Parker appears to have lost control and attacked another woman quite ferociously, leaving her with serious injuries.'

Joe groaned inwardly. Could his sister-in-law stoop any lower?

'How does this affect the trial? Will it go ahead as

planned?' He'd been dreading the trial and giving evidence which might support Pam's claims of David being an abusive husband. Yet perhaps now Pam was demonstrating her own violent personality.

'Ah, well.' Ted Armstrong cleared his throat. 'It appears that Mrs Parker may not be standing trial. Her solicitor has put forward a motion to dismiss the charges due to her precarious mental health.'

'Is that likely to happen?'

'It's too early to say but the judge has ordered a round of psychiatric evaluations which will take time. The CPS still wishes to proceed with the charges, but the assessments will have to be completed before a final decision is made.'

'So if the trial doesn't go ahead, will Pam just get away with it?' Joe was horrified to think David's death might go unpunished.

'I wouldn't put it quite like that. If Mrs Parker is declared unfit to stand trial, at the very least she'll be committed to a psychiatric institution for treatment. But then your guess is as good as mine, Mr Parker. I will, however, keep you informed of any further developments and if I can help in any way, please give me a call.'

Joe was troubled, unsure whether this was good news or bad. If the trial didn't go ahead, he wouldn't have to give evidence of David's attempt on his life, something he wished he'd never told Ted Armstrong in the first instance. But on the other hand, Joe strongly felt that Pam should be held accountable and the more he thought about it the more he wondered if she could be playing a part, or was she really insane?

After work, when Joe picked Liffey up from Phil and Diane's, he shared what the detective had told him earlier.

'Goodness, she must be absolutely mad,' Diane said, her husband nodding in agreement.

'Will the trial be delayed?' Phil asked.

'It could even be cancelled. DS Armstrong said her solicitor is asking for the charges to be dismissed due to her failing mental health. I don't know what to think. I was dreading the trial and having to give evidence which wouldn't help David, but the thought of Pam getting away with his murder is too shocking to contemplate. I don't know what'll happen now, but it's sure to drag on. These evaluations take forever. Pam could be faking this mental illness to avoid standing trial. What do you think?'

'Oh, Joe, we don't know her well enough to make a judgement, but if she is faking it, I shouldn't think years in a mental institution will be a better option than prison. And as she's proved to be violent, she'll surely be kept in some kind of secure facility. Who'd want that for who knows how many years?' Diane asked.

'Perhaps you're right. Pam's going to be locked away whatever happens. I'll have to be patient and wait to see what these evaluations throw up.'

Joe took Liffey down to the meadow before going home to feed her. The weather was still holding and the earth was parched, the grass scorched and bleached of its usual cool green colour. He thought about the year behind him, the ferocious arctic weather that had caused the fateful accident and changed so many lives; a cruel, indiscriminate ripple effect, stealing life, happiness and health from all involved.

And the contrast from such fierce winter weather to one of the hottest summers he could remember, was incredible. David came into his mind too, and the pain he'd added to Joe's already broken world, but David was still his brother and Joe wished he was still alive. How would the latter part of the year unfold? Undoubtedly he'd been allotted more than his share of misery, could there possibly be something left to make living worthwhile?

51

September made way for October, with signs of autumn bringing a welcome change from the hot, dry summer. Hannah couldn't remember there ever being such a contrast between the awful winter weather they'd experienced, followed by such a scorching summer. People compared it to the summer of 1976, long before Hannah was born, and there was much talk about global warming and if such extremes of weather would become the norm. But it wasn't only the end of summer which sat heavily on Hannah's heart – it was her children's impending departure for university which simultaneously produced pride and sorrow.

Kate's grades matched the requirements to take up an offer from Cardiff University to study journalism and media studies. Her excitement was off the scale. The university's reputation for excellence in her chosen field made it her natural first choice. Over the holidays, Kate's delight increased as she experienced more success in selling articles to magazines.

Particularly pleasing was the feature Kate had written on Cassie and Alan's venture of Keiron's Farm which sold to the first magazine she approached. As well as a little extra pocket money for Kate, it was great publicity for the farm. Cassie and Alan had agreed to be interviewed by Kate, and the resulting article was an empathic, human interest story of which Hannah was so proud.

Kate would be the first to leave home, her bags were packed and Hannah was driving her to Cardiff the following day. Sam would leave two days later, heading for Swansea. In Hannah's ideal world, her children would have found places at the same university, but this hadn't been an option as their chosen courses were so different. They would, however, be geographically close enough to meet up on occasions and even travel home together for weekends and holidays, a thought with which Hannah contented herself.

Sam's course was sports science, his passion in life, and his ultimate intention was to gain a teaching degree. Mike offered to take him to Swansea and he'd accepted; Sam was Mike's son too and the children were seeing quite a bit of him and Sarah, mainly due to being captivated by baby Isla. The divorce was proceeding amicably and Hannah's ex had recently moved into a new house where he appeared to be satisfied with his chosen life.

The twins celebrated their eighteenth birthdays at the end of August. Neither wanted extravagant parties for which Hannah was silently thankful. Instead, Sam asked for a new laptop and Kate an iPhone. There were a few nights out to celebrate with friends, but nothing riotous, or so they told their mother. They both appeared happy and had apparently overcome the impact of the accident and the divorce – a huge relief for Hannah. Her children were on the threshold of adult life and she hoped and prayed they would continue to make the right choices for their future happiness.

Hannah frequently reflected on the changes the year had presented. The negative ones were becoming easier to live with and she stubbornly determined to maintain a positive view of life. The grieving process for her lost leg gradually turned into acceptance; it would never be easy to live with and some days she suffered considerable pain, but Hannah was pragmatic – as with her divorce. They were events which no amount of wishful thinking could alter.

The shock of losing Mike had cut deeply into Hannah's core, although she occasionally wondered why she hadn't seen it coming. The affair being undiscovered for so long was a bitter blow, humiliating and hurtful but with hindsight her marriage was clearly fragile. Hannah and Mike had grown apart and left it too long before either of them admitted there was a problem.

Hannah truly wished Mike happiness with his new family. He would always be her children's father, and that would connect them forever. In time, who knows, she might even feel brave enough to meet Sarah.

And now, with the twins leaving home, Hannah faced another significant change, but not everything which was happening in her life was negative.

Hannah worked a couple of evenings a week with Cassie and Alan Lang and enjoyed organising their office. The couple were so busy caring for their animals, marketing and fundraising, that much of the everyday paperwork was a mess. Hannah's organisational skills soon produced a massive effect. She introduced systems for payment of bills, ordering of feed and other essential stock and generally kept the office running smoothly, much to the delight of Cassie and Alan. The three were quickly becoming firm friends.

Hannah intended to work the occasional Saturday morning once the twins left home, which would help to fill some of her weekends and she loved being at the farm. The atmosphere was special. As a team they were restoring health to neglected animals and the rewards were immeasurable. Sometimes a little love and care brought the most remarkable returns and the animals responded with a devotion which suggested they understood they were being helped.

Perhaps she was getting soppy in her old age, but Hannah was moved by many of the cases they took on and couldn't imagine life without being part of Keiron's Farm.

Another bright spot in Hannah's life was Joe Parker who was becoming a valued friend, someone she could talk to quite openly and she was sure he felt the same. They'd had several telephone conversations, and Joe rang most weeks just to catch up and chat about what was happening in their lives. They also exchanged occasional emails, something Hannah enjoyed writing, particularly at night when her leg troubled her.

Joe was always interested in the twins' progress and what was happening at Keiron's Farm, so there was plenty to write. In return, Joe shared what was happening in his own life. It seemed the most natural thing in the world for them to be open and honest with each other, something Hannah truly appreciated – she'd had enough of secrets and lies and wanted to carve out a different future for herself.

52

It was early November – the wind was bracing, but it didn't put man or dog off and at least it was dry. The meadow was much greener after being parched the colour of straw during most of the long dry summer and it remained Liffey's favourite playground.

During the hot weather, Liffey had splashed happily in the stream, which almost disappeared at the height of the heatwave, and then rolled enthusiastically in the long grass, drying off her coat and bringing a smile to Joe's face. He enjoyed their walks together and liked to think of Alison looking down on them during their frequent forays to the meadow; she'd loved this place, especially in the early morning. They'd so often laughed together at their dog's antics.

Joe no longer felt guilt at taking pleasure in the small things of life. Instead, a strange feeling wrapped itself around him like a cloak – as if Ali was encouraging him to live again – giving him permission to smile and laugh without that awful haunting sense of guilt hanging over him.

Clouds swirled in a moody grey mass in the sky above, but

rain would be a welcome change. It was Saturday. Joe had spent more time in the meadow than usual, with nothing special to get home for, but Liffey was tired after bounding around chasing shadows of rabbits, so he turned to walk home.

The telephone was ringing as he unlocked the door, and Joe was surprised to hear Detective Sergeant Armstrong on the line.

'Good morning, Mr Parker. I hope I'm not disturbing your Saturday morning.'

'Not at all. I've just come in from walking the dog.' The call would concern Pamela, and Joe almost dreaded hearing the latest development.

'I wanted to update you on your sister-in-law's situation. The psychiatric evaluations are complete and the recommendation is that Pamela Parker is unfit to stand trial.' DS Armstrong paused to let the news sink in. Joe's initial feeling was of relief – this meant he wouldn't have to testify, but on the other hand, did it mean Pam would get away with murdering his brother?

'What will happen to her?' he asked. 'Will she stand trial at a later date?'

'It seems unlikely. I've seen the medical reports but haven't studied them in any depth, it's not in my remit, but they suggest that Mrs Parker's violent episodes have continued to escalate. She needs long-term medication and supervision. The recommendation is treatment and detention in a secure institution. The report is quite lengthy and rather wordy as these things are, but I'm sure it could be made available to you if you wish to see it. It contains the usual jargon regarding biological and neurological reasons for her *condition* but doesn't offer much hope of change in the near future. As I say, my work on this case is now complete and I wanted to update you on what is, or rather, isn't, happening.' The DS sounded relieved to be able to put the case to bed, even without a successful prosecution which Joe thought must be somewhat frustrating for him.

'I don't want to see the report; there's no point in reading it as far as I can see. I'm sorry Pam won't be held accountable for her actions, but if, as it seems, she's had a mental breakdown, then we'll have to accept she's in the best place. At least she won't be able to harm anyone else where she is.' Joe was keen to finish the conversation and assimilate his thoughts on this latest development. 'Thank you for keeping me informed, DS Armstrong. I appreciate your efforts.'

The call ended and Joe smiled. *He's got me talking like a textbook now,* he thought. Joe briefly wondered if DS Armstrong regularly worked on Saturdays and if so, did the man have any life outside of work? In all the detective novels he'd read the job demanded a single-minded determination with the protagonists generally defined by their role and consumed to the point of exclusion of any personal life. Ted Armstrong could easily fit into that category from what Joe had seen of the man.

After making coffee, Joe sat in the conservatory to collect his thoughts. It rattled him that Pam appeared to be getting away with her crime lightly but a trial could have been awkward. Any evidence Joe could give would only sully his brother's character and may even have had the effect of strengthening Pam's defence. Perhaps this was the best outcome after all. Fed up with the worry and negativity of late, if this was the best he could expect, then so be it, he'd take it, try to let it go and hopefully put an end to this chapter in his life.

Joe needed to tell someone and his first thought was of Hannah Graham, so he picked up the telephone and tapped in her number. Since they'd met at Keiron's Farm open day, he'd rung several times and they'd chatted easily. A comfortable bond was formed between them as if they'd known each other for years rather than just a few short months. Hannah was a good listener. Perhaps he'd suggest they go out for a meal that evening if she was free. Listening to the ringtone, Joe relished the prospect of a night out with Hannah.

'I'd love to have dinner with you, Joe. What a lovely idea.' Hannah sounded genuinely pleased, making Joe wish he'd asked sooner. 'The twins left for university this week, so a bit of cheering up is in order, thank you.'

Joe picked Hannah up later that evening and drove to a relatively new restaurant which had been receiving rave reviews for its food. It was housed in a delightful conservatory addition to a traditional village pub. The Greyhound was bright and spacious with a delicious aroma wafting in from the kitchen. They were shown to a corner table, prettily set for two, with a single rose and a lighted candle. The room was full, but space between the tables was generous so they didn't feel their conversation would be overheard.

A waiter left menus and they took their time choosing. When the food was ordered and a glass of wine poured, they naturally fell into easy conversation. Joe described his earlier call with DS Armstrong while Hannah listened intently.

'Perhaps it's for the best,' she commented when he finished talking. 'I know how much you dreaded testifying in court, so this could be a good thing, couldn't it?'

'Yes, I suppose it is, but I hate the thought that Pam won't be punished for what she did.'

'She'll lose her liberty, wherever she's held, and I shouldn't think a secure institute is much different from prison. If it had gone to trial, she might have succeeded in painting David as the villain she said he was, and got away with a more lenient sentence.'

'You're right. I need to put it behind me. There's nothing else I can do, is there? Now, tell me how it went with Kate and Sam. Are they settled in?'

'Oh yes, and loving it by all accounts. They're both in halls of residence for the first year and I have to say I was impressed with the facilities. The room was small but well designed and maintained. Kate was making it more homely even before I left and although I didn't see where Sam's living, it sounds very similar. They're both good at making friends, so I know they'll be okay.'

'But you're their mother and you'll worry anyway?' Joe added, noticing the sadness creep into her eyes.

'Yes, you're right.' She smiled. 'But it's in the job description – I'm allowed!'

The conversation drifted to other topics. Hannah filled him in on her work with Cassie and Alan, a couple she increasingly admired as she got to know them better, and the evening passed far too quickly.

***

Not wanting their time together to end, Hannah invited Joe in for coffee when he took her home. It was the first time he'd been inside her house and it was warm and inviting enough for him to feel immediately comfortable there.

'Can I help?' he asked.

'No thanks, it won't be long.' Hannah worked quickly in the kitchen, not wanting to miss a moment of Joe's company. If she'd been alone, her prosthetic leg would have been off by now, it was uncomfortable but there was no way she'd take it off in front of Joe.

'Here we are.' Hannah smiled as she placed a full tray on the coffee table and sat next to Joe on the sofa. Their conversation flowed as before, now covering their respective plans for Christmas. Hannah would have the children home and she asked what Joe was planning.

'Nothing special. It'll be the first without Alison so I don't think I'll feel much like celebrating.'

Hannah pondered for a moment, then asked, 'Would you like to come here? It'll be strange for me too, but the twins will be home and you'll be very welcome. I'm not a bad cook either!' She gave a nervous laugh, hoping he would say yes.

'Are you sure, Hannah? I'd love to be with you but how will the children feel about it?'

'I'm sure they'll relish the opportunity to get to know you a little better.' They were not empty words; she knew the twins would enjoy the chance to spend time with Joe.

'In that case I can hardly refuse. Thank you, I'd love to come.'

During the evening they were both aware of a subtle change in their relationship. Hannah welcomed it but was unsure how Joe was feeling. She didn't want the evening to end but when Joe moved slowly towards her to kiss her, she felt a sudden rush of uninvited panic and pulled away.

'Joe … doesn't this,' she put her hand on her knee, 'repulse you at all?' She had to ask; to make sure he knew what he was taking on, but as she stumbled over the words and feared what the answer might be, Joe silenced her with a kiss. Then, as they drew apart, the look in his eyes told her everything she needed to know.

This man will never hurt me, she thought. *His love is solid, complete, as is mine for him!*

EPILOGUE
HANNAH

To say the last eighteen months has been a rollercoaster would be an absolute understatement. February's accident heralded the very worst time of my life, a time predominantly defined by loss and fear, a terrifying event which changed everything, not only for me but for so many others.

Waking up in a hospital bed to the realisation that I'd lost my leg was without doubt the biggest shock of my life and thoughts of being a burden to Mike and the twins terrified me. Independence is a gift which most of us take for granted, until it's snatched away.

For a time I was engulfed by self-pity and as I grieved for my leg and the effect of the injury on my family, having no recollection of the event and the full implications of the gap in my memory suddenly hit home. The aching fear was compounded by the possibility that I was somehow to blame for the accident, or at the very least, could have prevented it and didn't. To have any kind of culpability in the death of three people is a harrowing thought which at times was almost too much to bear.

The very real possibility of facing charges for something I couldn't even remember was utterly scary and life was in limbo until the inquest. Yet even after a no-fault verdict I couldn't settle, and constantly grappled with my thoughts, frantically trying to remember, for my own peace of mind. This was fearful enough in itself, but at the time I had no idea how close I was to losing my marriage.

Perhaps subconsciously I'd known things were not right between Mike and me, but finding out that my husband was seeing another woman suddenly presented another dread, one of being alone and rejected. Until my memory returned and I finally had the assurance that there was nothing I could have done to prevent the accident, I lived in a state of perpetual fear. The morning my memory returned was perhaps the watershed, the turning point for me and although difficult times still lay before me, I could once again hold my head high.

Kate and Sam have been the bright spot throughout all of this and perhaps they have coped with events so much better than me. My delight in them knows no bounds and I'm proud of their achievements, yet even more proud of the people they are becoming.

Yes, their leaving for university presented another loss but it's the natural progression of life, our children are a gift for only a season. I'm genuinely pleased that they maintain a good relationship with their father, but secretly delighted that they choose to stay with me during holidays rather than him. (Okay, it could be because I have the space to accommodate them, but I like to read more into it than that!)

And then there's Joe. I can't honestly say when I first realised how much more he meant to me than simply being a good friend, or if he became aware of it before me, but Joe has brought joy and passion back into my life.

Yet even our burgeoning relationship brought a different kind of fear and doubt. Were we drawn to each other simply through our need for love and company? No one wants to be a replacement for another person, a notion which niggled in the back of my mind as I'm sure it did in Joe's.

Friendship came first and built the foundations of what we now have. The falling in love followed quite naturally. We discovered we could talk openly to each other, held similar interests, hopes and dreams and eventually I admitted to myself (and to Rachel) that I couldn't imagine life without Joe in it … and didn't want a life without him. Our first date last November assured me I didn't have to live without him and over the next few months our relationship blossomed into something beautiful.

Joe proposed in March, almost fourteen months since that fateful accident and I had no hesitation in accepting. The twins love him too and are delighted for us. Sam gave me away at our wedding in June and Kate was my bridesmaid. It was perfection, a small affair with the twins, our good friends Rachel and Frank, Cassie and Alan, Phil and Diane and a few work colleagues from our respective offices. For the reception we took over the conservatory at The Greyhound, the scene of our first date and it was beautiful, decorated tastefully with masses of fragrant summer blooms, and excellent food.

So, I have now gained a husband and a dog, as Liffey is delightful and I'm completely besotted with her. I'd defy anyone not to love Liffey, she's gentle and friendly and so funny in her antics. Joe has gained children, the family he always longed for.

In the run-up to our wedding, Joe decided to get into contact with Alison's mother in a final attempt at reconciliation, with the idea of inviting her to the wedding in mind. Her response to our good news was unsurprising. Ethel accused him of never having loved her daughter and wished him nothing but ill. I don't think she'll be on our Christmas card list after such a vitriolic outburst! Joe's done everything possible to make things up with her, but she appears to enjoy wallowing in self-pity and there's nothing we can do about it. Ethel has no desire to see Joe again but that is her choice, and her loss.

We decided to move house, to make a fresh start, but the news came with a warning from Phil and Diane not to move too far away, or they may have to begin proceedings to gain custody of Liffey.

And now we're looking forward to our second Christmas together and our first as man and wife. The year ahead presents new possibilities, as our baby is due in late spring. Yes, it was a surprise to us both, but a more than welcome one. Joe assumed he could never father children, erroneously as it turned out, and I'd given up hope of ever having another baby, and so our delight knows no bounds.

Each day is a fresh page in our life on which to make new memories and record our many blessings. I thank God that out of the very worst experience of my life beauty and joy have blossomed and we can finally put the horrors of the accident to rest.

THE END

NOTE FROM THE AUTHOR

Thank you for reading *The Accident*. I'm often asked if the characters in my books are based on real people. The answer is yes and no. Character traits of people I've known over the years influence my writing, sometimes even surprising me, but generally I take snippets of reality to combine with imagination.

The Accident is the exception but not regarding people. Liffey is real, the rescue dog we adopted six years ago. She arrived from Ireland with forty other dogs, a skinny, terrified girl who, although happy in the home, remains scared of her own shadow in the outside world. The bravery and intelligence bestowed on Liffey in the book is pure literary licence.

The concept of ripples in a pond has always fascinated me – one action, one decision, and the whole future is changed. The weather event in February 2018, aptly named the 'Beast from the East' swept into the British Isles taking everyone by surprise. Sub-zero temperatures, unusually heavy snow and violent storms brought much of the UK's infrastructure to a standstill. We probably all have a story relating to that event.

The physical cause was a "sudden stratospheric warming" above the North Pole, dragging extremely cold air in from Siberia. But to most people it was simply inconvenient, uncomfortable, and finger- and toe-numbingly cold.

At its height, fifty centimetres of snow fell in some areas in just a few hours, leaving cars and their passengers stranded, rail and road links impassable, and bringing airports to a standstill. The country was on red alert, a rarely issued warning of danger to life, and the Ministry of Defence sent in troops to rescue hundreds of stranded motorists.

Weather-related deaths were at an all-time high as the cold spell continued, and power failures contributed to the misery of freezing temperatures. The extreme weather forced hundreds of schools to close their doors, the children perhaps the only ones to enjoy the snow and ice.

Most people battled on against the elements, facing icy conditions and freezing rain on a daily basis as they stoically endeavoured to reach their places of employment. But for some, the 'Beast from the East' was to change their lives forever.

Bereavement and life-changing injuries affect people in different ways, something I try to explore in *The Accident*. For Hannah the accident brings physical pain as she struggles to carve out a new life coping with her injuries, and emotional pain, living with the tyranny of the 'what ifs' and battling with guilt. The ripples reach out to her family, altering the future she'd always taken for granted.

Joe, who loses his beloved wife, is at his lowest ebb but the ripples extend to his wider family too and become the catalyst for greed and hatred.

Grief can appear to break us, but perhaps also remake us. I've always admired those who channel their grief into something positive, and so Keiron Lang's parents become the example to us all. Refusing to allow their son's memory to die, they decide to fulfil his dream and build a living monument to his lost life, to make his years on earth count for something. I so enjoyed writing their story; beauty from ashes.

ACKNOWLEDGEMENTS

As ever, my thanks to my husband and family for their love and support during the hours I spend writing. Many thanks to the wonderful Denise Smith, a truly inspirational lady, whose generous help and advice enabled me to create the character of Hannah.

And to the team at Bloodhound Books for their amazing help in getting this book out into the world. Each book is a collaboration and I truly appreciate their patience, dedication, professionalism and guidance throughout the process.

A NOTE FROM THE PUBLISHER

Thank you for reading this book. If you enjoyed it please do consider leaving a review on Amazon to help others find it too.

We hate typos. All of our books have been rigorously edited and proofread, but sometimes mistakes do slip through. If you have spotted a typo, please do let us know and we can get it amended within hours.

info@bloodhoundbooks.com

Printed in Great Britain
by Amazon